Death among the Dons

Dame Sarah Murchieson, characterful veteran of a long Civil Service career, finds herself with a real challenge when she agrees at the urgent request of her distinguished ex-lover to become Warden of Gladstone College. The Fellows are at odds over the future of this all-female nineteenth-century institution, the college buildings are being ravaged by damp and woodworm and the finances are in chaos. Dame Sarah's predecessor died suddenly, and it was never established whether this was accidental death or suicide.

Into this difficult situation comes a potential killer striking apparently at random, and adding further complications to the relationships among the all-female Fellowship, which includes a disappointed Deputy Warden who had hoped to get Dame Sarah's job and a brilliant young specialist in medieval studies, unhappy in her marriage, whose sexual affairs threaten further difficulty for the college. Even Dame Sarah's principal ally, Francesca Wilson, seconded from the DTI, and her policeman husband, Superintendent John McLeish seem to be unable to stem the tide of disasters threatening the college, its undergraduates and Fellows.

In this her fourth book, Janet Neel confirms her reputation, established by *Death's bright angel*, *Death on site* and *Death of a partner*, as a crime novelist of the first rank. *Death's bright angel* won the Crime Writers' Association John Creasey prize and *Death of a partner* was shortlisted for the Gold Dagger award in 1991.

By the same author

Death's bright angel (1988)
Death on site (1989)
Death of a partner (1991)

DEATH AMONG THE DONS

Janet Neel

Constable · London

First published in Great Britain 1993
by Constable & Company Ltd
3 The Lanchesters, 162 Fulham Palace Road
London W6 9ER
Copyright © 1993 by Janet Neel
The right of Janet Neel to be
identified as the author of this work
has been asserted by her in accordance
with the Copyright, Designs and Patents Act 1988
ISBN 0 09 472370 2
Set in Linotron 11 pt Palatino by
CentraCet Limited, Cambridge
Printed in Great Britain by
St Edmundsbury Press Limited
Bury St Edmunds, Suffolk

A CIP catalogue record for this book
is available from the British Library

For my son Richard Cohen

1

Dr Judith Symonds, Warden of Gladstone College, banged the door of her taxi with more force than was strictly necessary and snapped her umbrella up before rushing head down across the intervening strip of pavement to the high, awkward stone steps that lead up to the Combined Universities Club. It was an awful night, she thought crossly, cold even for early January, rain pouring down, and chill, the soaking pavement penetrating through her thin-soled elegant black suede shoes. Idiotic to have worn them: this was the end-of-term party for a Commission into the Funding of Higher Education, and senior and distinguished educationalists were not renowned for their elegance in matters of dress. Decent fur-lined boots and ancient raincoats would probably be *de rigueur* among the rest of the guests. She pushed through the heavy glass doors and stopped at the top of the steps to shake out her umbrella and hand over a heavy briefcase to the porter on duty. This was her club and the man recognized her, making meaningless, soothing conversation about the dreadfulness of the weather. Calmed somewhat by the ritual she turned and went down the dark, awkward stairs to the basement to leave coat and umbrella and tidy herself up.

She looked in the mirror above the basins dispassionately; her hair, expensively restored to its original dark chestnut, had been set that morning and was only a little flattened by the damp day. She had the clear colour and unlined skin of someone who had never smoked and who took good care of herself and, as usual, she looked younger than her fifty-three years, though the lines round the wide, round, brown eyes were looking heavier tonight. Applying lipstick carefully, with a brush, she decided she was looking tired. Christmas had been totally unrestful, with manifold worries coming at her from all sides about the physical condition and financial problems of the all-women college of which she had been Warden for the past five years. A poisoned chalice, and it had been from the beginning, she thought, suddenly prepared to acknowledge the depth of her difficulties; taken aback, she dropped her lipstick brush. She picked it up and finished the job, painstakingly.

She stepped back and looked herself over to check that her skirt was not too creased nor a stocking laddered, and considered her reflected image: a small woman, not more than five feet two inches, carefully and neatly dressed in a pale yellow fine wool suit, with carefully chosen jewellery, she looked reassuringly unlike the senior classical scholar she was and more like her expensively clothed contemporaries who had fought their way to senior, highly paid jobs in major companies, or who had married men who had done that. The suit was new and chosen to please Sir Neville Allason, Chairman of the Funding Commission and Permanent Secretary to the Department of Education and Science, as indeed all her clothes had been for the last two years since she had become his mistress. And therein, she acknowledged to the image in the mirror, lay another reason why Christmas had been a misery. It was, of course, inevitable that a married man would spend the Christmas holiday with his wife and children, but he could surely have found time to ring her more than once – and that a hurried five-minute call from his office on Christmas Eve. They had met just over two years ago, and over *that* Christmas he had pursued her with phone calls, leaving her in a state of excitement and longing that had meant she was in his bed at the earliest possible opportunity in the New Year.

The corners of her mouth went up involuntarily, remembering that period. She had been fifty-one, and while, then as now, she had looked and felt a good deal younger most of the time, she had insensibly become a *grande dame* having, she thought, outgrown any romantic adventures. Then she had met Neville, and all this careful accommodation to her age and circumstances had vanished, instantly. He had not seemed to think a woman of fifty-one was too old for passion; of course that was one of his most potent charms. A very young fifty-one then himself, he apparently preferred women his own age or older, rather than

8

twenty years younger as men of his age so often seemed to. This evening, although it was the first time she would have seen him for three weeks, she could not even be sure that they would have any time together; his wife might well be there as this was an official occasion. She sighed, checked her handbag and told herself not to be silly; at least she would see Neville, and she could legitimately demand his full attention for some part of the time to consider the thickening problems of Gladstone College.

She turned to go upstairs, content that she would not now be among the very early guests, and recognized, slowly, a slight, exhausted woman, leaning heavily on a stick.

'Sarah! How are you? I heard you had been ill.'

'Well, Judith, since it's you I'll tell you. I thought I was getting over this thing – it's a viral arthritis, just like . . . well . . . arthritis, but it's a bug, and they promise it will go away. Only it hasn't.'

'Can I help?'

'Yes, dammit, I mean, please. Could you hold the stick, and my bag, while I get my coat off?'

Dame Sarah Murchieson, distinguished veteran of a long Home Office career, and member of the University Funding Commission, eased her coat off stiffly and eyed the coat-rack doubtfully.

'I'll do it, Sarah.' Judith Symonds put down the bag and the umbrella and took her colleague's coat and hung it up, observing the older woman out of the corner of her eye. Dame Sarah was looking truly tired, more than her sixty-two years, her curly grey hair flattened and her skin lined, and Judith felt the weight of her own future. She could, she thought in a moment of panic, at any moment be ill, as Sarah was, and unable to work, or to keep Neville at her side; she tried and failed utterly to imagine that bounding, healthy dynamo supporting her in sickness rather than in health.

'How long have you had this?' she asked, watching Dame Sarah flinch as she dragged a comb through her hair.

'A couple of months. It is going away, but lifting my arms, or carrying anything heavier than a very small handbag, is still beyond me.' She peered in the mirror critically. 'Either I've changed colour or this make-up has rotted.'

'You look fine,' Judith Symonds lied, gallantly.

Sarah Murchieson had always been good-looking; even at over

sixty she was slim and well made with enviable springy hair and good regular features, but the point was her charm, which was direct, unaffected and entirely confident.

Judith, struggling with a complex of emotions and worries about Neville, felt a momentary pang of pure envy of Dame Sarah, ill or well. 'Can I carry anything up the stairs?' she asked.

'No, bless you. I hang this bag around me – so – and lean on this damned stick and go up very slowly indeed. Don't wait, you could be here for hours.'

Judith properly ignored this suggestion and both women arrived at the main door just as a tall, blond man shot in out of the rain, coatless and shaking off raindrops.

'Neville!' Judith Symonds felt her whole face lift with pleasure, and the man bent to kiss her cheek. She stood back to look at him; he was wearing his best suit and a new tie which she disliked instantly; his wife's taste had always run to yellow and small spots. Whatever he was wearing, however, he was a very good-looking man, just over six feet, curly blond hair, the bright colour only just beginning to fade, cropped very close to his head, blunt, regular features and green eyes, narrowed as he took in his surroundings. He would be fifty-four soon, she thought – his birthday fell in February, as hers did, and they had both been amused and impressed by the coincidence two years ago – but he did not look his age. It was the way he moved, in one piece and quickly, like the good athlete he had always been; energy in every movement, as he shook off the rain.

'No briefcase tonight, Sir Neville?' The porter, of course, knew him well.

'No, John, thank you. The car's coming back for me.'

Judith's heart sank; if Neville was using the official car it probably meant he was going on somewhere after this party, and her hopes would be dashed. He glanced at her companion and exploded into action.

'Sarah. Darling.'

'Neville. Be careful, I am totally fragile.' Dame Sarah was laughing as she was swept into his embrace. Judith watched them longingly.

'Let me carry you?' he offered.

'No, I'm *much* too fragile for that,' Dame Sarah said demurely, slanting her eyes at him. Judith realized that what she had always half suspected was true: Sarah, although obviously far too old for her Neville, was nonetheless another one of his past affairs.

'Well, let me walk very slowly upstairs with you then,' he suggested, and Judith found herself making an awkward third as Neville helped Sarah up the stairs to the main floor, using the peculiarly masculine force of his personality to keep her going. They paused on the main entrance floor in the two-storey high, galleried hall which is the centre of the club and one of its principal charms, to let Sarah collect herself, and Judith noticed enviously how many of the men gathered by the bar, or by the boards on which the Reuters print-outs carrying the latest news were displayed, came to greet Sarah Murchieson. Pale with exhaustion and leaning on a stick, she still drew them to her side, their faces alight with enthusiasm, and there was no hint of pity or patronage in the attention she was getting.

It was with an unusual sensation of relief that Judith recognized her Deputy Warden, Dr Alice Hellier, leaning over the balcony to watch their progress. She smiled kindly at Alice, past Sarah's bent head, and observed that she was indeed wearing fur-lined boots and a skirt of some much too bunchy material. Alice had never cared much about clothes and had cared less since she had rather unexpectedly married George, some ten years younger than herself, who was said to prefer women to be neat rather than gaudy – on both of which counts Alice had managed to fail tonight. Judith forgave herself for this piece of unkindness; Alice Hellier was not a helpful or supportive Deputy Warden. She had wanted the Warden's job herself and had spent the first full year of Judith's tenure in an academic sulk, applying conspicuously for other jobs, flouncing about the college and doing the minimum amount of the load of administration that she could possibly achieve. She had improved markedly since that time – under pressure, Judith suspected, from her husband, who had found a post as Deputy Bursar to the college, and was not prepared to allow his wife to undermine his career plans. She sighed as she thought of George Hellier, who would undoubtedly also be present, and decided she really need not discuss college business tonight. All that could wait until tomorrow when Neville Allason would not be on hand. Neville was chatting civilly enough to one of Sarah's admirers, but every line of him proclaimed impatience to get on, and she watched to see what he would do.

11

'Glad to have had a word, Jim,' he said easily to the distinguished older man who had buttonholed him, and turned decisively to Sarah. 'Ready?'

'Up to a point,' Dame Sarah said, with enviable firmness. 'You go on, Neville, you can find me a drink. And you, Judith – I shall be fine in a minute, and I'll make my own way.'

Neville Allason hesitated but Judith seized her chance, conscious in some uncomfortable corner of her mind that Neville was reluctant to be alone with her. They set off up the wide, plush stairs together, Judith moving fast to keep up with Neville's longer stride.

'Neville, darling. I need some time with you. I'm seriously worried about the college,' she said urgently, her real need – to go to bed with him, to get close to all that warmth and reassurance and energy – unstated.

'Mm.' He was not looking at her. 'It's the usual problem, I've come back to a mountain of rubbish at the Department. What *is* it about the educational world that causes them all to write pages and pages of furious vituperation of colleagues over Christmas?'

Judith refused to be sidetracked. 'Can we go somewhere after this party?' She meant, as they both knew, to his London flat.

'Darling, I am sorry, absolutely not possible. Jennifer is up for the night. She's having dinner with her brother.'

'I'm staying at my flat tonight,' Judith said baldly, and felt rather than saw his sideways, exasperated look.

'My sweet, I'd love to, but it just doesn't work tonight.'

'Can we have a quick dinner, then?' she asked, feeling slightly sick with anxiety.

'Why not?' he said easily. 'What is it now – seven o'clock? I'll have to do an hour at this party, then I'll come and find you. Eat here, shall we?'

'Why not Gianni's?' she asked through stiff lips. Dinner in the club, in the big room where everyone could see them and intimate conversation was likely to be broken up by friendly fellow members dropping by to talk to one of them, was not what she had in mind, and it frightened her that Neville had even proposed it.

'It gives us more time if we just stop here,' he said, consideringly. 'I'd like to talk about the college, too, and if we go to Gianni's it'll be a rush. I can't remember how to organize here.'

He looked gracefully helpless and she found herself volunteering to book a table. One of the first thngs she had learned about him was that, despite his brisk commanding manner, he liked, and always sought out, women who would look after him.

'Right, fine,' he said briskly. 'Susan. How are you, you're looking very beautiful.' He plunged forward to kiss the cheek of the bridling secretary to the Commission and was swallowed up, instantly, by the party, people drifting from every corner of the high-ceilinged imposing library, plush curtains drawn comfortingly over the tall windows. Judith watched him go, secure in the knowledge that she would be dining with him in just over an hour, and slipped out to book the table, resolutely ignoring the nagging knowledge that she had cornered him into this. She could, however, rely on his being there at 8 p.m.: he was used to doing what others organized for him, possibly as a legacy of his long-ago days as a regular soldier. He had joined the army at seventeen to get away from a miserable home, and found both friends and mentors. The army had seen past the good looks and the athletic prowess and, after two years in a nasty guerrilla war, sent him to university when he was twenty-one and watched unsurprised as he got a good First in Economics. After four years in the Intelligence Corps, he had been head-hunted into the Home Office, and from there a distinguished career had unfolded.

Judith took a drink from the tray held out by one of the waiters, one of the regular 'extras'. The library was always in use for evening drinks parties, to the point where any member trying to work there could have been seriously incommoded, but it was not that sort of club. Papers might not be brought into the club, except under special conditions and to particular rooms. Business, by convention, might not be discussed, though this was usually honoured more in the breach; most of the people at this party were actually working hard for their drink, having a word with a colleague in another university, promoting a private idea or sabotaging a rival's scheme. None of us, of course, Judith reflected, have any leisure interests any more; all of us work very hard and what we do when we meet is business, tiny bits of organization in our own field. She sipped her drink and concluded that if she or any of this distinguished gang wanted to do any real reading it would not be here but in their own establish-

13

ments or the London Library, just a step across the road in St James's Square.

She had just decided to go and join the group containing the Vice Chancellor of Cambridge University, when she was buttonholed by Alice Hellier.

'Judith, sorry to catch you like this, but I'm not in college tomorrow and I know you're not there the day after, and I *did* want a word.'

'Of course, Alice.'

'George has had a rotten Christmas, and I don't think he's ever stopped working. Day after day he goes into the Bursary and just comes back more and more discouraged. *When* are we going to do something about Phyllis?'

Phyllis Trench, the college's Bursar, was an acknowleged disaster in the role and before Christmas Judith herself had come to realize the extent of the problem. To do Lady Trench justice, she had not wanted the job originally, seven years ago when she was appointed, but it had been felt at the time that a mathematician who was no longer producing creative work would have the basic qualification of numeracy and could also be best spared to the task. It turned out that the ability to add two and two and produce the sum of four as opposed to some fascinating mathematical abstraction had been left out of Phyllis Trench's makeup, and she alternately neglected the job and interfered in every aspect of it. George Hellier, Alice's husband, unqualified, but with a background in commissary accounting in the RAF, had been hired at some fairly derisory salary to act as Deputy Bursar some three years ago, and some things had improved sharply – bills got paid, so that the college did not run out of food, and cheques were banked and logged. But evidently one man could make only limited headway with Phyllis Trench in place.

'Alice, I do assure you this is at the top of my agenda. I am very concerned about the accounts and I agree we must make a change.'

'George could do the whole job if Phyllis did not continually countermand whatever he had just done, and interfere all the time.'

Judith sighed; another aspect of the problem was that she herself was not at all confident of George's ability to do the increasingly complex job of a college bursar.

14

'There is the difficulty with the Statutes,' she said, lamely. The Statutes of Gladstone College provided that all the Fellows should be female, and it was felt to be inefficient to have a bursar who could not be an official part of the governing body.

'Oh, the Statutes. Ridiculously out of date – well, you know my views, Judith. I believe we should raise again the question of changing them.'

Judith, who remembered all too clearly the upheaval that had followed the last attempt to change the Statutes a year before she herself had been appointed, had no intention of attempting this process. It had soured the last years of the previous Warden's administration and set sister against sister to very little purpose. There would – there must – come a time when it was clear that Gladstone's all-female status was either illegal under the massive code being evolved by the EC, or impractical, and then would be the time to move. Alice Hellier, a physicist, had one highly respectable axe to grind: she feared that the college, unable to offer Fellowships to male scientists, would sink into second-class status. She also, naturally but inconveniently, wanted a better-paid job with the status of Fellow attached for her husband. And wanted it passionately: her late marriage to a man ten years younger than herself had obviously been fulfilling but, Judith thought disapprovingly, she was over-identified with her husband, each slight to him being felt as a slight to herself.

'We must, indeed, tackle the whole problem of the Bursary as soon as possible when we all meet next week,' she said firmly, in an attempt to conclude this conversation. 'I am having a quick dinner with Neville Allason after this party to seek his views.'

'What does he have to do with it?' Alice Hellier asked ungraciously.

'His Department has a lot to do with our funding,' Judith pointed out drily. 'And he has always been helpful; we are not alone in having trouble with our administration, and he will know how other establishments are managing.'

Alice Hellier shifted disbelievingly, and Judith felt pure exasperation. There were objectively very good reasons why she, an outsider, and not Alice Hellier, who had spent most of her working life at Gladstone, had got the Warden's job. Alice had no political skills, because she refused to believe they were necessary; she was still stuck in the seventies when governments, many of whose members had been the first in their families to be able to go to university, had funded higher education generously and unquestioningly. Her idea of a negotiation was to explain to the Department, in wearying detail, exactly what the college must have and to stare with uncomprehending arrogance at anyone who questioned that, or who suggested that the college itself could manage its affairs better. But you could not expect Alice herself to see this. Judith, watching her turn away in open exasperation, understood wryly that the woman still thought she would make a better Warden and, no doubt, still harboured hopes of getting the job this time round, when Judith herself left two years from now.

She shook off the depression engendered by talking to Alice and waved to an old friend, a distinguished historian who had been trying to attract her attention. He kissed her warmly and quietly invited her to dine with him, which she refused with real regret, despite the urgency of her need to be with Neville Allason. She glanced round, thinking of Neville, and saw him immediately. He was in a group with another Fellow of Gladstone, Louise Taylor, a young, dazzlingly clever medieval historian. Judith wondered, with a touch of jealousy, how Louise, only in her thirties, had got into this distinguished and senior party, then remembered that she had given evidence on the teaching of history to this Commission sometime back in November. No doubt, all those who had given evidence had been invited – or at least they had if they looked like Louise Taylor, who resembled not at all the popular conception of a senior historian, being small, slim and extremely pretty with a cloud of black hair and wide, blue eyes. She was entertaining Neville Allason, that was clear, all flying hands as she laughed up at him, and he was watching her, absorbed, listening with that careful unswerving concentration which was so much part of his charm. Judith watched them for a minute indulgently, liking the look of Neville's familiar, blunt profile and the strong shoulders, before her view was blocked by Louise's husband, Michael, slightly taller than Neville, and thinner, with over-long, blond hair flopping into his eyes.

Judith returned her attention to her own group and found that it had been augmented by George Hellier. Hoping that he, too, would not want to buttonhole her about the college's financial

16

affairs, she none the less regarded him with affection, as he stood, four-square and comfortable, easily coaxing a very shy female chemistry don into conversation. He was taller than he looked at first sight; his heavy shoulders and generally solid presence disguised the fact that he was nearly six foot. At forty-six he had a full head of thick, brown hair, not even beginning to go grey, so that at a distance he looked a good deal younger than his wife. Close up, the ten-year difference narrowed; George had lived an outdoor life and served overseas, so that his skin was reddened, weatherbeaten and lined, with patches of high colour on the cheekbones. He was a steady drinker, but she had never seen him more than becomingly cheerful in the three years and numerous parties of his time at Gladstone. He greeted her with affection, and did not attempt to tell her anything at all about the Bursary, not even to make the point that he had been working over Christmas. He confined himself to getting her another drink and making sure she had met everyone in the group. A comfortable man, Judith thought, warmed by the attention; not that she wanted one of those for herself, but they were nice to have around in the background.

She talked to various people, then noticed the party was beginning to thin out and was deciding to look for Neville, when she felt a familiar hand on her shoulder.

'Judith. Time to eat.' He beamed round the group, punctiliously greeting those he did not know, and Judith, warmed by his presence, surprised a gratifying look of pure envy from the shy chemist. Well might she be envious, Judith thought, her misgivings banished, retreating swiftly from the party with Neville, a star and very conscious of it. His stride checked just once as he saw Dame Sarah, grey with exhaustion, making for the door, but seeing three men of various ages spring to her aid, he went on.

They sat down at the quiet table at the far end of the members' dining-room and ordered swiftly. Neville, as usual throwing his full concentration into whatever he was doing, was charming with the middle-aged waitress and swiftly competent with the wine waiter.

'I don't know what we had to drink up there, but none of it was any good, so I decided I'd wait and have something with dinner,' he said cheerfully, and as he glanced at her enquiringly

17

she understood that he had not until that moment actually looked at her.

'How was your Christmas?' she asked, to give herself time.

'Oh, you know. Usual thing. Very busy, lots of family. Relief to get back to the office, despite the amount of paper waiting for me there. What did you do?'

'I rushed round family, like you.' She had chosen this formula to cover a holiday period when she had felt increasingly depressed and of no interest or importance to anyone. She had felt nothing but relief when, ten years before, she and her husband had decided to abandon a dull marriage in which, increasingly, both felt stifled; and she had felt no need to remarry. Previously she had not visited her family at Christmas, but had gone abroad to see old friends or new cities. This year, anxiety about the college, exhaustion after a heavy term, and a persistent, hovering influenza had decided her to spend Christmas in the middle of her younger sister's family. This had been a depressing mistake; the teenage children had been noisy and sullen by turns, totally uninterested in any grown-up, and she had found herself dealing with two of their joint aunts, both in their late eighties and both engaged, querulously, in falling apart, losing hearing, sight and ability to get out of an armchair. This disheartening vision of the future had depressed her, but she had buoyed herself up with thoughts of Neville. He now sat opposite her, visibly fidgeting and not quite meeting her eye.

'I'd have been glad of a letter or a phone call,' she said, as she had not meant to, and watched him put a glass down carefully.

'I don't know why, but there just did not seem to be one minute when I could sit down by myself,' he said earnestly. 'I think the last moment of peace was Christmas Eve, when I did ring. But tell me, what's happening at Gladstone to worry you so much?' He leant across the table to her, the green eyes alive with interest, and she felt momentarily immense exhaustion and misery. Not so long ago the full force of that personality would have been turned on *her*, not on the problems of the college. But these were real enough and she must get some help, so she took a steadying drink of wine and explained, as best she could, the muddle in the accounts.

'Well, that's *very* worrying,' he said energetically. 'That we have to fix.'

Her heart lifted at the 'we', but she saw that he was not thinking about her: his attention was directed to the problem that this might present for his Department.

'Judith, how much do you actually know about the detail of the college finances?'

'You mean am I just making a fuss? Neville, the auditors said in October that they cannot sign off the latest set without every kind of qualification, so I have made it my business to know how bad we are.' It was a relief to be angry with him.

'What about your Deputy Bursar? Could he take over?'

She sighed. 'I don't think so. We *all* like him, he's an asset to the college, but he isn't trained and, indeed, the most impenetrable muddle appears to be in the area he looks after – catering and housekeeping. It runs very efficiently on the ground, as it were, so it may just be that he is unable to cope with Phyllis Trench.'

'But he isn't an obvious successor? No, I see. And, of course, you really need a woman for the job. Leave it with me, Judith, I'll see what can be done. Now what else? Have you got enough support otherwise?'

Tears pricked again behind her eyes, but food arrived at that moment and in the bustle of it being assembled on their plates with much chatter between Neville and the attendant waitresses she was able to collect herself.

'I could do with a new Deputy Warden while you're at it, darling,' she was able to say, lightly, watching with longing affection at the way he was eating everything he could see, including anything she didn't want to eat.

'Alice Hellier still not being helpful? Of course, she applied for the job, didn't she?'

'Yes, she did. And she still hopes to get it, if I drop dead.'

'Well, you aren't going to do that, are you, love?' he said briskly, over a forkful of potato.

She looked back at him with despair, but he did not notice; he had put down the fork and was waving to someone at another table. She did not turn to look, sunk in misery.

'Judith, the Helliers and that delightful creature on your staff – what's her name? Louise? – are dining here too. I think I'll go over and suggest we all have coffee afterwards. Then you'll have someone to talk to when I have to rush off. Here, do have some more of this – I'll be carried out of here if I drink it all.'

Judith opened her mouth to say no; she had been warned that alcohol and the tranquillizers she had been taking for six weeks now did not mix well. But she stopped. There would be no surer way of driving Neville away than by confessing to such distress as to need drugs; his mother had lived on various early versions of the tranquillizers to enable her to cope with his alcoholic father. She felt suddenly utterly exhausted by the struggle and finished the glass of wine in two gulps. 'Neville, I'm wondering whether it might not be better if I left Gladstone early, at the end of this academic year. I'm finding it all too much. And I wouldn't be so far from you – we'd find it easier to meet. And Alice Hellier could have the job. She wants it, after all.'

She felt the wine hit her, turning her face and neck scarlet; she had never until this last term been much of a drinker, it did not suit her. She watched, hot and miserable, as Neville fidgeted with his fork.

'My love, you *have* had a rotten Christmas, haven't you? Look, don't weaken; I promise we'll sort out someone for the Bursary. You're doing fine, and you're far too young to quit early. You can't anyway – it'll spoil your chances of getting Vice Chancellor somewhere.'

'Could we manage a weekend away?' This, too, she had not meant to ask, and she heard with horror the hint of a whine. The doctor, she noted grimly, had been absolutely right about not mixing alcohol and whatever the active ingredient in these pills was called.

'I cannot see how for the moment.' Neville was studying the menu. 'I truly am terribly busy – I was going through the diary today and I would have difficulty finding a weekend that did not have some sort of official engagement. And, of course, Jennifer would rather wonder what was going on if I didn't spend a free weekend at home.'

Judith thought, through a haze of pain, that she had known the answer to that question, and it had been asking for trouble to push him to the limit. But a year ago, another part of her mind protested, official engagements had been moved or reorganized, and Jennifer Allason's views had never been mentioned to her. Neville was finding this affair a burden, while she still wanted to go on with it. She looked helplessly at the handsome man opposite her; his mouth was tight with tension. He was glancing at his watch, and she understood that she must collect herself; this was much too public an arena.

'I'll just go and tidy up,' she said. 'I don't feel like a pudding, but by all means let's have coffee with the Helliers and the Taylors. I'll see you there.'

She arrived in the basement Ladies and rushed into a lavatory. She found to her relief that she was not going to cry; she was shaking with anger and distress, but the tears had receded. She combed her hair, redid her lipstick, powdered down the high colour in her cheeks, and looked at herself in the mirror. Passable. And I am Warden of Gladstone still, she thought, resolutely, considering her shaking hands. She hesitated, but took another of her pills, deciding that somehow she had to get calmly and graciously through coffee and bid a collected farewell to Neville as he thankfully extricated himself from the evening.

It was as well she had taken time to collect herself, she thought, as she turned a corner and saw the group she had come to meet. The Helliers and Michael Taylor were talking in a constrained way, while Neville and the beautiful Louise Taylor were engaged in an animated tête-à-tête and getting on like the proverbial house on fire. The men stood as she came towards them and she found a seat opposite Neville, between the Helliers. She thankfully accepted a cup of coffee from George, who was looking anxious and abstracted under that calm façade, and decided the only dignified course was to leave Neville unimpeded to chat to Louise Taylor, and to engage the Helliers and Michael Taylor in conversation. After two minutes she saw this was an impossibly uphill task; all three of them were sulking, the Helliers presumably at not getting any attention from the great Neville Allason, and Michael, because his wife was getting far too much. Judith looked in appeal and reproof at Neville, who responded instantly, just as she had seen him do for his wife, and addressed himself easily to Alice Hellier, drawing them all into the conversation. She sat back, thankfully, watching Neville charm his way through.

'Can I get anyone some more coffee?' he said, just glancing at his watch, and she accepted, needing badly to stem the intense exhaustion which was starting to weigh her down. The extra tranquillizers had probably been a mistake, but at least she was calm and in control. She watched, as from a great distance, as Neville came back with the coffee, assisted by Alice Hellier who was talking to him with great animation.

'Judith? No milk, one sugar?'

'Thank you, Neville,' she said, grateful momentarily for the public acknowledgement that he knew precisely how she took her coffee, and just seeing Louise Taylor register the point. George Hellier took the cup from Neville and brought it round to her, very slightly spilling it in the saucer. Judith drank it thirstily. She looked up to see Neville watching her and met his gaze calmly.

'My driver will be waiting and I must go,' he said apologetically.

'Of course,' she said easily. 'I have a meeting tomorrow, so I am not going back to Gladstone. Would the Department's resources extend to dropping me in Notting Hill Gate? Not if it's a nuisance – I'll get a cab.'

'My dear Judith.' Neville did not hesitate, faced with this public demand. 'No trouble at all, Notting Hill Gate is nearly enough on the way to my flat. What is your meeting?'

She explained, calmly, wondering if she was going to manage to stay awake in the car, and said goodnight to the others, and made her exit with Neville, noticing sardonically that he had stopped to kiss Louise and – after only a fractional pause – Alice goodnight.

'It's the Department's driver, of course,' he said, neutrally, as they went down the steps.

'I know, Neville. I just need to get home,' she said wearily. She turned to him at the bottom of the steps. 'Does Jennifer know about us?'

She watched as he stiffened. 'No, no, she doesn't.'

'Or she doesn't want to?'

He did not answer, but stood back as the driver held the door for her. She looked up, just before she got into the car, and saw the Helliers on the steps above them, Alice looking more like a parcel than ever in a box-like winter coat that fell straight from padded shoulders to just above the winter boots, and George, who did not seem to feel the cold, in a light raincoat. She lifted a hand to them both and sank thankfully into the car.

2

Superintendent John McLeish dismissed the morning meeting of his senior officers and walked slowly back to his own office, uneasily conscious of a ringing in his ears. He hoped he was not getting the peculiarly debilitating virus which, combined with the excesses of Christmas, had decimated the uniformed force at Notting Dale, leaving it seriously undermanned on this cold, raw January day. He simply could not afford to have flu. Not only was he needed here, but he was also totally necessary at home. A much-loved, much-wanted five-month-old son, William, who never slept, had reduced his driving, ferociously competent wife to a pale-faced, unkempt, dependent, depressed ghost of herself, and if he failed her now he did not know what she would do. He stood, worrying, in the middle of his office, a big man, six feet four inches in his socks, with thick dark hair, regular features, marred by a slightly crooked nose, relic of a rugby accident, shoulders sagging with tiredness. He picked up his uniform tunic and shrugged it on, then buttoned up his coat and pulled up his tie. It was all right to hold the morning meeting with his more senior officers in some *déshabillé*, but it was no kind of example to young constables of either sex. He was, thus dressed, an impressive sight. His wife's expressive family had been uncharacteristically struck dumb by their first sight of him in uniform. 'There's such a lot of navy blue and so many buttons, John,' one of his four young and fashionable brothers-in-law had said faintly, rather too late.

He conceded privately – not having worn this, or any other uniform, since he was a rookie constable of twenty-three, just out of university – that it had been a shock to get back into one. But needs must; he had never expected to leave the CID, being

23

an extremely competent detective who had started his career, unusually, in the Flying Squad. Not normally tolerant of graduates ('What *use* would he be?' the senior officer had asked in honest bewilderment when it was proposed that McLeish, six months out of the University of Reading, should join), the squad had grudgingly admitted him on the basis of his several years in county-class Rugby. He had been a success and from there had risen meteorically and loved the work. He had nevertheless come to feel that the edict requiring CID officers to serve a term in the uniformed branch with each promotion rather than to spend their whole career in the CID was right. Whether in the Metropolitan Police or the regional forces, the CID was a close-knit group, and the consequences of this clanny independence had been unattractive and damaging; many forces had become élite groups which did things their way with no regard at all for the wider public interest.

The trouble was that, as his wife's family had implied, McLeish was too tall and too bulky to look reassuringly neat and soldierly on the TV, as the current Chief Commissioner did. And he had cut himself shaving; he had got the baby William off to sleep finally, persuaded his wife back to bed, and crept to the bathroom to get ready to go to work, only to be jerked to attention by hearing the miserable, grinding wail begin again. Well, it had probably been a choice between cutting his chin and hurling William out of the window at that point; the experience of having a child who cried virtually all the time had caused him to look differently at people who battered their babies. Not more sympathetically – he would himself willingly have died for the wailing scrap who clung to him half the night, the little knees pulled up in helpless discomfort – but differently. He peered into the mirror and decided he would look less battered without the sticking plaster than with it, and started gingerly to tug.

'John?'

His hand slipped, a small piece of blood appeared at the edge of the cut, and he cursed.

'What do you want?'

Detective Sergeant Bruce Davidson, framed in the doorway, raised his eyebrows.

'I mean, to what do I owe the honour of your company? Why aren't you in the CID room?'

Davidson grinned at him.

'Getting tired of the uniformed branch?'

'Experience of a management job is vital to any officer's career. I'm getting tired, end of sentence. Your godson does not sleep at all.'

'*Still* not?' Bruce Davidson sat on the edge of the desk, the better to chat, a clever Scot whose Irish descent showed in the very black hair, clear skin and blue eyes. 'How's the wee wifie?'

McLeish just let himself think for a treacherous moment how much his clever, bossy wife, five feet eight inches tall, would have hated to hear herself so described. 'Terrible. She isn't getting any sleep either. She says she hears William cry all the time, even when he isn't.'

'Ye'll need to watch that, John.'

'I know. I can't get her to go away for a couple of nights. I mean, I could manage. I'd feed the little brute solid whisky – anything. He'd sleep. But she won't let me.' Both men fell silent, considering the perversity of women. 'So why *are* you here, Bruce?'

'Aye, well. We've got a fatality in Southampton Place. I'd like you to come and look before we let them move the body.'

'Why me? What's happened to the CID?' McLeish was taken aback.

'We've two chief inspectors and two DIs off with flu. And MacAllister is on leave till Friday, and he *can't* come back. He's at a funeral in Glasgow.'

That did dispose pretty comprehensively of the senior CID staff, McLeish conceded, as he sat down behind his desk to try and decide where his duty lay. He was responsible for the day-to-day functioning and administration of Notting Dale police station. His superior, Chief Superintendent Beattie, was supposed to confine his attention to policy and, in pursuit of his aim, was at that moment attending a conference in Bournemouth on the young offender. In his absence, technically, the CID came under McLeish's command, but he himself had been CID for too long to try to exert day-to-day control over the independent, secretive clan housed in the four big offices on the third floor. Not that interference would have been particularly effective; the CID had their own separate entrance from the street, used primarily, according to the uniformed branch, for bringing in

25

women and wine. But it was sensible and careful of Davidson to get someone above his own rank of detective sergeant to take a look before the body was removed. Once you had shifted the corpse, no matter how carefully, you had lost a lot of direct evidence. He, McLeish, was moreover not just any superintendent; he had been once, and would be again, a detective, when and if he got his step to Chief Super.

'You're on,' he said, arriving at a decision. 'I'd better come now, I'll do the tour later. Hang on, I'll just tell Sally.'

He stopped to tell his secretary where he was going and when he would be back and to sign a couple of directives on duty rosters and tidiness in the canteen, both hardy perennials. He slid into the waiting car – one of the few advantages of this posting over any CID job he had so far held had been the ability to command a driver at any time – and sat in the back, with Davidson, looking out on to the sleety rain blowing nearly horizontally through the grey streets. They were heading for the richer end of his manor, where residential streets of tidy villas with fresh paint and polished brass on the doors alternated with streets of expensive little shops. It was one of these shopping streets they were driving down. 'Just off here,' Bruce Davidson said, as the traffic ground to a halt beside an expensive grocery store whose window was full of every kind of cheese, beautifully displayed. McLeish looked at it hungrily; he had eaten a hasty breakfast three hours ago, but the car moved a few feet to give him a less tantalizing view of a bookshop, with the latest hardback titles displayed, and next to it a small boutique, one coat and skirt carefully and expensively back-lit.

The car stopped abruptly and McLeish realized all the traffic ahead of them was being diverted to the left. 'It's the little alleyway there – see. We sealed it off to traffic. There's a primary school down there, we've got half the uniformed branch helping kids across roads.'

'Very proper,' McLeish said, quellingly, pondering again the vexed question of use of police manpower. The trouble was, it took a lot of police personnel in these crowded streets to enable the citizenry who wanted to go about their business to do that and to prevent those who had no business to attend to from getting in the way. The two policemen sat tight while the driver forced his way through and turned right down a short and narrow alley-way, filled, as Davidson had warned, with chattering under-nines in pairs, being herded by two brisk nuns. They made way reluctantly for the car.

'Isn't he big?' a small girl observed to another in awe, as McLeish levered himself out of the car.

'It's on the third floor, John,' Davidson said hastily.

McLeish removed his cap and stuffed it in his pocket before beginning the ascent. He walked up heavily, conscious both of the ache of tiredness in his legs and the unseen eyes behind the doors. Davidson had told him that the flats were arranged two to a floor, all either one or two bedrooms, in this 1930s building; the stairway was just not wide enough for comfort, and the ceilings were low. The whole building had obviously been put up to minimum standards and on the cheap, but it was clean, the stair carpet was newish and reasonably thick, and the doors to the flats were newly painted.

He paused on the turn of the staircase after the second floor to look up the stairs to where a door stood firmly closed with one of his young constables posted outside it. Jones, he recalled – one of two. This one was Edward C. as opposed to Gareth T.

'Doctor's here, sir,' the young Jones said, intelligently, as John McLeish arrived.

'Thank you.' McLeish waited for Davidson to catch up, then nodded to the constable to open the door. It opened on a poky hall, not more than four feet long, with a row of coat-hooks containing two old mackintoshes and a couple of umbrellas. Beyond that the door stood open and he moved into a small low-ceilinged living-room, nicely enough proportioned, with a small fireplace occupied by a large convector heater. Two armchairs faced the fire, and a big desk stood in the corner; a sofa backed against the wall occupied all the remaining space. A one-person flat or occasionally two, but there wasn't a lot of space. The kitchen, which he glanced at, was a narrow galley space, with a breakfast bar. Despite the vase of flowers in the kitchen and pictures on the walls, and a couple of magazines on the desk, the place was curiously impersonal. He waited a moment in front of the half-open door through which he could see Doc Brougham's stocky back and balding head, bent over the bed.

'Come in, come in. Good heavens, Superintendent McLeish! Wasn't expecting you.'

'CID is very thin at the top today, Doc. Bruce thought he'd like someone senior to take a look.'

'You've seen enough bodies, anyway.' McLeish had done a spell as a detective inspector at Notting Dale, and he and Doc Brougham knew each other well.

The bedroom was also small, barely large enough for the small double bed, single wardrobe and chest of drawers. A duvet, elegantly covered in a thin blue and white striped material, lay on the floor at the side of the bed, with a pillow encased in matching material. The body was on the bed, face down, head slightly turned to one side, he noted professionally, one leg sticking out from the bottom of a rather pretty long night-dress in white brushed cotton, and the arms turned awkwardly at the sides.

'A neighbour found her.'

'What time was this?'

'About eight thirty this morning,' Davidson said, consulting his notebook. 'The woman had taken in a parcel for her around seven thirty and around eight thirty she got to thinking that it would be reasonable to wake her and deliver it. She knew she was in, she said, because she had seen her on her way out to a party at six o'clock yesterday evening and had heard her moving around the flat later, around ten thirty. Thin walls. The neighbour has a key, because Dr Symonds – that's the deceased, here – only stays here the odd night, so the neighbour keeps an eye on the place.'

That accounted for the curiously impersonal air of the whole place, McLeish thought.

'What do we know about the lady here?' He bent to look at the profile outlined against the sheet.

'Dr Judith Symonds. Principal – no, sorry, Warden – of Gladstone College. All-female place over near Heathrow, part of London University. We've rung the college and they're sending someone over to identify her formally. A Dr Hellier.'

'No family?' McLeish asked.

'She's unmarried and there's no kin in London. A sister in Yorkshire.'

'What happened to her, Doc? She choke?'

'You noticed the dribble? No, I don't think so. I'm guessing, but I think she took too much of something and suffocated herself in the pillows. The bathroom cupboard's got an empty bottle of tranquillizers, and there's another empty one by the side of the bed.'

'Suicide?'

'Not necessarily. Like a lot of these middle-aged women under stress, just took too much of it.'

'Was there a note?'

The doctor turned a bright, brown-eyed look of enquiry on Davidson.

'None that we've found.'

McLeish nodded, and stood silently, feeling large and clumsy in the small room. He started to concentrate deliberately, narrowing his attention on the bed, so that soon there was nothing in the room but the woman who lay so quietly dead on her own bed, mouth slightly open, brown hair curling untidily over her forehead. A small woman. He bent closer to look; there were grey hairs among the brown, a web of lines beneath the closed eyes, the skin on the neck was a little crêpey, and there were three deep parallel sets of wrinkles running round the throat. The skin on the back of the hands was finely wrinkled, and dark brown spots clustered just above the base of the thumb. Probably in her mid-fifties, healthy, well-nourished, not fat, but the flesh looked smooth on the bones, and the skin was clear and supple. A woman who'd looked after herself too: her nails had been recently manicured, her legs were waxed, and her toe-nails were painted in the same clear pink varnish. Good-looking, even in death. He stepped back and looked carefully round the bedroom.

'Where is Gladstone College?'

'Not far from Heathrow,' Davidson said. 'About twelve miles. There's a flat with the job, the sister says, and she's got a little house in Yorkshire.'

'Wonder why she kept this flat . . . I mean Heathrow's not far, if you wanted to get back after a party.' He stopped, hearing his own words. 'Maybe she needed to meet someone discreetly.'

'That's about what I reckoned,' Bruce Davidson agreed promptly. 'Looked after herself, you can see, still in business. Having it away with someone she couldn't bring to the college?'

'No sign of anyone else here.' Doc Brougham was sounding disapproving, but Bruce Davidson was infallible in matters like this; his own career as a wildly successful womanizer had given him an eye like a knife for any form of sexual activity.

'So why am I here, Bruce?' he asked. Doc Brougham was an old enough friend of the house to be ignored for these purposes.

'I'm wondering about a boyfriend. Mebbe she topped herself, mebbe it was an accident, mebbe someone gave nature a wee bit of a hand, if he was getting tired of her.'

'No sign of recent sexual intercourse,' Doc Brougham said primly, and Bruce Davidson's mouth opened. McLeish scowled at him to forestall whatever homespun piece of sexual etiquette might be going to emerge to the effect that you didn't give the lass one if you were then going to top her, and returned his consideration to the body. Of course Davidson was right; it was obvious, although he himself might well not have seen the point of the place. Recreational sex, together with other luxuries like sleep, or even time to read a book, had become a dim memory since William's birth. He had managed to make love to his wife a few times in the last few months, but it had not exactly been a pleasure, more of a desperately needed relief for him and, he feared, yet another unexpectedly stressful and disappointing experience for her.

The phone rang, sharply, from the living-room, and Davidson ducked out of the bedroom to pick it up from the desk. 'John, Dr Hellier from Gladstone College is at the station now.'

'Bring him over.' He sent Davidson downstairs to dispatch the driver back and went into the bathroom to inspect that. It was a small, cramped room, with the minimal space between bath, lavatory with its overhead cistern, and wash-basin to allow one person to proceed cautiously, and it clearly proclaimed the flat's 1930s origins. But it had been recently redecorated and was bright and cheerful with a new cork-tiled floor and a pretty wallpaper in a small repeating design with matching curtains. A large fluffy towel overflowed the radiator. What taste and the expenditure of a small amount of money could do had been done. The bathroom cupboard, small, with awkwardly sliding doors to avoid encroaching on the limited space, held perfumed bath oil, scented soap, a large box of Anadin, another of Alka Seltzer, and the empty bottle of Valium that Dr Brougham had noticed. He padded into the kitchen and opened the refrigerator, using plastic gloves. Two bottles of a good white wine, one bottle of champagne, a carton of orange juice, some milk, eggs and butter. Very much the sort of thing his own refrigerator had held in his days as a bachelor, and Bruce Davidson had probably checked before he had done anything else.

McLeish heard the lock of the flat door click and turned in surprise, realizing that he had not heard anyone come upstairs. The answer must be that the stairs were built in concrete and didn't creak. He must remember to tell Davidson, tactfully, in case he had not noticed.

'Carry on, madam, please, straight through, both of you,' he heard Davidson say, warningly, and he went to stand squarely beside Dr Brougham in the middle of the small living-room, waiting to see who was coming through the door. Two people had arrived: a tall woman in her fifties, untidily dressed in a thick coat and heavy fur-boots, a too-bright headscarf round an anxious, thin, clever face, and a man, perceptibly younger than she. He was a square stocky person with a shock of dark hair and a curious roll to his walk as if one leg was slightly shorter than the other, but his handshake was firm and the blue eyes clear in the slightly reddened face, leaving an overall impression of a competent, confident personality, subdued by his surroundings.

'Dr Hellier?' McLeish said hopefully.

'No, no, that is my wife,' the man said, looking amused, leaving Dr Hellier to explain with a slightly mad laugh that she was, of course, a doctor of physics and no use at all in any medical emergency. McLeish watched her quietly, wondering if she was going to manage the task for which she had come.

'Dr Hellier, is it you who is going to be kind enough to try and identify the deceased for us?'

The woman gasped, and looked to her husband who stepped forward protectively.

'My wife is Deputy Warden of the college, Superintendent, but I also know . . . knew . . . Judith Symonds very well. I could do it.'

'That will be fine, sir, if you would prefer. Have you been to this flat before?'

'Yes, I have,' Hellier confirmed promptly. 'Several times, with my wife, and a couple of times by myself to pick up Dr Symonds, or to take her back after a function.' He hesitated, and looked anxiously at the bedroom door. McLeish nodded to Davidson,

31

who opened the door and went in ahead, leaving Dr Brougham to escort Mr Hellier. McLeish stayed with Dr Hellier; there was simply no room in the bedroom. He heard, against the hum of the London traffic passing thirty feet away down the busy shopping street, a stifled noise.

'Oh dear. Yes, I am afraid that is Dr Symonds.' The voice was husky and Hellier could be heard clearing his throat. 'Oh dear. What *happened*?'

'We don't really know yet, sir.'

'She looks as if she were asleep . . . no, she doesn't, does she, not at all. Sorry. It's quite different. She's not there any more.'

That's right, McLeish agreed silently. The person goes away, which is why the dead are not frightening, they're just gone. Even when they die in your arms, five minutes later they've gone, completely. He looked towards Dr Hellier who was standing absolutely still in the centre of the room, a handkerchief pressed to her mouth.

The party emerged from the bedroom. George Hellier was markedly paler and tears were standing in his eyes. His wife went to him. He pulled out a handkerchief and blew his nose thoroughly. 'Oh dear.'

McLeish had his eye on the man's wife. 'Dr Hellier, would you like to see? Would it help you?'

She looked at him, appalled. 'Oh no. Thank you. No.'

McLeish nodded and glanced at Davidson. 'Done everything else here, Bruce?'

Davidson nodded, and turned to Doc Brougham. 'All yours.'

'If you'd like to come with us, Dr and Mr Hellier, we'll go back and have some coffee and you can tell Sergeant Davidson here a bit about the deceased,' McLeish said.

'Yes, thank you. Of course.'

They descended the stairs, and George Hellier stood aside with automatic politeness for a woman heavily burdened with shopping bags, rescuing one neatly as it threatened to fall and deposit its contents. He restored it to her with a constrained smile and whisked on before she could formulate any questions. Brisk, competent and mannerly, even under stress, McLeish observed. Useful man in a women's college.

He decided on the way back that not only did he have no time to sit in on the interview with the Helliers, but that it would be tactless to do so. He had interfered in CID's affairs to the limited extent of going to see the body; no need to go further. Either of the Helliers could be reinterviewed by Davidson's CID seniors if they felt the need, whereas a viewing of the body could not have been postponed. He tidied his desk and made for the canteen with the dual purpose of eating lunch and finding out what was going on. As in any police station, the canteen was where all the conspiracies started and the gossip circulated; it was possible to pick up a great deal just from observing who was eating with whom.

He had piled his tray with food and was just deciding between a table full of uniformed sergeants and a larger table of young constables, when Davidson came up behind him.

'Wait for me, John? I need a hand.'

He waited, while Davidson piled his plate with whatever was closest to him on the counter.

'The Helliers not difficult, were they?' McLeish asked, as Davidson put down his overloaded tray.

'She was a bit upset, so we put her in an office with some coffee. He'd got over it. Very jolly, very easy, everyone's friend; knows the college inside out.' Davidson paused to fork in a mouthful. 'Not at all backward about coming forward, gey eager to assist us in every way.' The grinding Glasgow accent made willingness to co-operate with the police sound a circumstance deeply suspicious in itself. 'No, the problem is the boyfriend. He's a high-up in the Civil Service.'

'Not the Home Office?' McLeish asked, alarmed.

'Department of Education and Science. But they all hang together, don't they?'

McLeish, married into the administrative Civil Service, conceded the point.

'He's a Permanent Secretary, which means Head of the Department, apparently with a handle to his name: Sir Neville Allason. And he wants to come and see us – me – this afternoon.'

'Could he not wait till tomorrow, when, if God wills, Mac-Allister will be here?'

'I tried, John. I told him – or rather I told some young man who claimed to be his private secretary – that there was only me here, but he wasna bothered, he just wanted to talk today. And he's away to some conference in Stockholm the rest of the week.

So, I said to myself, I'd better have a wee word with the Superintendent.' He gazed, bright-eyed and villainous, at McLeish, who was chewing, gloomily, on half-warm baked beans.

'Yes,' he said, swallowing his mouthful. 'That *is* difficult.' He stopped to think, unselfconsciously. 'You have to see this bloke today, if he's that keen,' he decided. He glanced round the canteen: it was nearly 2 p.m. and there were only a few people eating, at a tactful distance from their table. 'Bruce, are you worried about this one? Doc Brougham thinks it's an accidental overdose, doesn't he?'

'Aye. He does. And Mr Hellier thinks the same, but he also made it clear that the lady was under a lot of stress, largely because of the boyfriend.'

'Hellier told you about a boyfriend?'

Bruce nodded. 'I asked where the good lady's husband was, and he told me that there was a divorce about ten years ago, apparently, and there had been a few men since them. Then he blethered a bit, so I just asked him who the current incumbent was, and out it all came.' He caught McLeish's eye. 'I'm summarizing, ye understand.'

'Indeed. Of course he'd not met you before – Hellier, I mean. Sir Neville is coming when?'

'Three o'clock. And he rang us before I had to decide what to do.'

'We don't yet know exactly when she died, of course,' McLeish pointed out.

'We do know she was alive at ten fifteen last night. She was at a party and she dined with Sir Neville and they met the Helliers and another couple, the Taylors, for coffee afterwards. Hellier said Sir Neville took her home.'

'Really?'

'In an official car, with an official driver.'

'So he's got a witness. Not a lot to worry about,' McLeish observed.

Bruce Davidson eyed him sideways. 'Depends what he thinks happened. If he thinks she topped herself because of him, then he's got a problem.' Silence fell between them while McLeish thought.

'You do the interview by yourself, Bruce,' McLeish said,

34

slowly. 'He can be interviewed again, next week, by MacAllister, or whoever, if the autopsy suggests any need. Just keep it routine and you can always call me if you need to. But I'd be a uniformed Super sitting in, and he'll know enough to wonder why me and not a senior CID man, and I don't want to get into *that*.'

Bruce Davidson gave him a look of wounded betrayal, but McLeish was immovable. 'You'll have MacAllister back tomorrow, and this way, you'll have the pleasure of having done the right thing in consulting me about the body but not letting me into the enquiry. You need him to get your recommendation for inspector, remember.'

'I canna wait for the blue uniform, and the wee cap,' Davidson said, with the privilege of long-standing friendship. 'Mebbie I'll be very lucky and get a job in Traffic,' he added bitterly.

At five to three, back in his office, McLeish got up from behind his desk, and padded to the window. As befitted the office of the man with overall responsibility for the station, it overlooked the entrance, offering an excellent view of any visitors. A black Rover was just drawing up at the kerb; nothing happened for two or three minutes, then the driver's door opened and a substantial man in the familiar nondescript uniform of an employee of the government car service got majestically out and opened the back door. McLeish got a good view of his passenger as he paused on his way out and ducked back into the car. Pale blond hair cut close to the head, no sign of thinning at the top; a blunt, solid profile, slightly snub-nosed with high cheekbones. Conventional grey suit, covering a muscular frame, tall – even foreshortened by the angle of vision, he looked six foot or better – and every movement was charged with impatient energy. He watched as the man issued a set of instructions to the driver and to a stocky, dark, much younger man who had got out with him, and thought with interest that it could have been a senior commander and his ADC; there was something crisp and military about the whole performance. As he watched, the senior man suddenly looked up; McLeish had stepped back abruptly before he remembered that he was invisible behind the venetian blind, but not before he had received a vivid impression of a whole personality very much on the *qui vive*.

He worked on until about four o'clock when some instinct alerted him and he went to look out of the window again. The black car was back, demurely (and illegally) sitting on a single yellow line, with the driver at the wheel. As he watched, Sir Neville Allason emerged with Bruce Davidson, shook his hand and darted down the steps. Led with his chin, McLeish thought, interested – head held slightly back. He'd seen rugger players like that: they were the ones who never gave up unless you flattened them unconscious

The winter afternoon was already closing in, and the street lights were shining yellow, but he could not decently go home until six, anxious though he was about his wife. He yielded to curiosity and by dint of some quick footwork managed to arrive at the internal entrance to Fortress CID at the same time as Davidson.

'Give me a cuppa in your office and I'll tell you.' Davidson had never been a man to bear a grudge.

'Yon was the boyfriend all right,' he said, taking off his jacket and relaxing under the yellow lights at the big table to which McLeish had motioned him. 'Made no bones about it. Came to clear himself, and to see if we had any letters.'

'Did he say so?' McLeish said, startled.

'Not in so many words.' Bruce Davidson was amused. 'That's an artist, that one. We were chatting like a couple of mates in a pub by the end, but he was watching his step every inch of the way. A chancer.'

'Tell me more.'

'Well, he said that he had been a close friend of the deceased, with all that that implied. As an opening bid.'

'Unusual.'

'Ye can say *that* again. Then he explained he'd dined with the deceased yesterday, and taken her to her London flat in his official car at about 10.30 p.m. Same driver as he had today. He thought it best to come in and see us straightaway when he heard the news this morning – from Mr Hellier, by the way, I asked. Anyway, I waited on and he said not a lot of people knew of the relationship but probably more people than he thought, that was always the case. Well, he's right there, isn't he?'

And exactly the right approach to adopt with Bruce Davidson, our local expert on sexual misdemeanour and the consequences thereof.

'I'm sorry I wasn't there to see this,' McLeish said truthfully.

'So then he explains to me that his wife did not, of course, know of the relationship.'

'Of course?'

'His words. Verbatim. So I said that we were waiting for an autopsy report.'

'What did he say to *that*?'

'That he had naturally assumed it was an accident, what else? So I asked him where the relationship was at – tactfully, you know – and he said that it was cooling a little. It had been going on for a couple of years, but after all he was married and had been for years, and there had never been any question of that position being changed.' Bruce Davidson took an enormous slug of coffee.

'What do you think, Bruce?'

The shrewd eyes flickered. 'He'd got tired of her. Another lass, I'd guess. So I said that we weren't interested in dragging out things better left, and he went home, not exactly rejoicing. *He* didna think it was suicide, though, and he'd given it consideration. He got a real shock when I asked him if she took Valium regularly.' Bruce grinned across at McLeish. 'Not when he was around, he said. Bit too good an opinion of himself, but a careful bloke. Won't lie where it's better not to.'

'Could he have spiked her drink over dinner?' McLeish asked, and Davidson looked aghast.

'Bloody hell, John, I'll talk to Doc Brougham.'

'It wasn't a serious suggestion,' McLeish said hastily, but the door opened on his protestations.

'I was told I'd find you here,' Doc Brougham said. 'Any chance of a cup of coffee? Thanks. What's the matter?'

'Superintendent McLeish here was wondering if our body this morning could have been fed something nasty at dinner earlier in the evening. What was it, Doc?'

Doc Brougham sat down heavily and produced a notebook. 'An overdose of diazepam. Eight tablets of Valium to you.'

'Not enough to kill her?'

'No. Short of a lethal dose. The standard dose is three a day, and that's what her doctor had prescribed. In fact, she suffocated.

Could have done that all by herself – if you lie on your face with that amount in you and go to sleep, that's what you're risking. What's this about dinner?'

'She had dinner with the boyfriend, as it turns out. When did she die?'

'I couldn't tell you within a couple of hours. But if she took pills with dinner and washed them down with alcohol they would work quicker. They interact. Rigor was fully established by the time I saw her around 10 a.m. That and the condition of the stomach – I'd say she died somewhere between 11 p.m. and 2 a.m., with a bias towards the earlier time.'

'She was dropped home about 10.30 p.m.'

'I'd reckon eleven to twelve o'clock, myself, but I'm not going to be able to swear to it.'

'Could it have been accidental?'

'Oh, yes. If you forgot what you'd taken and you drank too much – and she had – you could easily take extra.' He stretched, wearily. 'My report on this one will follow, but I can go with accident without stretching my conscience too far.' He departed, leaving McLeish and Davidson feeling vaguely anticlimactic.

'Ah, well. Just another busy day here at Notting Dale. Thanks for your help, John.'

'Not at all. And Mac should be back tomorrow – he can sort it out.'

3

Gladstone College was founded in 1873 by Alice Gladstone, a distant cousin of the Prime Minister, to enable women to follow a university career. The college was, from its inception, part of the University of London, but it was only in 1932 that women undergraduates were able to receive degrees awarded by that University. The college has currently 400 undergraduates, 100 graduate students and 32 Fellows. All are women by the terms of the Statutes. The Warden, Dr Judith Symonds, died on 2 January, this year, at the age of fifty-three.

Poor Judith, very young to die, Dame Sarah Murchieson, nine years older, thought with pity. She reminded herself sternly that while she herself had suffered a long, painful and debilitating illness, it was only viral arthritis; she was only sixty-two, and had no reason to suppose that any vital function was permanently impaired. She had never been beautiful; her face was too thin and her skin had the pallor inherited from her Dutch grandfather, which tends to look jaundiced in the winter. Her hair was grey now and looked flat, having lost some of its natural curl. But before this illness she had been a good-looking, small, rounded woman with a flat stomach and neat hips and a lot of male admirers. Nor had she been tired all the time, lacking the energy to spend time and money on herself.

Which was why she was here, at Ellenborough Health Hydro, in February, gazing out at a field of snowdrops, waiting to go to exercises, followed in seemingly random order by steam cabinet, massage, physiotherapy and peat bath. Lunch, such as it was, appeared somewhere in the middle of the schedule, but it was touch and go whether she ate it. After three days in the place she was still falling asleep at odd times and in odd places (the steam cabinet, for heaven's sake, not to say half-way through a yoga class). But all that could be counted as an expected consequence of months of viral illness, topped off with a bad cold. Today, for the first time in months, she did at least seem to be able to concentrate on the printed word. She returned to the papers before her, on the familiar Department of Education and Science headed paper. A short note, really – a crisp five pages with two annexes – but it was still an effort to read it, or to face up to the implications of what was written.

She fished her watch out of the pocket of her towelling bathrobe, gratifyingly thick, pink and fluffy, the gift of her sister, who had, unhesitatingly, vetoed the ancient, pale blue object she had had for the last twenty years. 'You'll look awful, and feel worse,' Mary had said crossly. 'I've been to one of those places and everyone has a new bathrobe – except the men, of course, but there aren't many of those.' Mary had been absolutely right, Sarah acknowledged. Nearly all the women, of whatever shape or conformation, were indeed wearing new, fresh towelling robes, brightly coloured new track suits, and neat, pretty, well-cut exercise clothes. She herself had been in the place for only twenty-four hours before she had thrown away her yellowing tennis shorts and crept into the well-stocked boutique, situated temptingly between the bedrooms and the swimming-pool, to buy herself a leotard, close-fitting and cut high in the leg, and to replace a ten-year-old bathing-suit.

Not everyone had made the same effort, however, she reflected, as a tall, dark young woman appeared in her sight-line among the snowdrops, head bent, hands dug deep into the pockets of a scruffy blue bathrobe which might have been the twin of the one Sarah's sister had vetoed. Indeed, it was rather worse, in as much as it had plainly been made for a slim man, so that in addition to its other defects it gaped unbecomingly over the young woman's substantial bosom. Sarah considered the hunched figure standing in the bright February sun; in a generally sociable atmosphere, the young Mrs McLeish had made no effort at all to join in, eating at a table by herself and answering any direct questions as briefly as possible. Sarah, childless herself but possessed of eight assorted nephews and nieces ranging from sixteen to thirty-five, had made a couple of efforts, but succeeded only in eliciting the information that her name was Francesca, and that she had one baby of the male sex, now six months old, who never slept – this delivered with a scowl sufficiently forbidding to preclude both sympathy and further enquiry. And no one had been brave enough to establish whether the baby's father was anywhere in the picture, or whether he had fled.

Sarah, an experienced aunt, had privately diagnosed a severe case of the sulks brought on by sleepless nights and the shock of having a privileged lifestyle disrupted. Despite the scruffy bathrobe there was something about Mrs McLeish that spoke of having had things hitherto much the way she wanted them. Someone else was looking after a six-month-old boy, so this young woman was not without resources.

Happily, this reflection had occupied enough time to mean that Sarah now needed to go quickly to the exercise class. The first two days she had found herself able to do very little of what she was asked, but she was philosophical about that. Months of struggling with serious viral illness did not leave you able to exercise on level terms with a brisk young woman in her twenties, who took four of these classes a day and apparently spent her evenings in some infinitely more demanding form of aerobic work-out. Which would probably kill me at the moment, Sarah thought, placidly abandoning one of the warm-up exercises which included standing on one foot and waving the other at knee-height.

She glanced sideways to see Mrs McLeish, who had not been in this class before, dressed in a greying ballet leotard and sagging tights. Scarlet with exertion, she was keeping up with the young teacher, every ounce of attention concentrated, watching herself in the long mirrors and making the small adjustments of the good athlete so that her back was straight and her spine pulled up. Sarah, who was herself managing this morning to do about one third of what was indicated, was intrigued by the determination and application evident on the mat next to hers, and resolved to try again to hold a conversation with her. But at the end of the class, Mrs McLeish, dripping with sweat, disappeared to the showers.

Sarah, following her in a leisurely way, decided she would sit at the edge of the pool and cool off before she went into the steam cabinet. She fished out the DES papers, nodding to the

41

pleasant women in bathrobes sitting in the uncomfortable wooden chairs waiting to be called for their next rendezvous with peat bath or physiotherapy, and plunged resolutely into Paragraph 2.

> The college is being run temporarily by the Deputy Warden, Dr Alice Hellier, who is also a university lecturer in physics. She is fifty-seven, and has been put forward as a candidate for the vacant Warden's post. She is being assisted by the Bursar, Lady Trench, who cannot continue in post beyond the end of this term; her husband, Sir Geoffrey Trench QC, is to head the Royal Commission on the future of the judiciary in Botswana, at the invitation of their government, and she naturally wishes to accompany him.

Greatly to everyone's relief, as the DES paper did not say. But the problems appeared to be more fundamental, even, than had so far been disclosed to her.

'The Trustees have commissioned a financial report from Kingsley, Williams which appears as Annexe I.' Not before time; all might well wonder what the Trustees had been doing for the past four years. They had, however, belatedly commissioned not only the financial report (Annexe I) but also a structural survey (Annexe II). Why, Sarah wondered, a structural survey? She read on, fascinated as the answer emerged from the sedate DES drafting. Lord Ryman, one of the most senior Trustees, had been the one to see the necessity. He had spent a January night in one of the college's guest-rooms and, just recovered from the shock of finding that the nearest bathroom was twenty yards away down an echoing chilly corridor, had sustained the further blow of finding water running down the wall into his pillow. This experience had evidently caused him to wonder whether the college was up to date with its repair-and-maintenance programme. It was clear to Sarah that the good Lord, having taken his responsibilities as Trustee fairly lightly up to then, had realized that he might well be open to censure, given the new emphasis on the duties of Trustees, and had hastened to cover his back by urging that the college's physical as well as its financial structure be surveyed and reported upon.

'Dame Sarah, please.'

42

Sarah looked up to find that she was being summoned by a brisk middle-aged lady in a white coat, and could not, for the moment, remember where she was or what she was doing. Then she recalled thankfully that she was being called to the steam cabinet. As she sat, uncomfortably hot and pouring sweat, she contemplated Gladstone College. Horribly fascinating though the papers were, she ought to read no further. Any fool – never mind an experienced administrator – could see that the job was an honour that she should pass up without hesitation, no matter how pressing the entreaties of Sir Neville Allason, Permanent Secretary of the DES. The place was a financial disaster and in a state of physical ruin, and Sarah knew from the academic grapevine that the Fellowship – as seemed increasingly common these days – was rent by schism, or rather by various different schisms: scientists versus arts people; major subjects versus minority subjects; feminists versus The Rest. Even as Sarah recited all this to herself, she could feel the powerful tug of a challenge, the lure of an institution that needed to be rescued and set right.

She looked restlessly at the clock by her side, but found as she turned her head that her glasses had slipped sideways. With her hands imprisoned in the cabinet she tried unavailingly to right them and was about to call for assistance when they were capably set straight on her face for her. She called her thanks, which were received only with a brisk nod of acknowledgement from the taciturn Mrs McLeish, who was standing damp and naked, considering herself critically in the long mirror, settling her spine and pelvic bones and sucking in flabby stomach muscles, so that the hip bones emerged. She sighed, then catching Sarah's interested gaze in the mirror, picked up her towel, scowling, and whisked out of the room.

Sarah grinned to herself, relieved by these signs of humanity, then thankfully found herself released from the cabinet into a shower, then to massage, in the middle of which she fell into a sound sleep. Wakened, apologetically, she pulled on her robe and walked limply along the side of the pool, and down the corridor, being overtaken by Mrs McLeish, her face shuttered and withdrawn under a cap of soaking wet short hair.

Sarah followed her slowly to the reception desk to check for messages, but found it unexpectedly impossible to attract anyone's attention. Both duty receptionists and half a dozen cus-tomers in track suits were gazing out of the wide windows beside the front door at an enormous brown Rolls Royce, from which two men were emerging. The driver was an overweight tough, with shirt bulging over his jeans and an incongruous pony tail; the other was a tall, graceful, dark, young man. He flipped a hand to the driver, and headed for the house with that indefin-able air of a celebrity, confident of his welcome and expecting to be recognized. He came through the door, stopped, and looked round. Elegant, in immaculate jeans with a padded patterned vermilion silk jacket and silk shirt, he was still totally and unmistakably masculine in the peacock clothes.

'Oh God,' a furious voice said from Sarah's right. 'I'm sup-posed to be left *alone*.'

'Frannie,' the young man said, happily walking over to kiss young Mrs McLeish, 'I've come to take you out to lunch. Or eat here, if you'd rather. Darling, what *are* you wearing? Isn't that one of my old ones?' He straightened the collar of the blue bathrobe for her, critically. 'Yes, it is, it's even still got the nametape, see – *P. J. P Wilson*. Come on, get dressed and we'll go and buy you a new one.'

'I don't want a new one. I don't want lunch.'

The onlookers drew in a scandalized breath, but the young man was unmoved by his hostile reception.

'Oh, darling. I've come all the way down specially.'

'Is that her husband?' a middle-aged lady who ran a taxi company said in Sarah's ear.

'No,' Sarah said, suddenly recognizing the situation. 'Her brother, surely?'

The young man had his arm round Mrs MacLeish's shoulder, coaxing her to laugh. As she grinned, reluctantly, the two faces were ridiculously alike.

'First time I've seen her even smile,' Susan Webb said, with interest. 'You're right, he's family. Look at that.'

'That' turned out to be Mrs McLeish, her scowl back in place, agreeing to change into clothes and join her brother for lunch.

'I've got an osteopath at two thirty, so we can't go out,' she was saying crossly, 'but I expect you can con your way into lunch here.'

The young man waved her off and turned a smile on the

receptionist. 'Can we move my sister's appointment to later in the afternoon? You are kind. I am sure lunch here would be delicious, but I promised my brother-in-law, her husband, that I would take her out.'

Ah, Sarah thought, having managed to ascertain from a still dazed receptionist that there were no messages, and proceeding upstairs, so there *is* a husband as well as a loving brother. She changed swiftly, and settled in a corner of the Light Diet room to eat her strictly calorie-controlled soup and salad. And perfectly nice, too, she thought, approvingly; one ate far too much in normal life, or at least in her normal life, which contained too many official lunches. Conscious of the duty owed to communal life, she looked round the room to make sure none of her week's acquaintance was sitting forlornly by themselves and, reassured, fished out her papers again. She knew absolutely that she ought to flee from this particular mess, but she could feel her professional fingers itching. If she took the job, she had a better chance than most of making it work – and perhaps she could at last produce her modest contribution to the debate on the development of European institutions? Anyway, surely it could not hurt to read to the end of this riveting story.

The financial and physical surveys appear as Annexes to this Memorandum [the text stated], but in brief the financial position is that the college has been operating at a deficit of some £300,000 annually over the last five years. The bulk of this deficit (some £150,000) is incurred on the tuition account; the college has found it impossible to charge its students the full cost of tuition now that government funds are increasingly being withdrawn. The residency accounts also show a deficit (£80,000), in as much as the full costs of accommodation are not charged to the students. A further £35,000 deficit appears on the kitchen accounts, and is currently unexplained; it has proved extremely difficult to extract proper cost and revenue streams for the last five years in this area. And finally, no charge for building maintenance has been carried to the accounts, and only the most urgently required items have been carried out. Kingsley, Williams, in reconstructing a profit and loss account at the Trustees' request, have stated that at least £75,000 a year should have been placed to buildings reserve.

To an experienced educational administrator this was all bad news. An imbalance on the tuition account was a familiar problem, and richer colleges at Oxford or Cambridge simply made it up from endowments – but even so, £150,000 was going it a bit. Not making the residency accounts balance was just poor housekeeping; but there was clearly something very far wrong with the kitchen accounts. And the lack of maintenance of the buildings was potentially the most serious problem; Gladstone College was under-endowed, being a nineteenth-century foundation that was limited to women, and it had probably been ignoring maintenance for years in order to make up some of the deficit on the other accounts.

Sarah turned, with anticipation, to the buildings survey, and found her worst fears were not far-reaching enough. Not only did the corridor walls run with damp, but the central heating (installed in 1865) barely generated enough warmth to raise the ambient temperature above freezing, even at an astronomical annual cost. Thirty or more years of inattention to the Victorian slate roofs had let rain soak into the Victorian timber, which over the years had become a home for thriving dry rot above the classic plaster ceiling of Tydeman Hall. It seemed all too likely that the college's student body suffered in winter from bronchitis, pneumonia and TB, in the best medieval style.

In any other society, the conclusion would be that the whole building should be demolished and its prestigious teaching force and highly educated undergraduates distributed to other corners of the University, while the valuable grounds at the western edge of London were sold to hungry developers. The very existence of the Note she was reading made it clear to Sarah that this logic had not obtained. Distinguished alumnae and their husbands in every field of endeavour had been badgering the DES, so that a set of proposals to rescue Gladstone College had been hastily put together and were here modestly presented. Characteristically of the Civil Service as a whole and of the DES in particular, these proposals started with People – in this case, inevitably, Female People. A new Warden was to be found – female, of course; of academic distinction, if possible but above all of proven administrative competence, and from outside the college. Sarah felt her eyebrows lifting to her hairline, but she contented herself with writing neatly in the margin: *Views of existing Fellows?*

A new Bursar, whose academic competence was not stated to be an issue but who ought to be a chartered accountant or near offer, and willing to work for half a professional salary, would also have to be secured. The confident writing faltered at this point, and confessed to some difficulty here, but went on to say that a temporary solution could be arrived at by a secondment from HM Civil Service or from one of the big accountants eager to establish good relations with HMG. A list of the Civil Service possibilities appeared at Annexe III, which was not yet attached but would follow shortly.

Financial provision for the buildings had been made; funds had been extracted from one of the DES Votes – there goes the stationery budget, Sarah thought, irreverently – English Heritage had promised a grant, and the American Friends of Gladstone College had found a million pounds to help. On the tuition side, two new Fellowships had been promised, one by Barclays and one by a Conservative Party supporter who had made his money in a hamburger franchise. Shell was producing two Research Fellowships. An appeal had also been launched, and the alumnae had already produced £400,000 for the buildings.

'Dame Sarah?'

Sarah blinked up at a flustered receptionist carrying a list.

'Dame Sarah, I *wondered* if you would be prepared to have your appointment with Mr Neal – the osteopath – at two thirty rather than four thirty? It's Mrs McLeish, you see. She wanted to change her appointment because her brother came to take her out to lunch.'

Sarah was momentarily annoyed, being absorbed in the affairs of Gladstone College, but decided good-temperedly that it really would not matter when she finished the papers, and that at least the osteopath would be over and done with. She put the papers away and changed back into knickers and a bra to receive the attention of Mr Neal, who at first sight appeared to be about seventeen years old, but on further consideration to be a capable young man in his mid-twenties. He was obviously well accustomed to this disadvantage, and compensated for it with a gruff and slightly pompous manner which evaporated as soon as he started to work. He questioned her carefully about the arthritis, and urged her briskly not to be stoic but to let him know if he hurt her in any way, because viral infection left weaknesses and

47

pain in unexpected places. There was just one nasty moment when he pushed on the base of her spine and she cried out at the unexpected sharp twinge, but he had good hands. When she got carefully off the couch at the end of the session, she felt lighter on her feet and her back felt much more comfortable. 'I'll see you again on Friday,' he said, steadying her. 'You may find you need to go to sleep now,' he added, looking at her carefully.

'I feel splendid,' she assured him gratefully, but once back in her room, the bed looked irresistible and she crawled under the duvet, deciding that ten minutes' sleep would be good for her.

She woke an hour later, thirsty, but relaxed and wanting tea. She pulled on her bathrobe and padded to the dining-room, feeling suddenly wonderfully well, relaxed and clear-eyed. A little cluster of people blocked the corridor, all watching something through the glass of the boutique. Sarah smiled enquiringly at nice Susan Webb. 'It's Mandy, I can't get her to come away.' Susan Webb was torn between embarrassment and amusement.

'Mm, it *is*.' Mandy, a pretty eighteen-year-old who had been sent off with her mother to keep her company, was jittery with excitement. 'It *is* Perry Wilson!' Sarah looked cautiously past Susan Webb, and recognized the young man who had come to collect the ingrate Mrs McLeish at lunchtime. He was laughing at his sister as she paraded in a white bathrobe, looking feminine and pleased with herself, so that Sarah saw an amused and attractive young woman, rather than the sullen, depressed creature of the past four days. 'Right,' he could be heard saying, 'that, then, and the slippers and the bathing-suit; and those two things there. No, shut *up*, Fran, the studio will pay – and you cannot go round looking like that. Don't pack the old ones up, Mrs Weaver' – how had he managed to learn the woman's name? – 'just give them to the deserving poor.' He seized three bags, smiled at the assistant, and collected his sister with his spare hand. A bravura performance – Mrs McLeish was a lucky woman, Sarah thought enviously. A key question occurred to her.

'Who *is* Perry Wilson?' she asked *sotto voce* of Susan Webb.

'He's one of these pop stars they all go for. He's a singer though, too – I mean a real one.'

So he was, Sarah remembered slowly. He had been the top treble at St Joseph's, then a scholar at that odd place in Kent, then a tenor choral scholar at King's, Cambridge, who had turned

48

rock star as a result of a famous recording of a couple of popular ballads. He was about thirty now, probably younger than his sister.

Mandy, unable to bear the tension any longer, had darted into the shop and was standing behind a rack of shirts, anxiety in every muscle.

'I hope she's not going to ask for his autograph,' Susan Webb said, horror-stricken; but Mandy did, and it opened the floodgates. Perry Wilson – an admirable young man, Sarah thought – signed bits of paper, treatment cards, and health hydro brochures with the utmost good temper, for everyone who asked, as he fought a graceful rearguard action towards his car. At the door he kissed his sister, loading the bags into her arms, and vanished into the vast waiting Rolls with a final wave for the attendant fans. Sarah felt like applauding. Even Mrs McLeish was smiling, her chin tucked down on the top of the pile of bags, as she watched him go.

Sarah finally tore herself away from the excited gossip and, deciding to skip the yoga class, changed into tidy clothes and took herself downstairs to sit quietly and finish the DES's careful essay, which was proving irresistible reading. Why was Sir Neville Allason taking such a lot of trouble with this problem? She had been told, somewhere, recently that the late Judith Symonds had been one of his mistresses – but then a lot of people had, including Sarah herself, briefly, twenty-five years ago. The experience, though painful, had not been ultimately damaging, despite the fact that Neville's enthusiasm had waned abruptly after a few months. Sarah, then thirty-seven to his twenty-eight, herself sexually very successful, and having even then decided never to marry, had confronted him calmly, pointing out that to seduce women with every evidence of enthusiasm, then to abandon them after a few months when his wife became suspicious, was not a way to treat grown-up people. Chagrined, he had at first run away, then had managed to return and apologize, so that she and he had remained friends and allies over the long years. The trouble with Neville, of course, was that he was, and always had been, extraordinarily good-looking, and he had never recovered from a severely deprived childhood. He looked like anyone else in the professional middle classes, but inside that good suit was a poor working-class child, son of an alcoholic father, who could not believe his success with middle-class women.

She returned to the papers: why had Neville or the DES not chosen for Warden the obvious candidate, the Acting Warden, Dr Alice Hellier, five years Sarah's junior? Sarah remembered her; married to someone younger than herself – ah yes, the papers had it reported without comment, to George Hellier, no doctorate, the Deputy Bursar. Why, come to that, was *he* not being suggested for the vacant post of Bursar? Here the writer had anticipated her question; the next paragraph explained that it was felt preferable that the Bursar should be a Fellow, which meant, of course, the post had to go to a woman. That explained a good deal: it would always have been difficult for the college to get a good bursar because the job paid far too badly to attract a good accountant. If, in addition, Gladstone College had disqualified half the human race, no wonder their accounts were in such a shambles.

'Dame Sarah.'

She looked up to see the receptionist beaming at her and gesturing towards Neville Allason, who was radiating energy from a corner of the reception counter.

'Sarah, my dear. You look very beautiful, as usual.' He advanced on her and she just managed to bury the papers under a magazine before he arrived at her side.

'It's lovely to see you too, Neville.' She kissed him back, warmed as usual by his compliments, even though she knew they flowed as easily and automatically as any courtier's. She looked carefully into the familiar, narrowed green eyes. 'But what are you doing here?'

'I was on my way to a dinner, at Marshlands. It's a conference on university funding.'

Plausible, Sarah conceded; Marshlands, the seat of many a prestigious conference, was only twenty miles away.

'So I thought, dear Sarah, that I'd come and see you, and to find out if you had had time to glance at the papers we sent you, and if there was anything you wanted to ask.' He beamed at her, bouncing with health and charm. But his hair no longer has any red in it, she thought, with a pang.

'I'm so sorry, Neville, I've not yet been able to summon any concentration,' she lied, out of long experience in dealing with this particular bulldozer. 'I've just flopped since I've been here.'

'Oh.' He looked openly and charmingly disappointed, and Sarah ruthlessly ignored the impulse to give him something to make him happy. Far too many women had wanted to give Neville Allason a present when he looked like that, and some of them, presumably including his wife, had come to understand that there was no way of giving him enough. He was always in need of something more: no doubt a legacy of that legendarily awful upbringing.

He glanced out of the window quickly, and she followed his eye. A black car with a government number plate was parked, insecurely, in the crowded car-park. Two people, a driver in the uniform of the government car service, and a woman with long dark hair blowing in the cold February breeze, were walking round it.

'One of your staff, Neville?' Permanent Secretaries in the big Departments typically had a private office, these days, with a high-flyer running it.

'No.' He lifted his chin a little, a gesture deeply familiar to her, used typically when he was in an awkward corner. 'No. That is a fellow guest at this dinner tonight, Dr Louise Taylor. I offered her a ride down, explaining that I would have to stop for a few minutes.'

'Bring her in,' Sarah suggested, delighted to have found a diversion. 'She looks cold.'

'She *could* just have stayed in the car, which is perfectly warm.' He looked back at her, defensively. 'Louise is a very distinguished historian, but she is a Fellow of Gladstone. I thought you might feel unduly pressurized if I forced her on you at this juncture.'

'It will not embarrass me, Neville, if you bring her out of the cold,' Sarah said crisply. 'I am neither more nor less likely to consider this offer seriously just because I have met another of the Fellows. I know three of them already.'

'Right. Well, I will, when I have handed over the last bits of paper.' He had always been good-tempered about accepting the inevitable; it was one of his many charms.

'Annexe III,' he announced briskly, sitting down, the long

hands busy in his briefcase. 'List of women, possibles for Bursar, none of whom I actually know. One looks very good, on paper.'

'Just tell me *one* thing, Neville – why me? Why not the obvious internal candidate?'

'Alice Hellier, the Acting Warden? She's very much wrapped up in her subject, which is physics, and not perceived to have . . . well . . . enough *breadth*. Not a high profile like you, darling.'

Sarah, who had been a minor celebrity since she had joined the Home Office in her mid-twenties, following five years in the Dutch resistance movement, inclined her head in acknowledgement. She rarely thought, or spoke, of her days as a young woman, but those wartime years in occupied Holland with her mother's family, helping to run a lifeline for Allied prisoners as well as resistance workers, had given her a disregard for inessentials which had stood her in good stead in the post-war Home Office. The assistance of her Scots father, who had ended his distinguished academic career as Professor of Greek at Aberdeen, had helped as well.

Neville Allason shuffled the papers together, as quick-moving and concentrated as he had been when they were lovers years ago. 'I'll ask Dr Taylor in for a minute, just to say hello, then we mustn't take any more of your time.'

'Or you'll risk missing drinks at Marshlands.'

'There is that.' He went to the door and made vigorous gestures indicating that his passenger should join them. She waved back, and came across the gravel, a small, slim young woman, with startling blue eyes against the black hair.

'Dame Sarah, this is Dr Taylor,' Neville announced.

'Oh, this does look comfortable,' Louise Taylor said enviously, opening up a black cloak and looking round the carefully arranged chintz sofas, the log fire and the brand-new glossy magazines. 'Much nicer than drafty Marshlands.'

Louise Taylor was preparing to brave chilly Marshlands Hall in low-cut dark blue silk, which clung to an excellent bosom and stopped well short of her knees. Sarah considered her with interest, feeling sneakingly glad of her new track suit and freshly done hair. A beauty, and intelligence crackling in every movement: no wonder Neville was charmed.

'You had arthritis, Neville was telling me?' Louise Taylor said, with easy friendliness; and Sarah explained that it was finally going away, and expressed condolences on the death of Gladstone's Warden.

'Yes, poor Judith, we were all so sorry,' Louise Taylor said conventionally. 'It is a very difficult job at the moment, being Warden there. And when a women's college is in difficulties, all the usual timid souls feel we should admit men.'

'You are against mixiing the college?'

'Yes, I am.' Louise Taylor paused and considered, but only, Sarah saw, the better to state what she meant, not to consider her audience's possible views. 'I am supported in this conviction by the more successful Fellows. Those in the lead in their field.'

'This is true also of the scientists?'

Louise Taylor looked suddenly furiously impatient and also extremely beautiful. 'They are a special case. Everywhere is short of good people in science, particularly in physics, and they don't understand that opening the college to men wouldn't help at all.'

'At the margins, surely?' Sarah said.

'Not enough to make it worth while accepting the other consequences,' Louise Taylor said firmly, and started to pull her cloak back round her, with an elaborately casual helping hand from Neville Allason. Charmed he was, Sarah observed – but surely Louise Taylor must be twenty years too young for him, cautious creature that he was?

She took them to the door, and returned Neville's accustomed goodbye kiss, just seeing over his shoulder the young Mrs McLeish motionless by the recepion desk, silently watching them.

She waved her visitors off, walked back, and smiled cautiously at Mrs McLeish, who was looking quite different in a well-cut new blue track suit and brilliant white sneakers, her hair washed and combed. She was staring after Neville Allason with fierce longing, and Sarah sighed inwardly.

'That's a government car outside,' Mrs McLeish said intently, in the tones of one announcing the appearance of the Holy Grail. 'And that chap – faded golden oldie – was carrying a government briefcase,' she added accusingly.

Sarah, trying not to choke on the description, said demurely that the man was a friend and a senior civil servant. The yearning look intensified as Mrs McLeish watched the black car's tail-lights flicker out of sight behind the dense evergreens lining the drive.

53

'Is your husband also a civil servant?' Sarah ventured, when even the sound of the departing car had vanished.

'He's a policeman.' Mrs McLeish was still looking longingly after the car.

Now *that*, Sarah thought crossly, was gratuitous. However little this young woman was prepared to reveal about herself, it was simply insulting to ask Sarah to believe that she was married into the beat, as it were. She compressed her lips and lifted the magazines under which she had hidden her papers.

'He is currently a superintendent at Notting Dale. He was a graduate entry and has spent all his career until now in the CID, but he's doing a stint in the uniformed branch.' Mrs McLeish was perched on the other end of the sofa, restlessly kicking its side.

'Ah,' Sarah said, somewhat mollified.

'*I'm* a civil servant, or was, until the baby.'

'Which Department?'

'Trade and Industry. I was a Principal.' The tone was remarkably final.

'Are you on maternity leave?' Sarah asked cautiously.

'Technically.' Mrs McLeish was not looking at her but was staring at her own hands, seeing defeat there. 'I went back after four months, but I couldn't carry on. The baby – William – does not sleep. Well, he does, but only for a couple of hours, and I wake at a touch, I always did. Then I can't get back to sleep.' She drew a long, despairing breath. 'So when I went back to the Department, I couldn't stay awake at all. I fell asleep – it was utterly uncontrollable – in the front row of the Secretary's briefing. They say I can come back when they find a part-time job for me, doubtless involving counting paper clips.'

'Did the baby sleep better when you stopped work?'

'No. Worse. So by popular vote I was sent here and my brother Perry – well, you saw him – has paid for an appallingly expensive nurse for ten days to help my Mum look after William.'

'And how is that going?' Sarah asked cautiously.

'The bloody child is sleeping for six hours at a time in the night. She must be doping him. Or Mum is.' She looked accusingly at Sarah. 'Various health visitors' – Mrs McLeish made it sound like a group of Hitler's closest associates – 'had suggested to Mum and to John – my husband – that it was all my fault, that William cried because *I* was in a fuss. It seems they may even have been right.' She kicked viciously at the edge of the sofa. Sarah tried to think how to proceed.

'Did you not have someone to help after he was born?'

'My mother, my mother-in-law, my daily help . . . many health visitors.'

'Not a nanny?'

'No.' There was a long, reluctant pause. 'I couldn't get my head round it. I didn't want someone living in, I have little enough of John as it is. But I must get my act together. This is ridiculous, even I can see it is – he's only a baby, for God's sake, not a monster.'

'I have no children, but I can imagine that one could feel totally invaded by a crying baby.'

'Yes.' Mrs McLeish stared out into the darkness, then turned to her in acknowledgement. 'That's how it feels . . . as if I have been invaded. But after even four nights' sleep I begin to feel human again.'

'And after some new clothes,' Sarah pointed out, feeling something was due to the brother who had paid for all this, and had taken time to visit and coax his sister out.

The young woman smiled. 'He's a good brother – much of the time. But I have four of them, all younger and all dependent on me since we were little. To find myself with a crying male baby was a blow, I have to say. Still, he could have been twins – two of my brothers are.' She got up decisively. 'I must go and eat. Perry has bullied me into the main dining-room, because he says I need to lose flab not weight. Nothing like a brother to tell you the odds. You are sticking it out on delicious rhubarb?'

She was indeed good-looking, now that the worst of the exhaustion had gone, Sarah thought, amused. 'Yes,' she confirmed. 'So I'll see you tomorrow, if not later tonight? My name is Sarah Murchieson, by the way.'

'I had got that, Dame Sarah. I've not been unconscious, just miserable.' She had real charm when she smiled. 'I'll see you tomorrow. At the moment I just fall asleep at eight o'clock, it's such a luxury without the baby.' She rose to go, flipping a hand in farewell.

Sarah watched her regretfully. Oh well, by tomorrow she, too, would be in the dining-room, having shed all the excess weight she needed to lose. In the mean time she could read the extra papers Neville had brought down with him. She picked up Annexe III: possible candidates for Bursar. It was a list of three only, their CVs attached at back. The first was a woman in her late forties, to be seconded from the Department of Defence; she had good project accounting experience but all too clearly an impossible personality. Then came a chief clerk from the statistics branch of the Treasury, aged fifty-five, not bad experience but a poor health record. And finally there was a Principal from the DTI, with a high-flyer's record of top policy jobs and a spell in Washington, who had spent the last few years engaged in deciding which ailing companies should receive regional selective assistance and which should be left to perish. She had no conventional accountancy training but was a whizz at figures, apparently.

This rising star, who sounded to be ahead of the other two by some distance, had not yet been consulted as to her willingness to accept the appointment, but was assumed to be available, being desperate for a high-quality part-time job to enable her to cope with the demands of a new baby. With a mounting sense of disbelief, Sarah read the personal note attached by the Principal Establishment Officer at the DTI.

'Francesca is an extremely able, conscientious and talented civil servant,' he had written, in a crabbed hand. 'She is having a difficult time in a new marriage – her second – to John McLeish, currently a superintendent in the Metropolitan Police Force. He, too, is a high-flyer, and is expected to reach the top ranks of that force. With a new baby, now six months old, she is seeking part-time work to enable her to settle in this situation.' There was a two-line gap, as if the writer had hesitated. 'She is my god-daughter, the eldest child of a family of five; her father died young after a long illness. She is not everyone's cup of tea; you would need to interview.'

4

Alice Hellier, Acting Warden of Gladstone College, sat in her room and gazed out on the college grounds, at lawns, still looking unkempt and lifeless after the snow, and at the high beech trees a good hundred yards beyond, still leafless, but just beginning to look fuzzy. The one splash of colour in the landscape on this blowy April day was the camellia bed, where white, pink and deep red bloomed side by side.

'May I come in?'

'Darling, of course.' Alice smiled at her husband, warmed as usual by his presence. She still secretly could not believe her good fortune in having found him, when she had resigned herself to not marrying. 'I'm not looking forward to this morning.'

'I know this is very difficult for you.' Her husband's voice was warm with sympathy and Alice surveyed him with affection. He was looking older, she thought with a pang; for years he had seemed to her inexhaustibly young, but he was forty-seven this year. His thick hair showed no signs of thinning, but it was much greyer suddenly, and the lines round his eyes and mouth were deeper.

'Personally, I hope Sarah Murchieson, having been given this job over my head, will feel able to get on with modernizing this place,' she said savagely. 'It is ridiculous that we had to import this chit from the Civil Service as Bursar, when you are here.'

George looked over at her with a smile. 'We've always known I probably wouldn't get past Deputy Bursar here, darling. I took the job because of you, but I'm not an accountant.'

'Neither is this girl.'

'No, but she's used to working with accounts, and she's got

one other great asset.' His wife looked at him enquiringly. 'She's new. She can close the books on last year's mess and start again. If she wants to make her name – and I'm sure she does – the thing to do is to forget about the past and concentrate on getting us on a straight path for the future. That's the way to get the money in.'

'Yes, that's true. If the government is not going to support higher education then we depend on industrial people, who aren't going to give money if they think we are incompetent financially. As we are, or have been – except in your area, darling.'

'Oh, I've made my share of mistakes.' George was looking tired, Alice realized, alarmed as he lit a cigarette.

'*You've* managed very well though, darling,' he was saying, hunting for the ashtray she kept for him. 'Two new Research Fellowships, quite out of the blue, with your name on them.'

'Yes, that was enormously helpful.' She looked at him carefully, but he was watching something in the garden outside. 'It made the difference between being able to keep my two best graduates and having to see them go elsewhere. And I can get perhaps eight hours' teaching out of the pair of them. We would have had to cut right back on girls wanting to read physics, without them.'

Her husband had switched his attention from the lawn back to her. 'Very lucky.'

'No,' she said reluctantly. 'The department here is quite good enough to get funding for fellowships in its own right, at any time. I am afraid, however, that, unfair as it is, Shell at least would have given theirs to UCL, without some intervention from somewhere.'

'You didn't tell me that.'

'Well, I'm afraid it's true. Neville Allason put them my way. To sweeten me for not getting Warden.' Her mouth twisted uncontrollably, and George Hellier reached across the desk and took her hands in his.

'Darling,' she said, close to tears, 'I'll get over it. At least I won't have to feel this department is evaporating – and I may even be here when Sarah Murchieson finds the job too much for her.'

*

Ten miles away, Sarah Murchieson and Francesca were stuck in a traffic jam. Francesca was driving them, in a large Volvo Estate. They had been seen off by Superintendent John McLeish and the paragon Norland nanny, who had been found by Francesca's brother Perry. Sarah, still not quite on easy terms with her formidable recruit, had not felt able to ask how Francesca's husband was receiving all this. She had liked the look of John McLeish and found him touching; he was enormously protective of his wife, and was obviously delighted by the baby, William, his huge hands gently cradling the small creature who had gone promptly to sleep. She hoped that he was simply grateful to anyone who had contributed to restoring his wife to health and strength. There was no sign of the strained, angry, over-weight, young woman she had first seen at the health hydro; Francesca, competently manoeuvring the big car through traffic, was bright-eyed, properly rested, tidily dressed, and obviously looking forward to every problem Gladstone College could provide.

'I am so grateful to you, Sarah,' she was saying. 'This job is perfect: not full-time, so I can get home and see William. God knows what we'll do when the wonderful Caroline is returned to her training college, but I guess we'll just order up another one. But William goes to *sleep* for her!'

Sarah murmured some acknowledgement, and they drove on in companionable silence. It had been a hectic few weeks since they had first encountered each other. Francesca had been so obviously the best candidate on offer for Bursar that Sarah had approached her on the day before they were both due to leave Ellenborough Health Hydro. She had watched as Francesca absorbed, with the speed of the starving, every word she was told about the college. 'Let me look at the numbers,' she had said, urgently stretching out both hands for the draft accounts that had been delivered by special DES messenger. 'That way I'll know the worst.'

By the next day she had extracted the key data from the general mess, and had laid before Sarah a very much clearer analysis than the DES accountants had produced. She had taken Sarah through it, breaking off only as one of them was summoned for a final massage, or to be weighed off. When she completed her explanation, she handed back the files, slowly and reluctantly.

'I could start very soon. If you wanted me,' she had said boldly.

Sarah, who had been formulating a careful invitation to her to see the college, sat up sharply.

'Are you sure you want it, Francesca? This is a bed of nails – worse than I realized before you went through the figures. I'm not sure that *I'm* going to take the job.'

'Please. You must. And please, please have me as Bursar.'

Sarah gazed at her, reminded strongly of a labrador puppy that she had owned years ago. 'You can't say I didn't warn you.'

'You gave me the numbers – what more could I want? Am I on, then?'

'Yes, you are. And as soon as possible.'

They had solemnly shaken hands, and Sarah had sat later, laughing aloud, at her bedroom window, watching Francesca run round the field with the snowdrops, leaping into the air. Whatever was to happen in the future, she thought, she was fortunate to have found someone so overjoyed at being invited to wade into the terrible mess that lay before them.

'Your husband was asking me about my predecessor,' she said now, to Francesca's profile.

'He met her, you see. When she was dead.'

'What?'

'Sorry. You can depend on me not to say that publicly. I thought you knew. The flat where Dr Symonds died is in his manor, and he got hauled out to take a look at her. Did he not say?'

'I think he was just going to,' Sarah said, in recollection. 'Only the nanny came in to take William.'

'Story of our lives at the moment. We never finish a conversation – either William cries or a nanny arrives.'

Sarah hesitated. 'Did your husband . . . John . . . did the police think there was anything suspicious about Dr Symonds's death?'

'No. But they always take a reserved view of people found dead in bed. There are lots of murders that go undetected – I mean, where no one ever realizes it's murder.' She glanced at Sarah. 'John didn't tell me about it at the time, and he wouldn't have to this day, if I hadn't been chattering away about you and the college. He said they had decided that it was possibly suicide, but more probably an accident. She had taken an overdose, but

60

it could easily have been a mistake, so they were happy with a coroner's verdict of "accidental death".'

Sarah wondered crossly whether the police were prone to decide that women in their fifties had reached an age where muddles over pills were inevitable. John McLeish, she decided on her brief acquaintance with him, did not look like a man prone to patronizing generalizations about older women, so his view had presumably been that Judith Symonds had committed suicide. He must equally have been sure that it was something other than the difficulties of Gladstone College which had motivated her, or he would otherwise hardly have acquiesced so cheerfully in his newly recovered wife's decision to join the college.

'Sarah, do I turn left here?'

'Yes, and left again.'

The big car swung neatly to a halt outside large iron gates in a high brick wall. Through the nineteenth-century ironwork green lawns and trees could be seen. The distant scream of a jet could be heard and the vapour trail was clear in the bright blue wintry sky.

Sarah explained their presence to the man on the gate, who, doubtfully and grudgingly, and after much consultation with a battered piece of paper, decided to admit them.

'Well, *he* can go, for a start,' Francesca said, wincing as the car took a bump a little too fast.

'Francesca, we have to proceed carefully.'

'We don't have time to do that, Sarah. This business is right on the edge of receivership. If someone doesn't do something fast, it'll go under. Sir Neville made that perfectly clear when he kindly gave me lunch.' She fell silent, manoeuvring the car slowly over the series of bumps put there to control traffic speed, thinking about the lunch with Neville Allason. It had been three weeks ago and she had dressed carefully, managing to squeeze into a plain grey suit and white blouse in which she hoped she managed to look like a senior civil servant, rather than a mother. She was extremely anxious; Sarah had made it clear that her appointment would have to be approved by the DES as well as her home Department. The latter had been easy, with a godfather in place at the top of the DTI, but the DES could be very difficult indeed. This appointment was obviously of particular significance; the fact that she was god-daughter to a senior civil servant

61

would not normally have meant she was interviewed by the head of another Department. In fact, the more she thought about it, the more peculiar it appeared and the more anxious she became. She had arrived at a small, forbiddingly smart French restaurant, Le Jardin, in a state of ill-concealed panic; she needed this job and she had not much idea how to cope with Sir Neville Allason KCB.

Her alarm had subsided rapidly from the moment when the handsome man with the faded blond hair had slid neatly off a stool at the bar, beaming at her. He had exerted himself to put her at her ease, accepting without demur her refusal of alcohol and plying her with olives, bread and the menu. He was known here, she observed; the head waiter was looking after them with careful deference which none the less attracted attention from the other lunchers. They finished their first course, chatting about current trivia, and Francesca managed to make him laugh aloud with her description of life at Ellenborough Hydro.

'Sarah did tell me a bit about it, but I suppose I didn't believe it,' he said, pouring her some more mineral water. 'Now. We need to talk about this job and how it can be done, or we shall find ourselves running out of time. You're not an accountant, of course.'

Francesca had swallowed the last of the bread and taken a sip of water and a deep breath. 'No. But I am experienced at dealing with the finances of businesses in a mess. Where the accounts are not, in fact, representative or helpful, as I know is the case at Gladstone. I've seen the draft accounts.'

'Which tell you not very much?'

'That's right. Only that the place is in chaos and making losses. But I do know where to start.'

'Where is that?'

'With the auditors, who are accountants. They'll tell me the general area in which the bodies are buried – and what sort they are. And considering the amount of money they've had out of the college over the years, they can lend me a couple of people to help for a few days. Or the people who did the financial report will.'

Sir Neville looked amused. 'On that basis I imagine the auditors will volunteer.'

'So do I.'

They grinned at each other, and Francesca, heartened by this exchange, decided to risk some of her own questions.

'How did the place get into such a mess?' She watched, interested, as the man poured himself some more water and fidgeted with his napkin. He looked up and met her enquiring gaze.

'I honestly do not know.'

Francesca, a policeman's wife, registered the use of the word 'honestly'. Along with 'frankly' and 'truthfully' it was a warning signal. 'I did not know Dr Symonds,' she said, neutrally.

'I knew her quite well and I confess I am surprised that the college finances are in such disarray. She did not have a good Bursar, of course.' Neville Allason was fidgeting again.

'Did you have a hand in appointing her?' The green eyes narrowed and she realized, rattled, that lulled by the atmosphere of easy communication between them, she had asked a question too far.

'No,' he said, recovering. 'No, I was still in the Treasury, not that I would necessarily have been consulted anyway. I met her, oh a year or so after her appointment. And no, before you ask, she did not ask me for help until just before she . . . died.'

'Sorry,' Francesca said, blushing. 'I guess I was trying to learn from someone else's experience.'

He looked at her indulgently. 'Well, quite right. And I cannot too strongly emphasize, Francesca, how important your and Sarah's jobs are. This is a mess, and one peculiarly difficult to explain to a government not fundamentally sympathetic to a very privileged corner of higher education.'

'Oh, I do see that.' Francesca was eager to make amends. 'Sell Gladstone and you could have a new polytechnic, or near offer.'

'Yes.'

She had not quite got the point, she understood, and considered him as he received their main course. 'It is thought', he said carefully, when the waiters had departed, 'that the DES is in general so prejudiced in favour of the older universities that it is prone to ignore truly staggering lapses of administrative competence.'

'And the situation at Gladstone is felt to prove the point.' Francesca had also had a sound training in the use of the Civil Service passive.

'That's right. So, if we can't pull this one round it will be a serious blow.'

To Sir Neville Allason as well as to the Department of which he was head, Francesca understood, with a surge of confidence. She swallowed her forkful of delicious fish, and speared a potato.

'If you are rescuing a disaster you have to go very fast and ignore all the screams of rage,' she said, watching him.

He looked back at her, alert, the personality fully engaged.

'*Yes*. Right. Absolutely, and as I have told Sarah, you will have my – our – full support. Where we can.'

The caveat was added conscientiously and without conviction, and Francesca thought about him as she worked her way through the cooling fish. Sir Neville himself had a lot riding on this particular rescue, that was clear. He must for some reason feel himself vulnerable. She looked up to find the green eyes flick away from her. For all he looked so young he was fifty-four and if he was to get the final step, Secretary to the Cabinet, head of all the other Permanent Secretaries, he had to get out of the DES without a stain on his record and back into the Cabinet Office or Treasury inside the next two years. 'He was lucky to get Permanent Secretary when he did,' her godfather, older and relaxed about his own future, had said. 'He's got enemies, but he was on the spot when James Finer died in harness so suddenly. But he could get the top job, he'll just have to hurry. And keep his nose clean.'

She smiled at Sir Neville and wondered if she had done enough to convince him that she was the person who, along with Dame Sarah, could be relied on to get his chestnuts out of the fire. 'In the medium term, Sir Neville, the college will need a real bursar – I mean, not a secondee. A proper chartered accountant, who is going to want paying properly.'

'That is absolutely true. But I can't do that in a hurry.' He looked at her carefully and she waited, heart pounding. 'You would be prepared to do two years?'

'Yes. Beyond that my own lot might get restive, and I have a career to consider.'

'Doing this one well will do you nothing but good,' he said earnestly, and she grinned at him.

'I do know. Am I on?'

'Yes.'

They surveyed each other across the table and she reached across with her right hand. 'Deal.'

He was disconcerted, but only for a moment, and she gave him full marks.

'Deal,' he said, solemnly shaking her hand. 'Now, what do you want for pudding? And do you operate as Francesca Wilson or are you using your married name?'

'Francesca Wilson. The name I was born with.'

'I should have known,' he said, straightfaced, and they had both laughed.

Francesca, arriving at the end of her recollections, discovered that they were at the porter's lodge.

'Now, let us find someone to help carry these files,' Sarah said briskly. 'Ah, good morning, Dr Taylor. I think you were at a conference when Miss Wilson visited the college?'

Louise Taylor heaved her briefcase out of the bicycle basket and came over to meet Francesca, presenting Sarah with an interesting contrast in type. Beside Louise Taylor's dark, petite neatness, Francesca looked like a refugee from the national hockey team, being a good five inches taller and a couple of stone heavier. Louise Taylor was also the more finished product, neatly made, tidy and contained. Francesca still looked as if she had not quite stopped growing. But both young women were formidable personalities, and much the same age, Francesca being thirty-four and Louise thirty-five, as Sarah knew from the briefing.

'Is there someone who could help carry all this kit to our offices, or do we make several voyages?' Francesca was saying, the first civilities concluded.

'We are dependent on volunteer labour here. Let me see if I can find some student help.' Louise Taylor lifted a hand lazily to a group of young women gathered, covertly watching, at the steps, and two of them came eagerly over to her.

'Dawn Jacobson and Susan Elias, Warden. Two of my pupils. Dawn, Susan, we need some help unloading the Warden, as it were. And our new Bursar, Francesca Wilson, who, I am sure, will tell you where things are to go.'

Louise Taylor watched as Francesca loaded up Dawn, Susan, and several others who had joined the group. Francesca picked

65

up the remaining load herself, wedging her chin on the top of the files, leaving Louise, unencumbered except for a briefcase, to lead Sarah to her office. A very neat demonstration of power for the alien visitors, Sarah thought, watching Francesca scowl as she, too, registered the point.

Once they had reached her office, Sarah, as befitted a Warden, thanked the undergraduate porters, and enquired names and subjects. All five were historians and pupils of Louise Taylor's, this unusual concentration of one subject being explained by the fact that they were her second-year supervision group, who had just had their weekly session with her. The five were a mixed bag: Dawn Jacobson was a beauty, with long, fine, pale blonde hair, ex-Cheltenham; Susan Elias was a dark, nervous Jewish girl from North London Collegiate School; Petra Greenwood, dark and plump, came from a comprehensive in Wales; Jenny Martin was a tall red-headed Scot from Edinburgh; and Celia O'Brien a green-eyed product of St Aloysius in north London. But they were all easy-mannered, answering Sarah's questions readily as they placed files in piles to her direction.

Francesca had withdrawn into the Bursary, leaving Sarah free to talk and to observe Louise Taylor's relationship with her students. She was obviously popular with them, treating them in a brisk, sisterly way as equals, and Sarah noted that this was one Fellow of Gladstone whose allegiance – or at least acquiescence – she would have to ensure.

'Thank you for your help,' Sarah said, as Louise Taylor detached herself. 'A very pleasant group of students.'

'Yes. And much more at ease with themselves and intellectually confident than when they arrived.' Louise Taylor paused. 'Well, Dawn Jacobson was always confident. Cheltenham does that if you are clever enough. But the others have come on a lot; Susan Elias had been much undermined by a public school sixth form, where the girls are treated as bimbos because the boys are threatened by them. Celia O'Brien was educated by nuns, and Petra Greenwood by the Welsh where she was one of the very few girls to survive the boys' teasing. Even the cleverest adolescent girl gets discouraged by the games adolescent boys play. Here, of course, they don't have to put up with all that.'

No, indeed, Sarah thought, amused and irritated by Louise

Taylor's losing not a moment before declaring on which side of the debate she stood.

'Where was the Scot – Jenny – at school?' Francesca had appeared from the Bursary, scenting battle.

'A mixed Scottish school,' Louise Taylor acknowledged the point promptly. 'But the Scots have a long tradition of educating women, and the girls there seem to survive teenage dominant-male behaviour rather better.'

Sarah watched Francesca think about teenage males. 'Were you the eldest, Francesca?' she asked, knowing the answer.

'Yes. I have four younger brothers,' she explained for Louise's benefit, 'but even allowing for that, I do not recognize these dominant teenage males. When I was young, I and all the girls I knew were infinitely more competent than the boys, who never seemed to know how to work and were always in some ghastly muddle, usually having to do with money or the motor car.'

Louise Taylor bent her full attention on Francesca. 'But none the less, boys are trained to self-assertion, and they band together very efficiently to impose their values and put down any young woman who threatens them.'

'Mm.' Francesca sounded unconvinced. Sarah watched, amused, as her Bursar worked out how to engage with this unexpectedly capable and competitive colleague. 'Do you have children, Dr Taylor?' she asked finally.

'Louise, please. Two, one of three, one of four.'

'Goodness,' Francesca said, daunted.

'Goodness had nothing to do with it.'

Francesca, taken by surprise, burst out laughing, and the atmosphere lightened at once. Remembering where she was, she gave Sarah an apologetic look as she started to struggle out of the sofa into which she had incautiously sunk.

'This'll have to go too,' she said cheerfully. 'Your visitors will stay for ever, trapped in this thing's embrace. You need something with an upright back and a hard seat, along the lines of a pew.'

Louise Taylor agreed, laughing. 'And I need my coffee-break. Do you have time, Francesca, or ought you to start reforming our finances at once?'

'Let me just tell the Bursary where I have gone.'

They retreated from Sarah's room to Louise Taylor's small

room, which overlooked the car-park rather than the green college lawns.

'It will take you no time at all to discover that room allocation is one of the most disputed areas in this college. I am in a poor negotiating position, since I do not live in the college and have only been here for five years.' Louise Taylor handed her a sizeable mug.

'I was thinking that five people and you in this room must be a squash.'

'It is, it is! And some of my supervisions are six or seven. I teach for UCL; we exchange two hours of me for two hours' supervision in physics and chemistry for our students.' Louise caught Francesca's enquiring look. 'Well, you were at Newnham, weren't you? It's the same infinitely complicated network of obligations, and exchanges – two hours of physics offered in exchange for an hour of Greek and another of geography. It isn't even a two-way system; here we are involved with two other colleges, and occasionally – if we have a student doing, say, chemical engineering – we have to involve a third. The three weeks planning it all before the autumn term are a nightmare.'

'I didn't think about that. I *was* indeed at Newnham, and someone there must have had to take young men from St Catherine's or Trinity Hall in "payment" for me, as it were. We had no law dons, so I was never taught in Newnham at all.' Francesca put her cup down, struck by a sudden, belated realization. 'I must have been the most frightful nuisance. I was due to read classics, where Newnham had plenty of people, but decided at the last possible moment – a week before term began – to read law.'

'Oh, you would have caused a major upheaval. Wretched junior Fellows would have had to supervise some lout from St Catherine's, probably for geography, so you could be inserted into the system. What did you need – four hours a week?'

'About that.' Francesca was still brooding on the past. 'None of those women ever as much as hinted to me that I had been a nuisance, much less tried to discourage me, although I was an exhibitioner in classics.'

'Well, that's because they were women, and concerned to give you the best possible chance to do what you wanted to do. The story would have been quite different if it had been men you were dealing with.'

'Men would have been just as awkward with a *boy* who wanted to do something out of the way. It certainly seemed to me that all-male schools ran for the convenience of the institution not the boy. Two out of my four brothers are singers of real ability, and not a term went past, once they were out of choir school, without Mum or me having to insist that Peregrine or Tristram could *not* just as well do geography and first-team Rugby, rather than piano and singing. Those teachers, placed in a Cambridge college, would have behaved just the same.'

Louise laughed, conceding the point. 'But young men are trained to dominance. At eighteen they would feel they had to get their own way, whereas young women are brought up to feel that they have no right to insist.'

'In short, Dr Taylor, you are an opponent of mixing the college,' Francesca said in the bright, enquiring idiot tones of breakfast TV.

'To the last barricade, if that is going to be necessary.' Louise was amused but undeflected.

'Cor Christmas, Louise, we've got enough on our hands here without starting that fight. I've got enough to do with the basics, like persuading people to keep invoices, and taming your outside contractors, including the caterers. Let us just lop off the worst excesses and get the roof debugged and nailed back on the building before we worry about the fancy stuff.'

'That impersonation of a simple hooligan is very good,' Louise Taylor said, with interest. 'I expect you use it a lot. No doubt we have managed our physical assets and our money in the most incompetent way – another characteristic of women. But none the less we are doing first-class work here, and rearing a generation of women who will change things, as I would ask you to observe.'

Francesca sat back, watching Louise with interest and pleasure. 'How do you manage your children? I need to know, I am making a nonsense of my only chick, where an eighteen-year-old Norland trainee is having no problems at all.'

'Yours is a boy?'

'William, yes. I knew I'd made a mistake there,' Francesca acknowledged.

'What's your husband like? Is he any use with children? I understand he's a policeman.'

'Yes – John. Superintendent at the roughest nick in London, and young for the rank – he's only thirty-eight. Which leaves him not much time in the week to be good with children but he gets up in the night for William. What's yours like?'

Louise busied herself with collecting books. 'Michael is an academic, the same age as your policeman. A Fellow of UCL in chemistry. Assistant Lecturer. Does some teaching for us here. This is him arriving now.'

The tone was remarkably dry and Francesca turned to look out of the window. A tall man with pale blond hair flopping into one eye was flinging open the boot of a battered car. He turned to respond to some summons, giving her a good view of a classic straight nose and rounded chin, then shook his hair out of his eyes and smiled. The beautiful Dawn Jacobson came into view, smiling back, and stood facing him, a little too close. Both, as if suddenly aware of scrutiny, glanced towards the window. Michael Taylor waved briskly, while Dawn smiled lazily. He was a chemist, Francesca remembered, and the girl could not therefore be one of his pupils. She sneaked a look at Louise Taylor who was watching the pair, unmoving, her expression unreadable, and decided it was time she started work.

5

On the third Friday of the Summer term, as the college Statutes ordained, a meeting of the Fellowship convened, following the traditional Friday lunch of cold meats, beetroot and wilting coleslaw. The weather was typical of late April, cold and rainy.

Sarah arrived just behind Francesca, and she considered her back view with affection. Francesca had disappeared into the Bursary two weeks ago, from where evidence of her progress surfaced like the mounds left by a particularly energetic and determined mole. People came and went. A ruffled partner in the college's accountants turned up on the first Monday, and returned on the Wednesday to add two of his assistants to the labour force in the Bursary. On Thursday, a junior Bursary employee resigned tearfully, and on the following Monday two new candidates were being interviewed. The college library had found itself working through lunch-hours in order not to disrupt undergraduates preparing for exams, Heads of Studies were struggling to recall year-old transactions and to find bills. Francesca was seen briefly at intervals watching the till operations in the self-service dining-room, and occasionally pouncing on some imperfection in operation. The whole college machine, not without substantial moanings and groanings, was being forcibly overhauled.

A major product of all this admirable activity was the discovery of a series of what an Evelyn Waugh character had described as 'Utter Nonsense.' It turned out that the building maintenance account had been kept in balance by dint of doing no maintenance and/or by failing to debit any sum which would enable maintenance to be done at any time. The consequence, in unrepaired roofs, in drainpipes left to decay and leak water all

71

down their lengths into Gladstone's nineteenth-century brick, was going to be amazingly expensive. The American Friends' million pounds had been properly and carefully placed at interest with Barclays, but no one, including Barclays, could for the moment find the college account to which this interest had been credited. The garden account had been credited with the proceeds of the Appeal Committee's garden party, which had a sort of logic, except that the money had been pledged specifically by those present for the purpose of putting a few of the thousands of the new tiles needed back on to the roof of Tydeman Hall rather than for putting plants in the garden. And the kitchen account had so far repelled even the dauntless Francesca who, as she said grimly to Sarah, was even now deciding how and where to cut the Gordian knot in which the supplies, invoices, receipts, conference payments and gratuities to staff had become entangled.

Sarah's heart had, however, been cheered by the way that the business of the college teaching and research continued efficiently. An organization that still fulfils competently (and better than that) its main business must be salvageable, she reflected, watching the Fellowship assemble, black gowns over the wild variety of clothing they had considered suitable for late April. This mixed array of women was lecturing in the University and teaching some 400 young women aged between eighteen and twenty-one, as well as turning out some very good research and writing. As always, too, the best, like Louise Taylor, were managing to do all these things at once.

She was at this moment bent over a draft – Louise did not waste a moment of her limited time – and Sarah recalled that she had today delivered two well-attended lectures on aspects of fiteenth-century French history, and taken two supervisions, both of which had run generously over their time, as well as attending a Library Committee meeting this morning, and getting home to lunch with two toddlers. And for this she was paid about the same as a new graduate in the Civil Service, with little prospect of any improvement, given this government's view of academics and their use – or lack of it – to society.

Sarah took a deep breath and summoned the meeting to order. Change was needed, or the whole institution, including the parts that worked so well, could be swept away. And to effect the change it would be necessary to win over the hearts and minds of most of the best people like Louise Taylor. If you got that right, then the others either fell into line, or removed themselves. She had done this before – it was not impossible, she reminded herself, as she launched into her brief prepared speech which neatly combined gratitude and pleasure at becoming Warden of Gladstone with the clearest possible warning about the state of the college finances, and the likely consequences if a grip were not taken on same. The speech concluded with a vision of the sunlit uplands in which Fellows of a well-managed and financially prudent college might wander; enough research students, lightening of the teaching load so Fellows had time for their own work, the best of the applicants to London University fighting to get through the doors.

Carefully constructed as it was, the speech was poorly received, and Sarah realized from the expressions, ranging from mulish obstinacy through exasperation to abstraction, that she had an uphill task ahead of her. This group had, she saw belatedly, been harangued about the college's finances many times before, and now heard the exhortations only as a noise, without feeling any responsibility, or any real ability to do anything about any of it. The problem would have to be attacked more specifically. She looked at Francesca, who was sitting tactfully three places away from her.

'The Bursar has spent her first two weeks here in the urgent task of getting last year's accounts into a form which can be presented to the University. Francesca, perhaps you would tell us how you are getting on?' She considered the Fellowship, who were openly registering total disinterest in any task Francesca might be going to waste her time doing. 'And what further help you will require from us.'

'I am most grateful for the help already given to me.' Francesca had been properly trained. 'I need to spend the next three weeks as well, with the aid of the Bursary staff and the auditors, going over all the raw data from which last year's accounts have been compiled.' Francesca in her turn considered her audience. 'Then we will have to redo the accounts at all convenient speed, given that the college is already late in its submission.'

'This happens every year,' Louise Taylor said impatiently. 'Not only to us – lots of colleges submits accounts late.'

'Interesting. If you can't get your accounts in on time it means you haven't got the faintest idea what you are doing, financially. As turns out to be the case here.'

The entire Fellowship regarded Francesca with varying degrees of hostility. Sarah decided to sit back.

'I had hoped,' Alice Hellier said, surprisingly, in tones of barely suppressed dislike, 'that a new Bursar was going to spend time getting financial support for the college rather than in fruitless post-mortems about the past.' She leant forward, trembling slightly with anxiety and anger, her hair, seriously in need of washing and cutting, falling raggedly forward.

'I intend to do that,' Francesca assured her, coolly. 'But until I understand the way the college's finances run, and until I can produce a set of accounts that communicate this understanding clearly, there is no way I – we – can look for outside funding. Or even get the DES to give us all that we are entitled to.'

'Why do you have to redo the accounts? I understood they were finished in draft form.' Hazel Bradford, a young, lively economist, whom the college was lucky to have kept and who had a lucrative consultancy with one of the City stockbrokers, asked briskly.

It was a helpful question, as Francesca's quick appreciative glance indicated. 'Because the draft came apart in my hands. The first four things I asked about neither the Bursary nor the auditors could explain or document.' She grinned at Hazel. 'And it got worse as I went on.'

'Can you not just start from where we are now?' Alice Hellier was sounding as if Francesca was a not very bright student.

'The difficulty is, Dr Hellier, that there is no way of determining where that is. There is no solid ground. Indeed, whatever the accounts for the year before say, I would doubt that they truly represent the position in July of the year before last. But that is what the college told the University and, as you suggest, I have to stop somewhere, so I intend to reconcile the figures back to there.'

'Are not some parts of the accounts straightforward? Like the tuition account, for example?' Louise Taylor was interested rather than hostile.

'If I had to rank the most difficult parts of the accounts, the kitchen account would be in the lead rather than the tuition account, yes. But not by much. As with all businesses, the income side is easy enough, both to count and to allocate to the right place. It's the costs that are usually all over the shop: what are they and against what should they be charged?'

The meeting considered costs, allocation of, in respectful silence, and Sarah decided to intervene before Francesca could suggest they not bother their pretty heads. Everybody around this table was going to have to understand the college's finances if change was going to be made, and no one was going to get away with the view that their fine brain should not be troubled by such things. 'The Bursar will report to this meeting with revised draft accounts in four weeks' time, at which point we will have a clearer idea of where we are and what we must do. Can we take the next item? The Raab Lecture. Dr Taylor, I believe you have the arrangements for this in hand, though it seems rather hard that you should be doing all that as well as giving the lecture.'

'Well, if I organize it, I actually get more or less the audience I want, and people get properly fed and watered. I have invited 550 people, of whom 400 have accepted.'

'This is to be held in Tydeman Hall, yes? Does it take 400 people?'

'No, more like 350. But around fifty drop out at the last moment. And there is room for a few more chairs round the outside. It all worked last time. We give them drinks first and supper afterwards. I've made the arrangements with the caterers.'

Sarah was contemplating this confident unfussy planning with pleasure when her attention was caught by Francesca's forbidding scowl.

'Bursar?' she said, returning to the formalities.

'Through you, Warden – Dr Taylor, did you fix the caterers yourself?'

'Yes, I have a budget.'

'Like when this lecture happened last year?'

'Yes.' Louise Taylor was sounding uncharacteristically defensive.

'It went twenty per cent over the specific endowment for the lecture, didn't it?'

'I hadn't remembered it was as much as that.'

'It was twenty-two per cent, to be precise. I gather there was some misunderstanding between you and the Deputy Bursar on costs?'

'Yes. The college charges its facilities out at a higher rate than I was expecting, and people drank more than we had thought.' Louise Taylor was ruffled.

'Warden, in a small operation, such as we are, the finance department had better handle everything to do with money, from getting quotations to dealing with invoices. It is the only way to keep control. I have not yet got anywhere near the bottom of the kitchen account – I may just have to draw a line there – but a lot of the problems have been caused by split responsibility for entertaining, and too many people commissioning caterers and signing invoices. The Bursary should take over the whole thing including the Raab Lecture.'

'That must be right,' Sarah intervened swiftly, to head off any expression of the discontent she could see simmering round the table. The Fellows were not financially sophisticated, but they wanted to have the fun of spending any money there was. 'Thank you, Bursar.'

Louise Taylor, on weak ground and too intelligent not to realize it, conceded the point, saying that she would welcome any lightening of the load, this with a look of mingled respect and resentment at Francesca.

'Repairs to the Tydeman Hall roof,' Sarah said, sounding brisker than she felt. 'Item 6. We have before us three quotations, the lowest of which is for £751,000 from Callaghan's, and the highest for £843,000 from Thwaite's, with the third at £837,000. All three have done a lot of work for the University.'

'The architects recommend taking Callaghan's bid, I understand, Warden?' Alice Hellier was bent on being unhelpful, and Sarah sighed.

'They do. Bursar?'

'I want to redo the tender process, Warden.'

'We've got three quotations already,' Louise Taylor protested.

'Sure. From people who regularly work for the University and who know each other. It is at least possible that they share out the work and this is Callaghan's turn. I'd just like to get the process opened up a bit.'

'I thought your background was in industrial matters rather

76

than construction, Bursar?' Alice Hellier, this time, had been too quick for Sarah.

'It is.' Francesca was unperturbed. 'I asked a Department of the Environment colleague, who is used to looking at bids to repair historic houses, about this. He says these three builders may well be a cartel, and he gave me a couple more names.'

'Dr Hellier, if we could save five per cent, which is £36,000 on this bid, it is a lot of money,' Sarah observed.

'It could buy a lot of drinks at lectures.' Louise Taylor had decided to be supportive. 'How long will it take to get another quote?'

'Not very long, but we have enough time. We can't start the roof until July, because we have a conference of chartered accountants till then, booked and paid for.'

The meeting proceeded steadily, with all matters financial being annexed in similar style by the Bursary. Louise Taylor, Hazel Bradford the young economist, and five of the younger Fellows had understood what was going on and decided to support it, given Francesca's obvious competence. A group of older dons were also supporting the Warden and Bursar, because they did not want to find themselves overworked with administration of finance. This left a sizeable minority, led unexpectedly by Alice Hellier, who wished neither to have the Bursary take over all matters financial nor to understand and take responsibility for their own finances.

'They'll have to go,' Francesca said darkly to Sarah as they made their way back to their offices, encumbered by black gowns and piles of files.

'Who will?' It was George Hellier, appearing from nowhere and stretching out his arms for Sarah's files.

'Not you, George,' she said, smiling. 'The entire financial affairs of this college – except tutors' travelling expenses, is that right, Francesca? – are now with the Bursary. I just hope you won't both collapse under the weight.'

'I left tutors' expenses alone, George, because it's only eight people at £150 a year each. I told them not to account it, however; we'll just have a black hole entry of £1200.'

'Oh, excellent idea, Francesca,' George said, laughing. 'Was it a trying meeting? Shall I find some coffee?'

Both women assured him gratefully that nothing would be more welcome, and he bustled off to get it.

'I can't tell you what I had to do to get men at the DTI into coffee-fetching mode,' Francesca said reflectively, collapsing into a chair. 'Nice bloke, George, very supportive.'

'Oh yes. Did his best with Lady Trench apparently, but she was too much for him.' Sarah glanced across at her Bursar, who was looking haggard. 'I hardly dare ask, Francesca, but how is the baby?'

'Kept us up last night. The wonderful Caroline had to go home for the funeral of an aunt, and that blasted baby feels his parents do not understand him as she does. Nor we do, I'm afraid. Caroline goes back to Norland at the end of July; we can fudge by in August, and in September I am in a hole again. But don't worry, Sarah, I'll think of something. Oh, George, you are *good*, I need that.' She seized a mug of coffee from George Hellier.

'Are you coming to the guest night on Thursday?' George asked.

'Oh yes, I'm looking forward to it. I mean, I know it's just us, but there are four husbands I'm going to be very interested to meet. Or whatever people are bringing instead of husbands.' Francesca slanted a glance at Sarah.

'I thought it was time Neville Allason saw the college again, now it is looking its best,' Sarah said placidly. 'When he was last here, in January, it must have been very depressing.'

'That is certainly true,' George Hellier agreed. 'Poor Judith's death, of course, had saddened us all. And the weather was terrible, half the Fellowship went down with colds after her funeral.'

'And in three months' time Tydeman Hall will be covered with scaffolding and will look dreadful again,' Francesca pointed out. 'Though it may, of course, be safer like that; having seen the specification of works, Sarah, I have to tell you I am a little uneasy about eating in there. Most of the rot is above High Table.'

'As opposed to at High Table,' George Hellier suggested slyly.

'Nothing wrong with the teaching, here,' Francesca said thoughtfully. 'We may be useless financially, but all these women are conscientious. And some are marvellous, like Louise Taylor.'

George Hellier beamed at her. 'I am so glad you and Louise get on. She is a real ornament to the Fellowship.'

78

'In every sense,' Sarah agreed. 'A future professor if she keeps on going the way she is. And a lot of style. I've only met her husband once, but he seems very pleasant.'

'He's not very supportive.' George Hellier collected coffee mugs. 'And Louise needs help; she has a huge load to carry, with her teaching and research and the children.'

The comment was made very forcibly, and Sarah sought to lighten the atmosphere by saying, 'George, however did you get here? As far as I can see, most of the university men are truly and utterly chauvinistic.'

George Hellier relaxed and smiled at her. 'Well, I came with Alice, of course. I was in the RAF for twenty years, then I had a job in a small school for a year. But I wasn't going anywhere there, so I came as soon as there was a vacancy in the Bursary.'

Neither of the Helliers had quite the spark or determination or political sense to carry them right to the top, Sarah reflected. And, of course, one had to allow for luck which always played an important part in anyone's career.

Francesca said restlessly, 'I must have a word with Serena. We need to get the minutes right for the governing body.'

'Thank God for a trained civil servant,' Sarah said, watching her go.

'She is very capable,' George Hellier acknowledged. He picked up the tray of coffee mugs and smiled at her. 'I must let you get on, Warden.'

'Thank you, George. And for the coffee.' Sarah watched him go and decided that she had earned a rest before tackling the in-tray. Good progress was undoubtedly being made and this job was not going to be the nightmare she had occasionally feared.

She should have known better, Sarah realized four hours later, when summoned by a phone call from Alice Hellier, who had just been invaded by panic-stricken, weeping young women. Susan Elias, the dark Jewish girl in Louise Taylor's supervision group whom Sarah had met on her first day as Warden, had been walking back through the college grounds after a late supervision, when she had been threatened at knife-point by a man. Too scared to scream for help, she had escaped rape only because a group, who had been passing quite close, had fright-

79

ened off the intruder. Susan was not unnaturally in shock, and her tutor had had her hands too full even to ring the police. Sarah proceeded to do it.

'We'll be there as soon as we can,' a laconic young man assured her. 'No, the attacker's probably gone by now, but watch it. Any more of your young ladies out? Better get them in.'

Sound advice, but not very practical, given the existence of 400 young women who were free to come and go, Sarah thought, summoning the college nurse from her house a mile away and leaving a message for the college doctor.

The difficulty was to decide whether to send warning messengers to every room in college. At ten fifteen at night the college would buzz like an ant heap, and hours of valuable work or sleep would be lost. If the news could be broken, unemotionally, in the clear light of the next day, people's worries could be dealt with in an orderly way. On the other hand, none of this sensible administrative reasoning weighed at all against the possibility of another young woman badly frightened, physically damaged or perhaps even killed – the man had had a knife after all.

The answer became clear: college staff in groups, with lights, would search the grounds; this should scare off any intruders without causing panic in college. The undergraduates, if they looked out into the dark, would probably just consider it some strange administrative ritual. And Susan would be put in the college sanatorium with the college nurse and a friend to keep her company, just as soon as she had told her story to the police. Sarah rang the porter's lodge to alert them to the imminent presence of whatever force the police would send, explained her plan to Susan, and asked which friend she would like. The answer turned out to be Dawn Jacobson; not in Sarah's view a particularly comforting personality, but there was no accounting for friendship.

The phone rang sharply as she was completing these arrangements and she picked it up, expecting it to be the porter's lodge announcing the arrival of the police. It was instead Francesca, ringing from home to explain where she had left the notes on the accounts for which Sarah had asked. 'I meant to leave them on your desk, but I forgot.'

'I'm not surprised,' Sarah said forgivingly. She explained the current emergency, emphasizing in return to Francesca's anxious enquiries that no physical damage had been done.

'Funny. First thing John said when he saw the place was that it was wide open to prowlers. Policemen see things utterly differently from us, you know. *I* just saw something like Newnham. You have called the local force, I take it?'

'Yes. We'll search the grounds – or they will – but we shan't tell the college till tomorrow.'

'George is still in the Bursary, conscientious bloke that he is,' Francesca observed. 'I've just talked to him. He didn't know you've got a problem. Do you need him in the present emergency? Comforting sort of man?'

Sarah considered. 'I'll call him if I need him, but I'd rather not. Or Alice will – she is coping at the moment with Susan. I am trying to raise as little alarm as possible.'

'Well, good luck with it all. I'm sorry I'm not there.'

'Don't worry, there are lots of people I can call out. Get a good night's sleep.'

Sarah, cheered by the telephonic presence of her ally, emerged to find that the police presence was even now at the porter's lodge. She went down to collect them, and found that the two men waiting there were not in uniform. They stood, tucked in beside the porter's lodge, talking to each other, inconspicuous and quiet. As she arrived to greet them, with Francesca's comments fresh in her mind, she saw them through new eyes and realized how vulnerable the college was. Both policemen, she realized, for all their calm, were absolutely on the *qui vive*, eyes everywhere, noting everything. Two young men, known to her by sight as regular boyfriends of third-year undergraduates, went past them, talking, utterly unaware of the two strangers, but Sarah understood suddenly that the policemen could have produced an accurate description of both young men from no more than the apparently casual sidelong glance they had given them. Fascinated, she noticed the older of the two consider, apparently fleetingly, the interior of the porter's lodge, which was a jumble of pigeon-holes for letters, cash box for emergencies, notebooks, pads and a chewed-looking list of vital telephone numbers. His glance had comprehended also the porter, a square, upright man in his sixties, whose military bearing and brisk manner Sarah, seeing him through a policeman's eyes, abruptly realized concealed a fundamentally disorganized personality.

'Warden,' the porter said brightly, tripping over a parcel on the floor. 'Two gentlemen to see you. And a package for Miss Wilson – I know her office is next to yours.'

'Just leave it for her, please, Mr James.' Sarah realized that in Francesca's words this one would have to go as well, suppressing the thought that the college would at this rate be denuded of staff.

'Do come through,' she said to the policemen. As they walked, she explained quickly that she was trying to contain the damage without putting any more undergraduates at risk, and both men nodded.

'We'll have a quick look.' The older one, who had introduced himself as Detective Sergeant Fields, spoke, so softly that she had to strain to hear. 'Where was the incident, madam?' As they turned into the garden, it was less dark than she had thought; there was a full moon, but clouds kept obscuring it.

'By the fountain – just here, as I understand it.'

Both men considered the fountain, an edifice given by a long-dead Gladstone graduate which featured an only just decently clad nymph holding up a circlet. With an absolute absence of expression that was more eloquent than any amount of artistic criticism, both men turned to look round.

'He'd have waited in those bushes there,' Fields said, and walked off towards them, the younger man, a detective constable, at his elbow. Sarah reflected that she would never be able to view the thick clump of lilac trees, so beautiful at this time of year, in the same way again. 'Three fresh fag-ends,' she heard the younger man say.

'Yes. He waited a bit.' Fields was obviously not a man to waste words. 'Find where he came in.' He turned his back on Sarah, without impoliteness, and pulled aside a bit of lilac, delicately, his torch flickering as he hunted, and Sarah decided to go and assist the younger man.

'Here,' he said, and she stooped and gazed at the metal fence. Two of the upright bars had been bent out of shape, so that a thin person could, just, get through.

'Oh dear,' she said inadequately.

'Looks as if that's been there a while.' The young man's tone

82

was studiedly neutral as he and Sarah contemplated the fence by the unwavering light of a powerful wide-beam torch. She decided reluctantly that he was right and that this particular gap was probably a well-known entrance to the college. 'Or he could have climbed – just,' the young detective suggested, kindly, as Sarah was crossly working out how to bend this particular stable door back into position at the earliest possible opportunity the next morning.

She paused by Detective Sergeant Fields, who had carefully bagged the cigarette ends and the wrapper of a chocolate bar. 'Better go and see the young lady now,' he suggested. 'The chap who attacked her won't come back tonight. If he waited around – which I doubt – he'll have seen us.' He handed the bag to his junior with exactly the air of royalty passing on a bouquet, and rubbed his hands down his raincoat. 'Will you lead the way, madam?'

Sarah led them back through the garden door, stopping to lock it, and turned to guide them through the maze of corridors, but was brought up short by Michael Taylor, almost running.

'Michael? Dr Taylor.'

'Ah, Warden.' He halted, disconcerted. 'I was delivering back a couple of essays to Louise's students. She's at home with the children.' He glanced uneasily at the two policemen, who under their masks of polite unconcern were soaking up every detail of his appearance. 'I was taking a coffee off Dawn Jacobson when your messenger reached her. I assumed there was nothing I could do to help, so I'm on my way home. Louise will want to know what happened, of course, since Susan Elias is one of her pupils.'

'Did you hear anything from the garden, sir?' It was the soft-voiced Fields who asked, and Michael Taylor flinched.

'No, no, nothing at all,' he said anxiously. 'Of course, I hadn't been there very long.'

'Perhaps Miss Jacobson will be able to help us?'

Fields's eyes had not wavered from Michael Taylor's face, and all three of them saw him flush. Sarah, both fascinated and deeply worried, forced herself to stay silent; this was not a purely social awkwardness, she reminded herself; Michael Taylor's excuse for being on college premises at ten-thirty in the evening was remarkably thin, and a student in her charge had been attacked by a man who knew his way around the college grounds. 'Dawn's room is on the street side,' he said stiffly, and looked to Sarah in appeal, clutching his document case like a breast-plate.

Sarah found her eyes impelled to the first and index fingers of his right hand, which were heavily nicotine-stained, and knew, without turning round, that Fields had seen them too.

'Perhaps we could all go up there together and talk to the young ladies?' The soft voice had no suggestion of request about it.

Michael Taylor hesitated, fidgeted with his briefcase and started to speak, but Sarah, cold with anxiety and shock, got herself back into action. 'Certainly, Sergeant Fields. I expect Louise will forgive you for another few minutes, Dr Taylor.' She set out firmly up the corridor, relying on Fields to sweep Michael Taylor along with them, and the little procession, in total silence, walked the hundred yards to the room where Susan Elias was presumably being given warm tea and sympathy by her tutor.

Sarah knocked and led her group into the small sitting-room with pleasant chintz-covered chairs that the college provided for its Deputy Warden. Susan Elias was indeed there, still weeping gently, wrapped in a blanket and clasping a mug of tea, with Dawn Jacobson sitting on the arm of the chair, bent in an attitude of sympathy. Alice Hellier, looking frail and miserable, was filling a kettle in the corner of the room. Sitting squarely in the only other decent chair was a large man in his fifties, with grey hair like stubble, a solid round jaw and a snub nose, his raincoat on his knee, and perfectly at his ease. Sarah felt rather than saw her police escort's surprise.

'Sir?' Fields said, in tones combining surprise and reproach.

'I expect you've got the whole thing sussed by now, Fields. I was called out by a colleague, John McLeish, the Super at Notting Dale.'

'Oh,' Sarah said, 'Francesca's husband.'

'That's right. Alan Toms, Detective Chief Superintendent.' The man had hauled himself to his feet and was extending a large hand. 'I was at their wedding. And I trained young John. Took him into the squad. So he rang me when he heard you'd got a spot of bother here.' He looked benevolently at Susan Elias's bent head and thoughtfully at Dawn Jacobson. 'I told him you were in good hands, but I said I'd also look in myself.'

Like a top hospital consultant, Sarah thought, in instant recognition – down to the courteous deference he paid to his subordinates. She turned to introduce Michael Taylor, but found herself pre-empted; the large man's attention had focused itself on him, and he was embarking, unasked, on an increasingly uneasy explanation of his presence.

'Oh, yes.' Nothing in the man's face moved, but Sarah found herself suddenly very conscious of Dawn Jacobson's staggeringly good looks. 'Miss Jacobson, is that right? You heard nothing, neither of you. How long was Dr Taylor with you, would you say?'

Sarah watched with a cold, uncomfortable tenseness in her stomach as Dawn looked for help to Michael Taylor, who cleared his throat to speak.

'Miss Jacobson will tell us, sir.' Chief Superintendent Toms raised a hand, fractionally.

'Oh, I'm not sure. I can't remember what time Michael – Dr Taylor arrived. It was after supper.' She looked round her, and Sarah kept her face still. 'About eight thirty, I think.'

And it was nearly eleven o'clock now, and it must have been ten forty-five when the messenger caused Michael Taylor to leave, Sarah realized. She sneaked a look at Toms.

'I'd not realized it was quite as long as that. I am sorry, Dawn, I didn't mean to get in the way of your exam revision.' Michael Taylor had rallied.

'Oh, not to worry.' Dawn Jacobson picked up the cue with the speed of relief. 'I wasn't going to work, I'd been at it all day and the worst risk is getting muddled at this stage.' She smiled prettily and hopefully at Toms, who gave her his careful attention without smiling back.

'Yes,' he said thoughtfully, and turned to Sarah. 'Well, there are too many of us here to be useful. Fields, you'll want to talk to Miss Elias, and she'll be wanting to get to her bed, so I'll leave you here. Miss Jacobson, you'll be wanting to get your things if you too are spending the night in the sick-room.'

'Perhaps I could give you coffee, Mr Toms?' Sarah said faintly, deciding that she really could not cope with Detective Chief

Superintendent Toms in the vocative case. 'Will you be wanting to talk to Dr Taylor again?'

Some imperceptible signal passed between the police representatives, and Michael Taylor found himself escorted to another study by the young detective constable to await Fields's attention, while Sarah, feeling heavily outmanoeuvred, led the way to the Warden's lodge, noting as she passed her study door the presence of a neatly marked-up folder of papers. George Hellier must have finished in the Bursary; well, when he returned to his own crowded hearth Alice could explain to him what was up.

'A very pleasant room.' Toms, coffee achieved, sat firmly on her best chair and surveyed the room calmly. 'So you have young Francesca working for you?'

'Yes. I am fortunate to have someone as competent and with such financial expertise.' Sarah suspected that every word would be relayed to John McLeish in one form or another.

'There's some very capable women around these days,' Toms agreed magisterially. 'I've got one or two working for me too. Did I understand that Dr Taylor's wife works here as well?'

'Yes, indeed.' Sarah was relieved to be able to make this point. 'She is, of course, Dr Taylor also. Nearly all our Fellows have PhDs – doctorates.'

'Funny to call them Fellows, when they are all ladies, as I understand they are.'

'You have a point, Mr Toms. The term is rooted deep in the college's history – but, of course, the college was set up in imitation of a men's college, and retains all the same terms.'

'Been married long, have they?' Toms swallowed his coffee in a gulp. 'Dr Taylor and Dr Taylor?'

Sarah considered him and decided that he was not deliberately sending her up. 'Some years, certainly. They are both in their mid-thirties and there are two small children.'

'I see.' He let a silence fall, and Sarah found herself impelled to speak.

'I cannot see Michael Taylor as a prowler, preying on young women.'

'No, no, that's not what he was doing, or not tonight.' The verdict was delivered with complete and unconscious authority. 'He was having coffee with Miss Jacobson, from eight thirty

86

onwards – well before the attack on Miss Elias.' He picked up his replacement coffee. 'Very good-looking lassie.'

Sarah looked across, found him peeping at her over the coffee cup, and decided not to misunderstand him. 'You think that's why he was looking so shifty?'

'Yes. Mind you, I'm not saying they were doing anything they shouldn't, if you take my meaning. But that's where he was and that's what he wanted. Fields – he is one of my best, but I'd be obliged if you'd not say that to him or he'll be after promotion – will go through it again, but that's what it was.'

'A problem for me, not for you.'

'That's right. Your prowler is our problem, however. We've got a few nutters around whom we know about, and we'll find out what they were at tonight. And I'll get the uniformed branch to patrol, on those little Noddy bikes, noisily like they always do, so no one can miss them. Either we'll find him or he won't bother you again.' Toms rose to go, leaving Sarah feeling that it was she who had been dismissed.

'I'm most grateful, Detective Chief Superintendent.'

'Mr Toms is fine. Or Alan to any friend of Francesca's. Give her my best, will you?' He shook her hand firmly and walked out. Glancing at the window, Sarah saw the lights of a waiting car flicker on as he appeared, and a driver scramble out to hold open the back door for him.

6

Louise Taylor, huddled in her raincoat against the blustery rain, rounded the corner of the quiet Pimlico street and walked up it, trying to look brisk and competent while wondering feverishly whether she was too early. Her heart missed a beat as she saw a familiar figure fifty yards away turn into a doorway. She walked on sedately and rang one of the three bells of the flat-fronted, small house. Her host bustled her through the door and closed it behind her before taking her in his arms.

'God, that is nice.'

'I feel the same.' She stroked the thick blond hair, stretching to rub her cheek against his. 'I thought I would burst if I didn't see you again soon.'

Neville Allason looked down at her, tenderly. 'Oh, so did I.' He hugged her and released her. 'We must try and find a way of meeting more often. Better to meet publicly sometimes – it puts people off the track. I'm coming to the college guest night later this week, you know.'

'I didn't. Oh good, I was wondering how to duck it, but now I don't need to. Wonderful. Won't you be bored?'

'Well, not with you there. Come and have a drink.'

She followed him through to the kitchen, at the back of the house, small, modern and with venetian blinds drawn down, even on this sunless day. Discretion, she thought, indulgently; of course, he doesn't want the neighbours to know. He poured her a glass of wine – he had one already half drunk. He toasted her silently and watched her over the rim of his glass as he drank, and she looked back at him, entranced and longing for him.

'Are we going to bed?'

His green eyes opened wide in surprise, and he laughed, in pleasure. 'Absolutely. Now, just as soon as I defridge the food.'

'I thought it was my turn to suggest bed,' Louise said demurely. 'You usually do the asking.'

In fact, their affair was a mutual passion, she thought, with deep pleasure, watching him efficiently extracting lunch from the refrigerator. But he had certainly started it; she had been amused and flattered by his instant demonstrative interest in her when she had appeared as a witness on a day when he was chairing the Commission on University Funding. She had not been looking for a lover, but watching Neville deal incisively and gracefully with all the difficulties of that afternoon had brought sharply into focus all her unhappiness with her husband. Michael had been intolerable for months; distressed by his academic failure, he had reacted by distancing himself from her and all household concerns, leaving her overworked and tied down by domestic problems. Even given the situation, she would probably not have sought to take the relationship with Neville further, but she had had little time to consider, and she now smiled to herself as she remembered Neville's definitive move.

'What are you laughing at?' He had turned to look at her, filling the doorway, elegant in shirt-sleeves.

'I was remembering Marshlands. How did you dare?'

'Nothing ventured . . . you know. Besides, I couldn't stand it any longer, I wanted you so much.'

She had not hesitated to accept Neville's offer of a lift to the Marshlands conference in February, flattered by the attention and enjoying her colleagues' envious looks as the DES car turned up in the Gladstone car-park. She had been prepared to read or sit quietly while he read or telephoned, but he had turned all his attention on her. By the time they arrived – after an unexplained stop to visit Sarah Murchieson in a health farm – she had told him a great deal about herself under pressure of his intense, unfeigned interest. She had found herself diagonally opposite him at the dinner, placed rather higher than her position in that distinguished company warranted, and had had a wonderful time, aware throughout of his attention. After dinner, seeing him occupied, she had taken herself to the bar and had waited in the middle of a group until he arrived at her side and offered her a tour of the library. They had stood together under the high nineteenth-century basilica, nodding courteously to other conference members who had had the same idea. More or less in the middle of a sentence about the long-dead but fashionable architect, Neville had said, lightly, that he wanted very much to kiss her but not, for God's sake, here. Louise, in a high state of excitement and pleasure, had taken him for a brisk walk round the tennis courts, and they had kissed behind the thick beech hedge which kept the worst of the wind from the players. They had ended up in bed twenty minutes later – hers rather than his, since he was worried about phone calls from the Department. They had been meeting regularly since, though not as often as she would have liked; he was lovely in bed, inventive, untiring and intuitive, and always entertaining out of it. She was, she understood, totally in love with him.

'Come through to the living-room,' he was saying. 'Let's just sit and chat for a while.'

Another of his most attractive characteristics was that he did not rush; he never bustled her into bed while she was still recovering from the long, mental journey from the children and the college. She followed him into the small, immaculately neat living-room, not elegant but pretty with gentle colours and small patterns. His wife's taste, she thought again, as she had when she had first seen it.

'We were reasonably careful at Marshlands,' he said, putting his arm round her, and she laughed.

'I wondered if we hadn't overdone it at breakfast the next day,' she said drily.

'What happened? Oh God, yes, I was longing to see you, but I was nobbled. So I had breakfast with the Durham people about a hundred yards away from you.'

He had, of course, gone back to his own room that first night, after an hour or so, getting fully and correctly dressed to do so, grumbling that in these days of bathrooms in every room you could not, credibly, be found wandering along a corridor in a dressing-gown. They had spent the next day decorously avoiding each other until the day's proceedings ended at five thirty, when they had repaired to her room. She had arrived late and slightly flurried for dinner, to find him ahead of her, immaculate, showered, and looking pleased with himself, entertaining a group by the bar. She had been charmed; the easy expressive confident masculinity was such a sharp contrast to the anxious depression and hostility that emanated from her own husband.

She finished her wine, carefully, and leant against his shoulder, and he turned her face to his and started to kiss her, gently, sliding his other hand under her jacket to stroke her breasts until she felt soft all over with pleasure. She moved her right hand downwards and felt him breathe in sharply.

'Never mind me, my love, I'm always ready when I'm anywhere near you. But I'd be more comfortable in bed, I admit.'

They moved to the bedroom, still holding each other and afterwards they both slept briefly in each other's arms.

Louise woke first, cramped. She preferred to sleep on her back with plenty of space around her while Neville, all too obviously, preferred a warm body to wrap himself round. She tried not to think about him and his wife in this small double bed. He had explained that Jennifer preferred to be in the country, so that was where the family house was, but she came up two nights a week to join him in the flat. After ten weeks, Louise knew Jennifer Allason's schedule as well as her own.

Neville, feeling her fidget, woke and uncurled himself. 'How long have we got?' He reached across her, stroking her hair as he paused and found the clock. 'My love, we ought to eat. I need to be back by about four thirty.'

'What are you officially doing?' she asked, stretching. She had come to understand that every hour of a senior civil servant's working day was meticulously accounted for.

'Buying a suit.'

She burst out laughing. 'What do you do when you really need to buy one?'

'Oh, I go on a Saturday morning.'

With Jennifer, Louise silently supplied, and felt a painful stab of jealousy, as she understood that she would like to buy a suit with this man, or any other domestic, peaceful, married activity for that matter. She slid out of bed and started picking up clothes, but he reached after her and pulled her towards him, kissing her stomach. 'Don't do that, my love. Oh God, I wish we had more time and could do ordinary things together.'

She stood stiffly, holding him, caught by the speed and certainty with which he had picked up her thoughts. 'We'll just have to find another conference,' she said, as lightly as she could, and he pulled her back on to the bed.

'I'm not sure that's going to be enough,' he said, looking down at her, face relaxed and young. 'Oh, Louise.' He kissed her and she moved against him.

'No, I'm showing off. Not a chance of any further action till tomorrow,' he said into her collarbone. 'But you *were* all right, weren't you, my love? I mean, that we can do something about.'

Louise assured him that she had been more than all right. 'Even with you I wouldn't fake it.'

'Not ever. You mustn't.' He sat up and looked at her carefully, and she looked back, longingly, hearing the implied promise of continuity. 'OK?' he said gently. 'Lunch?'

They moved to the kitchen to eat and Louise found she was starving. Neville Allason ate sparingly, as he always did, and she teased him gently.

'I lead too sedentary a life. I don't get to bicycle from place to place pursuing students, as you do.'

Louise swallowed a lump of smoked salmon. 'I nearly forgot. I was so desperate to get off to see you this morning that everything has gone out of my head. We've got a prowler on top of everything else.' She told him about Susan Elias's narrow escape, and was interested to find he was horrified.

'My poor Sarah. I talked her into this one, you know. I must ring her.'

Louise considered him. 'Why Sarah? I mean, why not dear old Alice Hellier, who was dying to be Warden?'

'Do you not like Sarah?' he asked, sharply, and she understood that he was anxious.

'Yes, I do,' she said slowly. 'And I like her more as time goes by. A *very* cool customer, and doesn't get rattled as Judith Symonds did. She was another of your friends, wasn't she?'

He picked up his plate and washed it neatly, putting it back in the rack. 'I had actually nothing to do with her appointment, but yes, she was a friend. I'm sorry to hear she rattled easily.' He threw the tea-towel across the sink, where it caught, neatly, on its bar and she applauded.

'The thing is,' he said, sitting down again, 'that if you find an institution is in a mess you don't appoint someone who is already there – I mean, you assume they are part of the mess. You get someone from outside.'

Louise considered this matter-of-fact verdict. 'Yes, I see that. And it's just the sort of reasoning Alice Hellier would never in a million years understand.'

'Is she very sad?'

'Oh yes. She felt it was unfair that Judith Symonds got it three years ago, and she was fit to be tied when it was somehow indicated that no one but Sarah was being considered. She really thought she was going to get it this time.'

He sighed. 'Pity. There are a few people like that in the Department, and it's awful having to try and explain to them. They just cannot see it. I suppose they go to their graves feeling it was all totally unjust.'

Louise leant round him to dispose of her plate, deciding calmly that she was a guest and need not wash up. 'Well, I can't imagine *you* being very good about not getting something you want.'

He got up to wash her plate and clear the table, and she watched, luxuriously.

'Is it that you have never failed to get what you wanted?' she asked, amused.

'Something like that. Or it might be right to say that I have never wanted anything I did not have a very good chance of getting.'

'You presumably have it all now?'

He hesitated, and his mouth tightened. A rising star in her own field, she recognized and was interested in ambition and held her ground.

'What else could you want?'

'Oh, well, we all want the top job, you know. Secretary to the Cabinet.' He got up restlessly, and she realized that his voice, normally light and husky, had changed colour and tone. He turned back to her and kissed her.

'There are only twenty-three of us in the field, so I don't worry about it too much,' he said lightly, making it a joke, but she was not fooled, even though she was wrapped warmly in his arms.

'How many really? In the running, I mean?'

'Three for sure, maybe five.' His answer was absolutely unhesitating and she understood that he had thought long and hard.

'My money is on you,' she assured him, rubbing his back.

'Bless you. But I have to avoid the myriad booby traps that the DES is prone to throw up. It is *the* most accident-prone Department, save perhaps the Home Office, where I have also been. My love, I need to go. I am seeing you on Thursday so it isn't *too* long to wait.'

Sarah sat having coffee in her office after lunch, looking on to the rainswept garden, feeling harassed. The attack on Susan Elias had been an unwelcome addition to what were already heavy responsibilities. Two of the college's third-year undergraduates were already folding under the strain of final exams: one had had to be sent home, and the other, resident in the local psychiatric hospital, needed visiting and every possible encouragement to attempt her final examinations as best she could. Three other potential disasters threatened. One mathematician who had simply ceased to understand what she was being taught – not that this was an unprecedented situation – would need counselling and a change of subject. Then there was a talented student of English, whose participation in the university dramatic society meant that she had covered less than half the course, and who was likely to fail her first-year exams altogether, requiring difficult decisions as to whether she should be allowed to return next year and, if so, upon what terms. And, inevitably, one shy geographer in her second year had turned out to be five months pregnant and unwilling to have an abortion, wishing instead, passionately, to complete her degree without any support or co-operation from the father of the child, or her parents. The precedents here were unhelpful; young women in that situation usually dropped out unless their parents were willing and able to assist.

She scowled at the papers, then slowly understood that she could hear children's voices, and they were getting closer. Just then two small creatures, aged something under five, dressed in raincoats, rushed shrieking across her sight-line with the Bursar and Deputy Bursar in hot pursuit.

'We'll have to take the little brutes out to the park, George, or no one will get any work done. I'll strap them both into a pushchair, same as Louise showed me.' Francesca's clear voice sounded uncharacteristically harassed.

'I'll do it, Francesca, I'm used to these children. Clare, Andrew,

come here. We'll go and get an ice-cream and go on the swings.'
George Hellier, invisible behind a hedge, was taking charge, to
the noise of children's chants of approval. 'Francesca, *leave* the
kitchen account ledgers; you need two of us. I'll be back in an
hour and a half, then they can watch TV.'

'You wouldn't like to marry me, would you, George? I mean, I
know we'd have to think of something for our current spouses,
but you are what I need. How am I going to cope when William
is this size?'

Motherhood was obviously not coming easily to Francesca,
Sarah noted. Against a background of George Hellier rallying the
children, Sarah heard a knock at her door, which opened to
admit Alice.

'Those are Louise Taylor's. She had to go to London, apparently,' Alice said, in response to Sarah's query. 'She left them
with Francesca, but they are extremely spoilt. I'm not at all
surprised Francesca cannot handle them.' She hesitated, chewing
her lip. 'George is very good-natured and is always doing things
for the Fellows, particularly for Louise, whom he very much
admires.'

'She is, of course, an admirable young woman,' Sarah said,
cautiously.

'Academically, that is certainly true. But I am sure that her
husband and children pay a price for her success. She is capable
of being very ruthless.'

Alice Hellier might well feel a twinge of jealousy about a
woman more than twenty years her junior who was managing to
teach and publish and have a family, Sarah reflected, searching
for a way to turn the conversation. 'I wonder if we should be
thinking in terms of a college crèche, Alice? Some of the best of
our young Fellows are struggling to keep going at all with
children.'

'When we were young, Warden, we expected to make sacrifices
– either to give up the idea of family, or to give up an academic
career to bring up children.'

'I know, I know,' Sarah agreed. 'That's probably why I never
married – I never could see how to combine a career with a
marriage in which I expected to have children,' she added, in
deference to Alice Hellier's marital status. She considered the

95

Deputy Warden warily. 'And how are your pupils holding up, Alice? None of them seem to be on my worry list?'

'Two of them should get Firsts. They would be safe candidates indeed, but our supervision arrangements broke down in the Michaelmas term. John Beattie got a Fellowship at UCL, just before term started, and told us, very late, that he could only give us four hours a week. So I have been supervising them for one paper, but I hadn't really done the particular subject for thirty years. I have had to read a lot to stay ahead of them.'

'I suppose this is always a problem with male supervisors?' Sarah asked.

'Yes. When they get a Fellowship elsewhere they lose all interest in us, inevitably. And we cannot get enough women Fellows in physics. We ought, of course, to open the Fellowship, if not the undergraduate body to men, Warden.'

'Alice, I am sure I do not have to explain to you why I would rather not undertake that particular task at this stage. There must be some female physicists about, and we should be able to attract them. Would the promise of child-care by the college help?'

'Yes, I think it might.' However sore a spot this was, Alice Hellier had far too good a mind not to give weight to the balance of the evidence. 'Indeed we considered it – oh, four years ago. The problem, then as now, was that we have no suitable space in which to house a crèche, and we could not make it pay. Only a few Fellows would have used it, and they could not reasonably have been expected to pay the full costs. It would have required a continuing subvention from the college.'

Discouraging, but it rang true, Sarah thought, and dismissed the problem from her mind in favour of establishing why Alice Hellier had originally come to see her. When Alice left, after a good discussion of a knotty question of tutorial pay, she turned her attention back to the complex administrative problem represented by one of the older Fellows, who had been on sick leave for almost a year. When approached, as she had been several times, she invariably declared her intention of returning to teach German literature – badly, by all accounts – in the immediate future. Looking up her background, Sarah discovered she had served for a couple of years on a committee chaired by Neville Allason, and decided that his view could reasonably be sought. Besides that, she needed to make sure that Neville was coming to the guest night and that he had the dinner following the Raab Lecture securely in his diary; he had promised her his support and it would be a useful forum in which to display that the DES at the highest level was interested in the future of Gladstone.

'I am sorry, Dame Sarah.' The private secretary who answered the phone sounded defensive. 'Sir Neville has not yet come back from lunch.'

'By four o'clock? What is the DES coming to?'

'I understand he is buying a suit, or possibly two.' The young man at the other end knew exactly when to be indiscreet, and Sarah laughed.

'*Is* he coming back?'

'Yes. Shall I ask him to ring you?'

'Tomorrow will do, if he is in a rush, but I would be grateful.'

Sarah put the phone down, nostalgically amused that Neville was still using the same codes. In the days when they had been lovers he had used the necessity of buying a suit – or a shirt – or a tie – when he could find no other reasonable explanation for escaping from the Treasury to her flat. She felt a momentary pang of jealousy, stifled instantly as she remembered, across twenty-five years, the agony of trying to run an affair with Neville, and how much time she had spent waiting for him and planning for him, in relation to the time she had actually had with him. She was fortunate to have managed to keep him as a useful and loving friend; let some other woman struggle with being his mistress, fitted in between the demands of her career, and his unswerving determination not to let his wife know what was happening.

She worked on steadily through her list, interrupted only by the return of Louise Taylor; and listened with sardonic amusement to the hand-over process which appeared to be happening outside her door.

'They slept for an hour, Louise, but honestly not more. We couldn't stop them.'

'They always sleep for an hour, Fran, you've done brilliantly.'

'So did George. He was ever so much better than I was. We did it in shifts. I tell you, though, Louise, you're right about the crèche. We'll do that.'

Sarah opened her mouth to shout a comment, then decided that Francesca could find out the financial facts of life for herself.

'How was lunch?' she heard Francesca ask.

'Very interesting, thank you.'

'How was the shopping?'

'The shopping? Oh, I couldn't find what I wanted. But I had a good time. Have a drink?'

'I dare not, I am driving. And your little ones are filthy dirty and need feeding.'

Farewells followed, and car doors slammed, and Francesca's big Volvo pulled out of the car-park, making at speed for husband and son.

Sarah, undistracted by domestic commitments, worked on, interruped only by Neville Allason returning her phone call.

'Did you find a suit?' she asked demurely, and listened, unsurprised, to his explanations of the difficulties of finding suits anywhere in a hurry. Whatever he had been doing, his attention focused swiftly on her problem and he confirmed quickly her view that, courteously but inexorably, the college should explain to its failing sister that a second medical opinion would be required on her condition and likely ability to return to work.

'People try to hang on, very naturally, and just need to face up to the facts. In the DES we would have insisted on a medical done by our man after six months.'

'So would any well-conducted establishment. I just thought you ought to be warned, in case she came to you.'

'Thank you for that. I look forward to your guest night and the Raab Lecture. I really want to hear Louise Taylor speak. But Sarah, tell me about this prowler.'

'How did you know about him? Mercifully the girl was not hurt, only frightened. And the intervention of Francesca Wilson's husband has secured us some very senior police help.'

'I always forget he is a policeman. Not in your area, surely?'

'No, no, another bit of the Met.'

'But *apart* from that, Mrs Lincoln . . .'

She laughed and he chatted on for another ten minutes, leaving her insensibly soothed.

7

'Boy, oh boy, oh boy!' Francesca hauled off a long, black gown crossly, getting herself hopelessly caught up in her briefcase, sighed, put it down, and crouched awkwardly to disentangle her gown from the straps. 'Three mortal hours. Where *were* these people trained, Sarah?' She scowled, blackly, after the people in question, grandees of the University, their retreating backs in their dark gowns with flashes of colour on the sleeves making them look like great birds outlined against the massive colonnade of the Senate building. They looked totally alien in the press of Londoners fighting their way into the small sandwich bars for lunch. 'My life went past me like a drowning person, only very, very slowly.'

'It was rather protracted,' Sarah agreed, amused, and deciding that some of Francesca's strictures sprang from a slight hangover following the guest night which had taken place the evening before. 'I suppose you have never been to university meetings?'

'I thank God, as I have many times, that I do not work in the Department of Education and Science. Not that I ever would have, mind you – furnished as it is with those who couldn't make the grade in *real* Departments. But I could find it in my heart to pity even those deadbeats if they have to go to that sort of meeting often.'

'Well, they don't, quite.' Sarah was sidetracked. 'When university grandees attend the same meetings as DES people, it is the DES who has the money.'

'So the university people have to be civil, not bitch and whinge at everyone as they did all blasted morning?'

'They do all of that, but not for so long, because the DES are running the meeting. While I accept many of your strictures about the DES, Francesca, they *are* trained properly in that respect.'

Francesca, momentarily silenced, her gown awkwardly locked under one arm, followed her through the noisy streets to the car-park. It was a bright, windy day, making the early lunchtime throng move more briskly, and blowing the London litter in heaps.

'The university lot here weren't very nice to us either, were they?' Francesca said, as they waited for the lift in the car-park. 'Considering you and I are new, and the college is struggling?'

'That is because the college is insisting on remaining all-female. They think we bring our troubles on ourselves. I had to explain to no fewer than six other Heads of House that there were good and sufficient reasons why mixing the college was not at the top of my agenda. Our Fellows have been gossiping.'

'That must be right. I was surrounded by bursars being snottily superior about our buildings maintenance, lack of,' Francesca said, brooding. 'Not a lot I could say in our defence.'

'No,' Sarah agreed, noticing with pleasure the use of the possessive. She watched her subordinate with affection, as Francesca rolled up her gown into a ball preparatory to forcing it into an overloaded briefcase. 'Is that going to work, Francesca?'

'No, it isn't,' she said, chucking the whole thing in the back of the car. 'Let us go back to my house and get drunk.'

They were going to lunch at Francesca's house, she having explained with some embarrassment that a set of domestic crises rendered it necessary that she went home for an hour. Sarah had elected to come with her rather than go back to college on the tube; she was still not steady enough to be able to strap-hang if there was no free seat. The car came to an abrupt halt well short of Francesca's house.

'Oh heavens.' Francesca sounded extremely apprehensive.

'What?'

'It's Perry. Or, at least, it is his car which is blocking the street. And Tristram as well. That's another brother. I didn't realize they were back.'

'Back?'

'From America. Tristram's only just been allowed back in; he had an unfortunateness there three years ago. Here we go.'

The big brown Rolls had deposited two young men on the

doorstep of the pretty Victorian terrace house and moved smoothly off, unplugging the traffic jam, and Francesca slid her car on to the forecourt. Both young men turned to greet her with cries and kisses, then both rushed to help Sarah from the car. It was like having a family of labradors, she decided, gripping the handrail of the steps up to the front door while the three Wilsons ran round her. The door was flung open to reveal John McLeish, with William clamped to his chest. Both uncles reached for him, but William, tactfully, increased his grip on his father.

'Where's the nanny I got you?' Perry said crossly, stamping into the hall as if it were his own house.

'At the dentist. With an abscess. Come to that, what are you and Tris doing here?' Francesca reached her arms up for William who threw himself at her, gurgling.

'I was wondering that myself.' John McLeish, disencumbered, was helping Sarah with her coat. He hung it up for her and gazed, reflectively, at his hall which was entirely full of his brothers-in-law, strewing paper and packages around as they dug to the bottom of various bags.

'We dropped in on our way back from Heathrow,' Perry said, looking up from his bags. 'We wanted to see William.'

'And to check up on us,' John McLeish agreed evenly. 'Are you staying?'

'Oh, *darling!* Of course they must stay for lunch.' Francesca gave him back William and disappeared.

John McLeish grinned at Sarah. 'Very fine party last night, Dame Sarah.'

'Wasn't it?' she agreed, pleased, as she followed him through to the living-room, picking her way through the brothers who had now managed to find their offerings, and were rattling fearsome, garishly coloured plastic objects at William who plainly adored them. John McLeish put his son on the floor with his brothers-in-law and found her the weak mixture of wine and soda that suddenly seemed to her just what she needed.

It had been a good party; Neville Allason had been on his best form and particularly socially useful. Traditionally, the older, retired Fellows were invited to college guest nights and about a dozen had accepted on this occasion, wanting to see the new Warden. This could have made for a sticky party, since at least half a dozen of these distinguished figures from the college's past were heavily reliant on the hearing aid, and one or two were so frail as to make entertaining them at all an anxious business. Neville Allason had done more than his duty; Sarah had firmly not put him at her side, giving that place to a retired professor of Greek from Dundee, and had surrounded Neville by four of the older guests, all of whom had had a wonderful evening; Neville, crackling with vitality and apparently tireless, despite a heavy day at the Department, had coaxed even the very shy and infinitely distinguished ex-professor of chemistry, a dusty bundle of clothes held together by safety-pins, into real animation.

Francesca herself had been very good value; brought up in a large, competitive, social family, she had talked to, and persuaded to talk back, many of the less glittering guests. Louise Taylor had looked ravishing and been on particularly good form, and Sarah had felt, smugly, that at least two of her senior staff had very much raised the level of both looks and ability.

There had, in fact, only been one moment of discord and discomfort, and that was due to the presence of the large man sitting back opposite her in the high-ceilinged Victorian room, sardonically watching his brothers-in-law crawling on the floor with the baby. She had forgotten that John McLeish had been called in to view the body of her predecessor and that he had met both the Helliers on that gloomy day. George Hellier had greeted him over drinks before dinner, rather over-heartily, and had insisted, no doubt out of nerves, on recalling the occasion. Alice Hellier had shied, uncontrollably, and wrapped her black gown tightly over an unbecoming party dress in pink rayon. Neville Allason, overhearing the conversation, had stiffened and gone silent, rousing himself to say to her crossly that he had no idea Francesca's husband was involved in Judith's death, how very *unfortunate*. Sarah, roused by the Civil Service's strongest term of disapprobation, had cornered John McLeish, introduced him formally to Neville and listened while he explained, placidly, that he had in no sense been involved; it was a CID matter, now disposed of, and he had only been asked, in an emergency, to view a body. It had chilled the atmosphere for a bit, but Neville had recovered quickly.

'Lunch,' Francesca shouted from the floor below and the Wilson boys, indefatigably courteous, helped Sarah down the stairs, while John brought up the rear with William.

'You don't mean John had to stay home this morning?' Perry, not a hair out of place, barely even pale after a night's journey, had finally caught up with the situation. His sister regarded him with hostility.

'You mean it should have been me? Sarah and I had a critical meeting.'

'No, he means you should have some magic emergency stand-by.' The younger boy, Tristram, ridiculously like both Perry and his sister, dark-haired, hollowed eyes under high-arched brows, passed her a quarter of lemon, unasked.

'It's called Mum. She'll be here at two o'clock if you lot want to hang on. The trouble is, *she's* had things to do this morning as well.'

'What you need is a crèche, Dame Sarah,' Perry said through a mouthful of bread.

'I think we've considered it, Peregrine, under my predecessor. We couldn't make it pay – the Fellows do not have enough children between them and we didn't want to throw it open to the world for fear of letting ourselves in for administrative hassle.'

'I had a go at the numbers,' Francesca confirmed. 'We'd certainly lose money even on a cash basis in year one and, probably, year two. And we don't have a penny to spare anywhere for the building.'

She was watching her brother, Sarah saw, and Perry was thinking.

'Well, listen, darling,' he said, pushing his plate away, 'I am not, even for you, *ever* going to ring up that old bat at the Norland again. She was bad enough about talking to a man at all, but when I had to explain it wasn't my baby but my sister's, I thought she was going to bang the phone down.' His eyebrows went up exactly as his sister's did when he laughed, Sarah noticed, amused.

'What can she have thought you wanted an eighteen-year-old trainee nanny for?' Francesca asked wonderingly, and her brothers and her husband all looked at her.

'Oh, all right,' she said crossly, 'I always forget about men. I suppose the uniform would have been a great incentive.'

'And the black stockings,' Tristram confirmed, longingly, as he stuffed another mouthful of soup into William.

'Anyway,' Perry said, over their laughter, and getting up to

103

find himself another drink, 'I can't face all that again, and I suppose you and John are going to go on doing this?' He waved a glass at William who was gently spitting back his soup. 'Let me have a look at the numbers, Frannie. I guess I could help. Anything to avoid a shambles.'

'Thank you very much, darling,' Francesca said promptly, and Sarah marvelled at the speed with which siblings close in age operated. Francesca had not known she would see her brothers today, but had seized her opportunity starting from cold, as it were. 'If it comes out ridiculous, I won't hold you to it.'

'Deal.' He reached past William to shake her hand and the baby laid a sticky paw confidingly on the arm of his suede jacket. 'There's my lovely nephew,' Perry said happily, apparently unmoved by the prospective cleaning bill. 'So what else is new? Is it all otherwise going smoothly?'

'Up to a point,' his sister said cautiously, and told him about the prowler. Susan Elias had been too shocked and frightened to be able to offer the police any useful description of her assailant, being not at all secure on items like height, age or colour. All, indeed, she had been able to state with any conviction was that her attacker had been a man a little taller than herself; not noticeably young or old, fat or thin. The police had, not unreasonably, indicated that the chances of finding him on this basis were slim. They had not been censorious, taking the line that shock usually prevented assault victims from noticing any usable facts if the attacker was unknown to them, but there it was.

'Are you in on all this, John?' Perry asked.

'Of course he is,' Francesca said impatiently. 'He rang up a mate instantly – one of those terrifying old fascists who run these outposts of the Met. You know what they're like.'

'I never understood how a Mafia worked until Francesca married into the force,' Perry said, thoughtfully, to Sarah. 'None of us four brothers dare put a toe out of line now, for fear of large men descending on us or telling our brother-in-law. You've had it now, Dame Sarah, you know: you're family. You'll all get a great deal more support and encouragement than you actually want from huge men in Terylene raincoats.'

Amid general laughter, Francesca decided they ought to get back to college and organized her brothers into clearing the table into the dishwasher. She kissed her husband and the baby and asked, apologetically, if he would be all right.

'You couldn't take the boys with you?' he had said, laughing.

'I heard that,' Tristram said balefully. 'Come along Perry, we're not wanted.'

'You were, but I have to get this one to go for a rest and he won't while you're here,' McLeish said equably, and in the end they all left together, the brothers to find the Rolls, and Francesca and Sarah to drive back to college.

'It was actually George who did the crèche figures for me,' Francesca said, straightening the mirror as she pulled out.

'A tower of strength. Of course he hopes to be Bursar when you go.'

'Don't encourage him, Sarah.' Francesca's hands moved sharply on the wheel. 'Look, I'm sure he was messed around from here to Christmas by Lady Trench, but the accounts were a shambles. What he is, I think, is a very nice man who tries to make everyone happy and not quite consciously bends figures so that everybody can have a bit of what they want. What you need is someone with proper training who doesn't much mind about pleasing people.'

Sarah sighed, accepting the point. 'The difficulty has always been that we can't pay enough to get someone like that.'

'You want a zealot who took early retirement. I'll see what I can do. Bit early to be trying to get rid of me, isn't it?'

'I do beg your pardon, Francesca, I'm just trying to think ahead. I'm signed on for three years, you remember.'

'I do.' Francesca hesitated and flicked a glance at Sarah. 'Do you still feel it was a good idea?'

'Oh yes. I confess that the degree of chaos and mismanagement of our physical assets is worse than I thought, but the academic standards are very high. People of the calibre of Louise Taylor are not found everywhere. It really is a pity that some of our best Fellows are so uncompromisingly against mixing the college. Between ourselves, I do not see how Gladstone can go on, financially or academically, without mixing.'

'Tell me,' Francesca invited.

'We don't get the best undergraduates – though we do wonders with the ones we do get. The cleverest want to go to mixed colleges. And we cannot pretend to provide enough teaching for our scientists.'

'You are saying that if we don't mix we may end up as a liberal arts college, on the American pattern?' Francesca was thinking it out.

'That is what I am worried about. But I am not going to pluck that nettle for a year or so, if I can help it.'

'Alice Hellier would support you.'

'Very nearly two thirds of the Fellows wanted to mix, three years ago, which was not quite the necessary number under the Statute. But the argument tore the college apart and is one of the reasons people forgot about the accounts. Louise Taylor, in particular, opposed mixing.'

'I know. And she is a formidable opponent. A real star, and so good-looking.'

Francesca's tone was completely untroubled, and Sarah reflected that it was unusual to hear someone sound so ungrudging about a highly successful contemporary of the same sex.

'I always find really clever people a pleasure to work with,' Francesca was saying, sunnily. 'My best friend at school was like that, and I was supervised with the girl who got three starred Firsts and the Whewell Scholarship at Cambridge. It's relaxing. It's like having a Rolls Royce, you just sit and admire, you don't have to feel competitive.' She looked sideways at Sarah. 'And I've got a better husband than Louise has.'

'Your John seems to me an excellent man,' Sarah said, amused at this evidence of a competitive spirit.

'Louise's Michael is a real male chauvinist. Doesn't think the children should be his responsibility, expects his slippers ironed – even though he is doing a lot less well than Louise.'

'That is perhaps why he wants a bit of deference.'

Francesca considered the point. 'Yes. Perhaps women ought not to make the same arrogant statement as men have been making all these years: I earn more money than you, so you have to run round *me*. I'll think about that. Louise does express her impatience a bit openly.' She brooded on the question, flicking up a left hand signal. 'Actually, Sarah, I understand they are getting on quite badly.'

Sarah, who had decided not to tell Francesca that Michael Taylor had spent over two hours alone with Dawn Jacobson on the night of the attack on Susan Elias, changed the subject. 'While I do feel confidence in Detective Chief Superintendent Toms, I find him terrifying.'

'Alan Toms is a dinosaur,' Francesca said definitively. 'I just hope he is not at the moment fitting up some favoured suspect for the job.'

'He said he had trained John.'

'He did, in the sense that John learned a great deal from him, including what not to do. I'm rather cross with my lovely husband for bringing Alan down on us, but all police, even the modern sort like John, do that for each other's wives and associates.'

'Might it not be useful to have the protection of the top man, as it were?' Sarah asked.

'It would be, if we thought that Susan's attacker was a habitual criminal. I imagine we are now safe from regular thieves, which will be very handy when the builders are here and Tydeman is covered with scaffolding; the word will be round the profession. But the sort of chap who lies in wait for young girls with a knife isn't a member of that fraternity. He'll be a loner and will not know that the great Detective Chief Superintendent Toms has thrown the protection of his cloak around us.'

It was a sound analysis, Sarah conceded, and one which did nothing to dispel her worries.

'I'll tell you another thing,' Francesca said after a silence. 'In the coffee-break, my fellow bursars were being exceedingly snide about – and I quote – "the close relationship between some of our senior Fellows and the DES". Do they mean the Golden Oldie? Is he unusually close to us? I thought the implication was that he was close to Dr Symonds, but I wasn't sure . . .'

'I understand they were friends, yes,' Sarah said carefully.

'But he's still around.'

Sarah, not quite knowing how or what to reply, let silence fall, then became suddenly aware that Francesca was staring ahead, frozen rigid in the driving seat, blushing from the collarbones up. 'I am sorry, Sarah. Please forget I spoke,' she said, constrainedly.

'Whatever there was between Neville Allason and me was over not long after it started, twenty-five years ago, my dear.' Sarah reached a swift decision. 'But we were friends before and afterwards, and it is true that he guaranteed me his support if I took this job. I am sorry it seems to be causing comment, but academic circles are always malicious.' She glanced at Francesca who was still suffused with embarrassment. 'I do wish you wouldn't call him the Golden Oldie, though.'

'I won't. I've stopped,' she said, gabbling in dismay. 'I'm sorry. I can't think why I do. I had an affair myself with someone not much younger than him, just before John and I married.'

'Why did you?' Sarah asked with interest, because surely the dashing Francesca could never have been short of admirers of her own age?

'John, with reason I have to say, had gone off with a dazzler and I suddenly found someone like my father. Not that I thought of David like that at all, but I understood it afterwards.'

'He was married, I take it?'

'Oh yes. No question of not being.' Francesca opened her mouth to go on, and all too obviously decided not to.

'Neville Allason has been married for over thirty years. Even twenty-five years ago I never thought he would leave his wife, and I don't think anyone would realistically expect him to now.'

'Except my fellow bursars,' Francesca said slowly. 'Having gone this far out on a limb, Sarah, I'm going to go on. One particularly horrid little man implied that we were close to a scandal. He could just have been fishing, so I did my *grande dame* act. And prattled on about my policeman husband and new baby, just in case anyone thought it was me who fancied Sir Neville, or any other top DES official.' She glanced cautiously at Sarah.

'Well, I don't know who they have in mind,' Sarah said robustly. 'And we have other things to worry about. Do we not have our own Finance Committee this afternoon to discuss your draft accounts?'

'Yes, but that ought to take about ten minutes.' Francesca was glad to get away from difficult ground. 'The only people who are interested in getting last year's accounts right are thee and me, Sarah.' She turned the car into the gate at Gladstone, waiting patiently while the gatekeeper did his usual performance, passing from incredulity at finding anyone actually wanting to enter the college, through lip-pursed resignation at having to open the gate, to final, deliberate slow recognition of the car, the Warden and the Bursar.

'Good as a play,' Sarah said, to defuse Francesca's obvious exasperation as they drove through.

'I cannot see it that way. I sit there imagining, blissfully, the moment when I break it to him that we are replacing him with an electronic device.'

'Are we?' Sarah asked, startled.

'No, of course not. I thought about it, believe me; but in cash terms – and cash is what we're talking here – it's cheaper to go on paying old Rumpelstiltskin there. Louise, now, she thinks he's more like Charon – she says she can see him ferrying people over the Stygian river in just the same way he handles the gate – you know, not able to believe anyone wants to cross, grumblingly finding the oars, taking a very long time indeed to consider the coin he was handed, and finally, infinitely slowly, rowing across, whingeing all the way.' She stopped, neatly aligned with the hedge. 'I'll see you at three thirty, Sarah.'

The Finance Committee of the governing body gathered just after 4 p.m. in the big dining-room in the Warden's lodge. Sarah took her seat at the head of the table in the confident expectation that the meeting would be over, if not in twenty minutes as Francesca had predicted, at least by five that evening. There were only two items on the agenda: approval of the college accounts for submission to the governing body, and formal approval of the revised estimate for Tydeman's roof. Neither, she thought, should be difficult. It was a working-sized committee; Warden and Bursar ex-officio; Alice Hellier, Louise Taylor, and Hazel Bradford elected by the Fellowship. Sarah had suggested to Francesca that George Hellier, as Deputy Bursar, might be invited to assist the discussion on the accounts. Francesca had said no, without explanation, and Sarah had not sought to argue the point.

She took the revised estimate for Tydeman's roof first. Francesca's DoE contact had provided alternative bidders who had between them taken £70,000 off the lowest bid already received. The college architects had been inclined to be huffy, because, as Francesca pointed out, the client's new management had forced them to do something they should have been doing all along. Sarah had intervened in time to prevent Francesca saying all this to the senior partner and had given him lunch privately instead, with the result that the man now thought it was his own idea to go outside the charmed circle of the regular university contractors; she had also gently reminded Francesca of Edith Cavell's saying, that you could get anything done if you did not mind who got the credit.

Yet this indisputably valuable saving was not, Sarah noted, being received all that kindly. Alice Hellier was disposed to be critical of new builders whom the college had not used before. Sarah watched Francesca draw breath to denounce her for conservatism and deference to established ways, and called on Hazel Bradford to speak instead.

'Very interesting to me,' Hazel said sincerely, her brown eyes sparkling. 'Wonderful demonstration of market forces. Even with an apparently free market, you have to work all the time to prevent cartels forming. It's all right for educated women like us, because we can understand the mechanism, but it just goes to show that the price of economic efficiency is eternal vigilance.' No one, unsurprisingly, was prepared to take arms against economic efficiency, so Sarah seized the opportunity to sum up.

'I found it very interesting too. The architects are pleased with the quality of these people as well. So, can we recommend this bid to the governing body? Thank you.' She nodded to the college secretary, who logged the agreement, and went briskly on to the accounts, hoping that any resistance to the new financial management had fizzled out with item 1.

Not so, it rapidly transpired. Francesca produced a concise, dry, exposition of the accounts, detailing the major changes from the last draft and the reasons for them, but as she sat back, clearly feeling that was that, Louise Taylor and Alice Hellier leant forward, uncovering notes in various degrees of detail.

'I see that the kitchen account is £30,000 further in deficit than when we last saw these accounts.' Alice Hellier opened first. 'Could you explain that?'

'Not entirely.' Francesca, never one to be neutral about people, did not like Alice Hellier, alas. 'Or, rather, I can tell you that we found a further £10,000 of expenditure that should properly have been debited to that account. It turned up in the garden account and the building account. And £20,000 more of depreciation and replacement costs should have been taken, which weren't. If your question is directed as to why the overall deficit is so large, then I do not know the answer, but the size of the deficit is clear.'

'I am a little surprised that the Deputy Bursar is not present, Warden.'

Francesca had by now understood the difficulty of the situation. 'George has been extremely helpful, and I am confident I know everything he does about this account. The best we can both do is to say – to you and to ourselves – that there have been serious failures arising from split responsibilities and poor control.' She hesitated. 'And that those failures have certainly been exploited by our outside caterers. A proposal to change them will come to this committee just as soon as George and I have found some options to offer you.'

The group considered this in silence.

'We were careless and the caterers are crooks,' Hazel Bradford summarized helpfully, and Francesca eyed her, narrowly.

'That is as close as we can get, yes. There'll be more of this in the current year's accounts – bound to be.'

'What form does the caterers' villainy take?' Louise Taylor, always intellectually curious, asked.

'I haven't tried to analyse it all. But in a system where one person puts in the order, a second person takes delivery without cross-checking, and a third person, also without cross-checking, pays for it, there is substantial room for leakage. For example, perhaps the caterers don't send what it says on the order form, but they charge for it – and no one can prove otherwise. Or maybe they do send it, and when they come to take away the empties they filch a couple of unused cases, and charge us for them, and we can't prove a thing. Never mind all the single bottles that vanish. Gets even worse with large kitchen deliveries.'

Sarah wished heartily that Francesca would remember the objective of the meeting was to get the accounts approved rather than tear plasters off open wounds. Everyone else round the table was now looking offended and, interestingly, somewhat hangdog, and Sarah seized her opportunity to propose the accounts be recommended to the governing body. The motion was seconded with gratifying promptness by Alice Hellier.

'Any other business?' Sarah asked, in tones expecting the answer No; she got it, and declared the meeting was closed, aware that at least two of her audience were suffering from some undisclosed reservation. Alice Hellier, twitching her gown, hurried off without talking to anyone else; Louise Taylor and Hazel Bradford were, however, hovering, and Sarah realized that they were trying to speak privately either to her or to Francesca. She hesitated, then decided she had to ask who they wanted.

'Both of you, Warden, please,' Louise Taylor said, looking extremely uncomfortable. 'Hazel and I have something to confess.'

'So do most of the other Fellows, I expect.' Hazel Bradford was looking both impatient and embarrassed.

'What?'

'It's about the kitchen account.'

Francesca put her files down wordlessly, a living question mark.

Louise, rather pink, sighed heavily. 'You know you suggested the caterers mopped up a few bottles at the end of parties?'

'Yes.'

'Some of it is us. Dear George always keeps a few back and sneaks them to Fellows. Not just Hazel and me – all of us.'

'Damn.'

'Oh come on, Fran, it's not *that* serious. We're not talking about thousands of pounds,' Louise protested.

'The point is, Louise, that bang goes control and bang goes your ability to behave professionally towards caterers. If you can't admit to your accounting department what you are doing, you certainly can't sort anyone else out.'

A depressed, hostile silence greeted this trenchant analysis, and Sarah decided a more emollient approach might be useful.

'This was presumably to help you, Louise, to entertain people who might be important to the college?' she suggested hopefully.

'Up to a point, Warden,' Hazel Bradford said sadly. 'It has become a bit of a perk. It's not George's fault – we've all got into the habit.'

Sarah rallied, firmly. 'Well, it seems to me the answer is to decide, now, what we can afford for entertaining, and to stick to that. I expect we had clamped down unrealistically.'

'Now that's true,' Louise Taylor said, brightening, her clear skin returning to its normal pallor. 'We had reached the stage where we couldn't even offer distinguished visitors a glass of wine without buying a bottle out of our own pockets.'

All three turned to Francesca, who was looking like something off Mount Rushmore. 'I'll give this one thought, Warden, but we have to fire those caterers. We'll never get them back on the straight and narrow now.'

'I agree,' Sarah said meekly into the awkward, embarrassed silence. She considered her colleagues. 'Come and drink with me, I brought it back duty-free – honest, Bursar.'

Francesca relaxed and grinned at her, and said she would but it was only quarter to five, what about some college tea instead? Hazel and Louise left, clearly preferring to put some distance between themselves and this confession.

'Is that why you were against putting George up as Bursar?' Sarah decided she had better know the worst.

'Yes. I don't mean I saw this particular nonsense – I didn't – but, as I said, he is over-anxious to please people. You need someone in charge of your accounts who behaves like Sam, the American Eagle – *you* know, Sarah, that character in the Muppets who is always complaining of Falling Standards.' She sighed. 'I suppose they've all been benefiting. I mean, Alice Hellier nipped off a bit quick, didn't she?'

'I think she was offended by George's not being invited,' Sarah said repressively.

'She'd have been excessively embarrassed if he had been, given these revelations. Sorry, Sarah, what have I said?'

'Nothing really. God save me from zealots. Ah, well, at least that's over. What are you doing now?'

'Making a note. I shall count them all in and count them all out again at the Raab Lecture. The bottles, not the guests. They shall not pass.'

8

'Francesca! Psst.'

'Do you know, I have never heard anyone make that noise before. I've only seen it written,' Francesca observed, swinging long legs out of a Mini, and cursing at the blustery wind as it blew the door back at her.

'I need to talk to you,' Louise Taylor said crossly.

'Come in.' Louise, who had waited impatiently while Francesca unloaded the car, shut the door of her room decisively behind them and busied herself finding coffee. 'It's about George. I feel I must tell him that Hazel and I ratted on him last week about the accounts. We just didn't want you nursing unnecessary suspicions.'

'I wasn't.'

Louise looked up at her sharply, her dark hair falling perilously close to the coffee. 'Good. Old George is a pal.'

'You nervous about tonight?' Francesca enquired, considering her friend who was looking pale, strained and a little feverish.

'No . . . yes . . . not particularly.'

'I see.' Francesca took the proffered coffee. 'Oh dear, well, I shall have an awkward morning with George while he explains to me why he felt he had to help you all to a bottle or two.'

'Don't be rough with him, Fran. He doesn't have that much self-confidence. You were a blow to him, anyway. I mean, he's no worse than a lot of people who are bursars.'

'No, indeed. Not a decent qualification among the whole gang I met last week. The point is, Louise, universities are going to have to improve their financial control, and hire properly qualified people. Hard men in charge of government funding, such as are being drafted into the DES, will otherwise not play.'

114

Louise put her cup of coffee down, got up and walked to her desk, fiddled with papers and sat down again. She was wearing a long black skirt and a scarlet shirt, and Francesca, waiting for her to arrive at whatever the point was, thought admiringly how the clear red lit up the pale skin. 'George was a bit more than a friend at one time. That's why I feel badly.'

'Louise! You didn't!' Francesca was too startled to control her reaction.

'Oh yes, I did. Clare and Andrew were tiny, bloody Michael had gone on a conference, and I'd had virtually no sleep for a week. *You* know. George dropped round and found me screaming at the kids, so he jollied us all up, made me sit down and eat, stuffed the kids into the pram and told me he'd be back in three hours.' She smiled in memory, looking soft and pretty. 'When they came back, they were ready for an afternoon's rest; I'd had two hours' kip, and George helped me tidy the house.'

'And then?'

'Not what you're thinking. He said why didn't I go to the library till the kids' bedtime?'

'Ah. Yes. I do see. He fixed it so you could *work*.'

'That's right. I did two and a half hours, finished an article, and felt like a plant that had been watered just in time. George went back home after supper, but he'd given the kids such a good time that they both slept – oh, till something like six in the morning.'

'Which seemed, of course, like a long lie-in. I know it well.'

'Yes.' Louise sighed, looking at her hands. She looked up again. 'Anyway, Alice was away that week and dear George popped round after lunch every day so that I could get some sleep or get to the library, whichever I needed most. So on about the fourth day he stayed to supper, and we went to bed.'

Francesca watched her friend stirring coffee, looking a good deal younger than her thirty-five years, the straight-nosed, delicate profile outlined against the bookshelves which filled three walls of her small room. 'What happened when Alice came back?' she asked, having discarded several other questions.

'Michael came back home as well, from his conference, so we stopped. It all got too difficult.'

'Did George feel that too?'

'No.' Louise suddenly looked weary and impatient and har-

115

assed. 'No, he didn't. He kept trying to start again. And I felt like a pig, as if I'd used him just because I was so desperate with the children.'

'You used each other,' Francesca said firmly. 'You can't have four brothers, like I have, without knowing men are tremendous opportunists. You don't have to feel bad.'

'I do, though. He was rather smitten, while I just thought, Oh well, that was nice, but I don't want to go on doing it.'

'Neatly reversing the usual male-female feelings about an affair,' Francesca pointed out. 'You *are* lucky – I always used to come off worse, when I had affairs with people.'

A knock at the door startled them both.

'That's my supervision. I'll go and see George after it, so be ready to be gentle with him.'

'I'll do my best, Louise. See you.' Francesca rose, and opened the door, stepping back in surprise as she saw Michael Taylor, rather than several undergraduates. 'I know you're teaching in a minute,' she heard him say apologetically as she went down the corridor. She hesitated at the door to the Bursary, unwilling to face George Hellier, and decided that she could legitimately spend time with Serena Copley, the college secretary, squaring the notes of the Finance Committee meeting.

She passed a profitable hour and a half in the college secretary's office, getting another part of the college routine into her head. She had been so immersed in the Bursary that much of the work of the rest of the college had passed her by: the endless correspondence with schools, the University and the DES seemed to be occupying another useful woman virtually full-time, so her tentative hope that the college secretariat could be deployed on the Appeal was obviously not going to be fulfilled. She walked back to the Bursary, soberly considering, and drew breath sharply as she found George Hellier hovering at her desk.

'George, sorry, I was with Serena in the office. I should have told you.'

'No, no, I knew where you were.' George did that sort of thing very efficiently, Francesca reflected. His natural friendliness and curiosity meant he always knew where people were and what they were doing. She watched him as he fidgeted, trying to imagine him as Louise's lover, noticing the deep lines on his neck and round the eyes, the thick hair just beginning to recede above the square, reddened face. A comfortable fatherly chap, and so he must have appeared to her friend Louise. Not nearly clever enough for her, but then few men were, including, apparently, Michael Taylor.

'I've been talking to Louise,' he said heavily.

'Yes. She and Hazel Bradford told us that some of the wine bought for big occasions has been finding its way into the mouths of our Fellows.'

'I shouldn't have been doing it.'

'Nor should they, George. If we need our Fellows to entertain – and we do – then we must budget it properly, not tuck a few away at the end of parties. And so I told them.'

George Hellier, though plainly relieved at this wholesale allocation of responsibility, said gloomily, 'I should have said so at the time.'

'Yes, you should. I'm afraid we have just been inviting our caterers to join in. We'll have to get rid of them as soon as we can.'

'Yes.' George was looking miserable still, and Francesca considered him.

'Could you ask around and find us . . . what? . . . two or three different catering firms? Get some quotes? We'd better agree exactly what we're asking them for, then we'll see them together.'

'Oh yes. Thank you, Francesca.' He managed to get his head up and look her in the eye, and she was relieved to see the message that what was past had been received and understood. 'I'll do that right away.'

'We can't change this lot until September, mind. I haven't had time to look at the contract, but I'm sure we have to give three months' notice at least.'

'We do. You're absolutely right.' He hesitated at the door, and she hoped he was not going to make a speech of gratitude. 'I'm afraid it's rather the way we did things at the school I was at before I came here. It's not a mistake I'll make again. It has been quite a jump to here from St Aidan's, but I think I could manage as a bursar, in the end.'

Francesca, at thirty-four, was senior enough in the Civil Service to have had to disappoint subordinates older than herself, but she still found it difficult. She hesitated, fatally, and saw George

Hellier's face fall. Belatedly she found a formula. 'George, I just don't believe there is going to be such a thing in the future as a bursar without some formal financial qualifications, not for a college of this size. I am leaning heavily and expensively on our auditors in order to get by.'

'No, you're not,' he said bitterly, 'you're telling them what to do.' He walked back from the door, closing it after him. 'I should have done another training after I came out of the RAF.'

Francesca was now feeling wretched, but knew, grimly, that this was one of the prices of power and responsibility. 'George, there's more than one job to be done here, and we haven't even worked out how to run the Appeal. I haven't brought myself to look at those accounts.'

'Nor have I,' George said, usefully diverted. 'Or rather I haven't been allowed to. Patti – that's Patti Davis, an old Gladstonite – would never let me near them.'

'Oh God. Say no more, George – sufficient unto the day.'

'Yes.' He hesitated again at the door and she sat, waiting for him to leave. 'The caterers are coming at noon to set up for the lecture. I just want you to know I'll check everything as it arrives.'

'Thank you, George. I was wondering how we could do that without offending our own people.' Her genuine relief drew from him a wry smile, and finally he went, closing the door with his usual care.

Across in the Warden's lodge, Sarah was also having a busy morning. Susan Elias's parents were, perhaps inevitably, being a good deal less cool and sensible than Susan herself, particularly her father, an excitable, over-protective Jewish businessman who was disposed to feel that armed police should now be patrolling every corner of the college grounds. Sarah had been driven to bring into evidence the name and reputation of Detective Chief Superintendent Toms, which had unexpectedly exerted a calming effect. Alan Toms had appeared on TV the week before, modestly explaining how his men had dealt with a young man holding his estranged wife and mother-in-law hostage: his reputation would not necessarily deter a prowler, but it did appear to have given

Mr Elias pause. She must remember to tell Francesca, who would be amused; she would drop in on her way over to lunch.

She walked out on to one of the college's expensive gravel paths and saw Louise and Michael silhouetted against the impressive archways with which the college was generously provided. They were standing well apart; as she watched, Michael Taylor moved closer to his wife, who took a sharp step backwards. He said something, and she turned away, anger and impatience in every step. Not a good moment for a quarrel, when in seven hours' time Louise would be giving a show-piece lecture on medieval trade to a distinguished and critical audience. Sarah set her path to miss both of them, but failed to avoid Michael Taylor who started in one direction, decided against it, and changed course abruptly, so that he almost walked into her.

'Good morning, Michael,' she said firmly. 'Have you had lunch? Do join me.' It would keep him out of Louise's path for a while, and with luck would defuse whatever row they had been having.

'Warden, yes, I mean, no, I haven't had lunch.' There was a fleck of pink across his cheekbones and he was looking tired and thin – one of those men, thought Sarah, who fade away to skin and bone when they are unhappy or under stress. He was hesitating, plainly embarrassed, but she swept him along, ruthlessly, asking questions so that by the time they arrived at the hall he was talking with some animation. They queued and, being early, found that the 'special' was hot and plentiful.

'Francesca Wilson tells me that the essence of cost-effective catering is to provide some version of mince on blotting paper,' Sarah said into a silence, as Michael Taylor looked at the display, obviously not interested in eating any of it. 'As in spaghetti bolognese, or hamburger on a bun.'

'Or shepherd's pie.' Michael Taylor roused himself to contribute to the discussion.

'Or chilli con carne, which is today's offering. The beans count as the blotting paper, I expect.' She was pleased to see him ask for a plate of today's version of mince and a slice of apple pie and cream. Nothing could be gained by Louise Taylor's husband being hungry as well as at odds with her. She watched him covertly while he ate with the appetite of real hunger, not distracting him with conversation.

119

'Sorry, Warden,' he said, pushing back his plate. 'I missed breakfast.' He leant back to dispose of the empty plate, casting a would-be casual look round the dining-room, and Sarah could not decide whether he was relieved or disappointed that Dawn Jacobson was not there. She considered him as she ate her yoghurt, wondering what she could usefully say. Any entanglement between a supervisor and an undergraduate was always highly undesirable even if, as in this case, the undergraduate was not one of his pupils. He should have more sense. In the charged atmosphere of the feminist debate in the University, he was risking accusations of exploitation and sexual harassment. She had been weakly hoping the entanglement would evaporate over the long summer vacation, but something about Taylor's glance round the dining-hall made her feel that intervention might be necessary, for the college's sake.

'Do you have lunch here most days?' she asked, deciding to work obliquely towards her objective.

'No. Yes, I suppose I do. I am here teaching two days a week, and I fell into the habit of coming to join Louise.' He looked over at her, uneasily. 'We seem never to see each other alone; as soon as I come in Louise needs to hand me the reins and go back to the library, or her room here. We just don't have space for all her material at home.'

'It's difficult trying to keep papers in two places as well – I always seemed to come back to keeping it all together in a college room. You, of course, presumably need a laboratory?'

'Yes. But I'm not doing much at the moment.'

And Louise Taylor was; hard-working and naturally prolific, she had turned out five articles for academic journals and a well-received book in the last two years.

'It must be very hard keeping it all going at once – children and an academic career. I never tried.'

'I wish I hadn't gone in for an academic career.' The statement came straight from the heart, and Michael looked appalled as he heard what he had said. Sarah calmly went on with her yoghurt and waited, busying herself with passing him the sugar for his apple pie, which he took mechanically. 'I'd like to do something else, only I don't know what,' he said slowly.

'Teaching? In a school, I mean?'

'I don't particularly like teaching.' That, as Sarah knew from

120

reports, was true; Michael was uninspired and pedestrian, but in the highly fact-oriented first-year chemistry course, it did not really matter. 'I should have got out some time ago, but I had an idea – about crystalline structure. It didn't work.'

The best academics, of course, like this young man's wife, would have turned up another workable hypothesis; but Michael lacked Louise's confidence and the ferocious drive needed in the anti-academic climate of the day to keep one's place in a shrinking market. And Louise Taylor, who was brilliant, ambitious and focused, was not going to be supportive and spend hours talking out his problem with him. Neither, indeed, was Dawn Jacobson, if that was what he had hoped; Sarah's experienced eye saw that young woman as a hard nut, and unlikely to waste a lot of time on a thirty-eight-year-old failed academic.

'What about the Civil Service? It recruits people at your sort of age directly into the Principal grade. Or there are openings in the technical services?'

'I don't think the Civil Service is what I want. Anyway, it's pretty difficult to get in, isn't it? Their people seem to have commercial or legal training. Like Francesca Wilson.'

'Francesca is a one-off,' Sarah reassured him.

'Very ambitious, isn't she.' It was not a question. 'I couldn't imagine how her husband coped, until I met him. She can't push *him* around.'

Sarah recognized that this was the complaint he did not want to voice about Louise. 'I imagine it is easier for people, both of whom want careers, to marry people in different fields.'

'Yes. The competition is not as direct, and you aren't faced with someone who knows exactly how well or badly you are doing. But I still don't think the Civil Service is what I want.' He paused, stirring his coffee, and looked up at her. 'Louise seems to be meeting some of the senior DES people – I haven't liked them at all; they seem very obsessed with politics.'

'Internal politics are a hazard in any organization. But the DES has been very supportive of Gladstone.'

'Sir Neville Allason is an old colleague of yours, I understand?'

Sarah took some sugar to give herself time to recover; this rumour that Francesca had picked up from her fellow bursars appeared to have some general currency, but it was ridiculous. She and Neville had been discreet at the time and that was

121

twenty-five years ago. 'Yes. I have known him – oh, for ever, and he has been most helpful.'

'Louise sees a lot of him, of course.'

Sarah forced herself to continue stirring her coffee, carefully. All the college's formal dealings with the DES were mediated through her or, in extreme cases, through Francesca, as Bursar. In an official sense, Louise had no reason at all to meet Neville Allason. She remembered, as if it had all been many years ago, that Louise had been with Neville in February when he had come to see her at the health hydro, but that had seemed unremarkable at the time. 'Neville said that he was looking forward particularly to hearing Louise speak tonight,' she said, cautiously.

'Is Lady Allason coming?'

'No, unfortunately she can't – I'd have liked to see her myself.' Sarah had rung up Neville Allason's office a week before, having noticed that the invitation to the Raab Lecture did not include husbands and wives, to explain that Jennifer Allason was more than welcome. He had been effusively grateful, but briskly clear that she would not want to come. All this now took on a sinister air in the light of Michael Taylor's persistent questions.

'He's heard Louise speak before, of course, at a conference in February.' Michael picked at the sugar with a spoon; it had set into a white lump at the bottom of the bowl. 'And she had lunch with him recently, in town.'

Sarah was disconcerted to feel a faint, reminiscent, pang of pure jealousy, as the full implications of what she was being told struck her. She considered the young man opposite her and decided that he was not trying to denounce his wife to her Head of House – he was feeling his way blindly towards a frightening fact he did not want to recognize.

She sent him for more coffee for both of them while she thought about Neville Allason. In the long years she had known him he had always had an affair on the go, but they had invariably been conducted with women of his own age, or older – like herself indeed. An involvement with Louise, twenty years his junior, was a break in that pattern. Perhaps, Sarah recognized with an inward pang, the women of Neville's age or older were no longer a match for a dynamic, physically active, driven man of fifty-four. There was a lot of circumstantial evidence to suggest that Michael Taylor's worst fears were justified.

She could scarcely reassure him by pointing out that Neville's affairs lasted for about eighteen months before he ran to Jennifer Allason for cover; this explanation would hardly be comforting, and, worse, it might be wrong. This time, with an ambitious, beautiful woman nearly twenty years his junior, that pattern might not repeat itself. It was, in fact, exactly the kind of situation that could break up a long-established marriage. In a small, instantly suppressed, moment of self-pity Sarah found herself thinking that, given Gladstone's difficulties, Neville Allason might have chosen someone other than a Gladstone Fellow with whom to conduct a mid-life crisis.

She returned her attention to the young man before her, who was carefully putting cups on the table, his fair hair flopping and his mouth set.

'Where are you going on holiday?' she asked.

'I want to go to Italy, but Louise says she is too busy and can't make plans.' His mouth suddenly turned down and she realized he was close to tears.

'I should insist if I were you,' she said, abandoning caution. 'Everyone needs a holiday.'

He would not look at her and his mouth squared at the corners with the effort not to cry as he spoke. 'I have tried to insist. She doesn't want to go away at all. Or not with me.'

'Try again when the exams are over. It's a bad time now, and she must be nervous about the lecture tonight.'

'Not Louise. She knows she's good – unlike me. Sorry, Warden, you don't want to hear all this.' Michael put his cup down, looked at his hands for a moment and left her without a farewell.

She watched sadly as he walked out into the bright sun, head down, heedless of the warmth – then stopped, as someone called to him. It was, inevitably, Dawn Jacobson. They spoke for a few minutes, then turned and went off together in the opposte direction, towards the hall of residence.

By five thirty that afternoon the preparations for the Raab Lecture were virtually complete, at least in a material sense. Francesca, having carefully stayed away while the food and drink were being delivered, put her head into the hall in search of George

Hellier. As she had hoped, he was in the thick of it, carrying a clipboard full of papers, in earnest conversation with the dark man in his thirties who was the prime mover in Greenlees Ltd, the catering firm. Francesca made no move to go and talk to them; if her supposition was right Mr Greenlees had been responsible for milking cash from the college for all of the five years he had held the contract, and even if she was wrong, he still had to go since the college could not afford the risk. Mr Greenlees, interestingly, made no attempt to come and talk to her either; George Hellier must have decided to bite the bullet and warn him that notice would be given on this contract as soon as the college lawyers had cleared the letter. Her opinion of George rose again smartly; it was only right to warn them of the letter, but it could not have been a pleasant task and he had already had a bad morning. It was a great pity he had no formal training and had not had proper supervision. She looked past him to Louise Taylor who was on the platform, professionally checking the height of the microphone and testing the sound system, her lecture notes laid tidily on the rostrum.

Francesca joined her by the small table set in the middle of the platform and laid out four name-plates, for Louise herself, Sarah Murchieson, Jennifer Raab, granddaughter of the donor, and the Vice Chancellor as star visitor. Neville Allason, in this university gathering, rated a front row seat but not the platform, it not being his patch. Francesca herself had argued for putting him on the platform as the taxpayers' representative, but, to her exasperated amusement, this had been received as being in remarkably poor taste.

'You OK?' she said companionably to Louise.

'Up to a point.'

'What's wrong?'

'This bloody place. I've just had a stand-up row with Alice Hellier – why does one say a stand-up row? Would it have been better sitting down, I ask myself?'

'What a time to choose. I take it you didn't start it, though? What was it about, or would you rather just come and have tea?'

'Tea I need. It was about George, fundamentally, but disguised as a row about the Future of Gladstone.'

'I suppose you insisted on taking the real issue?' Francesca said, interested, descending the platform stairs and leading her friend towards the Bursary. 'My best friend at school was just like you. I would have been quite prepared to keep the row to Whither Gladstone.'

Louise hooked an arm in hers. 'Nonsense,' she said, with affection. 'You don't pull any punches either, you just do it differently.'

'So what happened? How did you get into a fight?'

'It broke out at the Library Committee meeting this morning.'

'The *Library* Committee? Sorry, Louise, do go on.'

'It was the usual argument about "Do we keep all the basic textbooks or do we reckon students have to budget to buy those anyway and we only keep the more esoteric stuff?" Now, some of my students can barely afford to eat, never mind buy textbooks, so I always argue for buying the basic stuff. But Alice Hellier, who was at Newnham around 1863, argues that everyone can afford the basic textbooks so we shouldn't keep them.'

'Every time? I mean, you both do this every time?'

'Francesca, being in college is like being in a convent. You're all stuck in it together. The names don't change and neither do the views.'

'Sorry, I distracted you. Tell me how you got from there to George?'

'By no straight line, believe me.' Louise had started to enjoy herself. 'It went, roughly, that it was ridiculous we should be so strapped for funds that this argument was even necessary. If "certain" Fellows – meaning me among others – had only agreed to mixing the college three years ago, then funds would have poured down on us, along with male Fellows and male undergraduates. And when I pointed out that this was a non-sequitur, Alice said, at least we could have had a sensible bursar like George, rather than Phyllis Trench who I conceded was a weak sister and a poor advertisement for women Fellows. So I produced you as an example – but it transpired that *you* haven't been very nice to George, and *I* have made it all worse by confessing to you our little customs and practices.'

'Oh dear, does she know that you and George were more than colleagues?'

'I hope not,' Louise said soberly. 'But I do sometimes wonder. If she knows, however, she presumably also knows it stopped not long after it started.'

'Presumably.' Francesca looked at her watch, anxiously. 'Louise, are you not on in just over an hour?'

'Yes. I must change. See you later.'

An hour later, Sarah, dressed and gowned, was waiting with Alice, Francesca and Louise to receive guests, all four of them very aware of being on show.

'At least I don't have to demonstrate academic distinction,' Francesca had pointed out. 'I can just look like the imported hard man.'

'Not a tremendously successful impersonation,' Louise said, straightening the gown on her shoulder for her.

Louise herself was looking slightly feverish, not surprisingly, but extremely pretty, and not at all nervous. Sarah returned her attention to the door and warned, 'Here we go! Peter, how nice. And Professor Barker.' This to a bent and hobbling figure of unimaginable distinction in a field of mathematics that she could only just spell.

Neville Allason came in and waited his turn to greet them; for once Sarah was not at all pleased to see him as he stood, glittering with health and vitality, his blond hair shining in the evening sun. Today, he made her feel old and tired instead of distinguished, and she resented him for it. He was looking a touch feverish too, she noticed with misgiving.

He kissed her, then Alice, then Francesca, then Louise, observing impersonally that they all looked beautiful, it was a pleasure to see them. Sarah was maliciously pleased to see Francesca receiving this with a whole carton of salt. He was, however, in top form, teasing Francesca about the sherry. 'I have to say that using up stocks, if they are all like this, is going to be a false economy,' he said, consideringly. 'You give this to a potential donor and you risk souring the milk of human kindness.'

'Either that or they will understand immediately how much we are in need of help.' Sarah was quite prepared to play along while they were still in private, and he turned to her, laughing.

'No, no, Sarah, they're used to men's colleges and decent drink. I wouldn't pioneer the 1980 gooseberry or whatever this is with the City.'

'Wait till you see what we're having with dinner,' Francesca

126

said, straightfaced. 'I was assured it was a great bargain, and they had a lot of it left.'

'Oh God,' Neville said, without impiety. 'As a matter of fact I can see that the drive to control costs must be biting deep, Francesca. I take it some other young woman is wearing the rest of that skirt.' He waved his glass at Dawn Jacobson, who was one of the paid student waitresses on duty, and who had acquired a uniform black skirt that fitted on the hip, but had plainly been made for a much shorter girl.

'That is Dawn Jacobson. One of my pupils,' Louise said. 'A very capable girl.'

'Hardly needs to be,' Neville Allason said cheerfully.

'Neville, what a thing for a Permanent Secretary in the DES to say,' Sarah said.

'I wasn't speaking professionally, dear Sarah. Hang on, is that not Professor Woinarski?'

'It is, indeed. I must go over.' Sarah went to greet her distinguished contemporary, and after a minute glanced back to summon Neville. He was at Louise Taylor's side, saying something to her in tones carefully pitched below general audibility. Louise looked up at him and blushed becomingly, and he gazed back at her, his expression momentarily unguarded, looking ten years less than his real age. Sarah looked away, uneasily, and found herself face to face with Michael Taylor who was watching, expressionless. Louise put a hand on Neville Allason's shoulder for a second, a gesture so intimate that they might have been alone, and went over to greet another guest. Neville watched her go, with a look quite unlike the careful public friendliness he had always displayed with his other lovers.

Sarah was momentarily furious with him; his looks and larger-than-life quality were causing heads to turn and a lot of distinguished and malicious observers might be drawing conclusions from that vignette. No wonder the University was gossiping. She glanced at Francesca who was looking blank, a clear sign with her of intense thought; well, perhaps she could reason with Louise, they were the same age.

Putting these considerations resolutely aside, Sarah led her group firmly across the lawn to join the rest of the audience in Tydeman Hall. Turning from the task of sorting out the front row, she found Francesca gazing balefully at the massive plaster rosette above their heads. 'Found your seat?'

'Yes. I am however being distracted by the thought of the woodworm chomping through the beam just above the front row. Hopefully it will come down on the Golden . . . sorry . . . Sir Neville, rather than on me.'

'Do not even think such things, Francesca.'

'You would, if you had spent the afternoon with an architect. Hadn't you better give the Vice Chancellor a bunk-up the stairs, poor old thing?'

Thus admonished, Sarah went over to assist Professor Sir William Tatten, only a couple of years her senior, but much incapacitated by arthritis in both knees, and arranged him in one of the platform chairs. She placed him between herself and Jennifer Raab, and sat down and waited for the stragglers to file in. At the very last minute, as the lights dimmed slightly and the audience settled, clearing their throats and rustling papers, John McLeish slid into his seat beside Francesca, who gave him a look of mixed reproof and relief. McLeish patted her hand, comfortably, looking pleased with himself, and nodded to Sarah on the platform as he caught her eye. She smiled at him, amused, and rose to her feet to introduce Louise and 'Some Problems of Medieval Trade'.

She had not realized quite how good Louise Taylor was, she thought humbly, ten minutes later, watching Louise's profile as she spoke. This slight dark creature was making medieval trade seem as alive and real and current as anything in the business sections of the Sunday papers, without in any way over-extending the known facts about it. Her hypotheses were clear, sharply argued and well supported; she had used three months in the libraries in Avignon last summer to good purpose; and Sarah could guess, from the reaction of the professional historians in the audience, that she was breaking new ground. And Louise made it fresh and not dusty; she made the audience see the medieval traders, hard men breaking open new markets and new transport routes, going bust or dying in the attempt. No wonder her students loved her; she was a born communicator who wanted to share her considerable knowledge and her pleasure in the subject. A future professor without a doubt, and an ornament to Gladstone. Whatever mess she was creating in her personal life would have to be tolerated or dealt with.

After a neatly timed fifty minutes, Louise arrived at a set of tentative conclusions, offered modestly but firmly, and told an enthralled audience where her research was going next. It was not the sort of occasion where audiences rose and stamped, or threw roses, but they were not far off, Sarah felt. The applause continued for a full three minutes, as Louise stood on the rostrum, flushed and smiling. While everyone was still clapping loudly, she looked down to the front row and smiled, for Neville Allason alone, who unguardedly raised both hands to clap her. Louise looked away quickly, then bowed again, and walked over to sit down in her place of honour, leaving Sarah to wait out the applause, and give the college's thanks from the rostrum.

As the audience rose to go, Sarah stood beside Louise, waiting courteously for Professor Tatten to be lowered from the platform and watching the milling groups below. 'A triumph, Louise,' she said quietly. 'A wonderful lecture.'

'Thank you.' Louise barely turned her head. Her whole attention was concentrated on Neville Allason who was standing by the steps, beaming at her. She came down like royalty, her eyes fixed on Neville Allason's face, and he greeted her with a kiss which could only just have been passed off as a salute between colleagues.

It was Louise's night, and she was deaf and blind to the conventions. All anyone could do was to try and bring the wilder excesses within the confines of suitable behaviour. To this end, Sarah resolved, Neville Allason and Louise would be kept busy, being introduced to as many of the distinguished company here present as possible. She appropriated Neville herself for the Vice Chancellor, and as he turned away from Louise to acknowledge the introduction, was able to introduce her to the Professor of Medieval Studies at Aberdeen, whom she had personally invited, and who was bursting to ask Louise about Avignon. Francesca was, she could see, doing her bit as well; as Neville finished his conversation with the Vice Chancellor, she was at his elbow with a Provost of King's, Cambridge, and a talkative German historian. It should be possible to keep the whole thing within the bounds of decorum until such time as twenty-four of the assembly could be swept away to the Warden's dining-room to eat – and *that*

129

would be all right, because Neville Allason and Louise Taylor were seated at different tables.

And so it proved. As gossip and scandal were averted, at least for the evening, Sarah began to relax. The soup and the main course passed without any of the undergraduate waitresses dropping anything, and pudding was on its way. A disturbance at the third table, at which Francesca was hostess, caught her eye; one of the undergraduate helpers was saying something urgently to Francesca, who was excusing herself and leaving at speed with the girl. Disaster, no doubt, in the kitchen – but no one could still be particularly hungry, and the infinitely efficient Francesca would cope with whatever it was.

Sarah went on with her conversation and, sure enough, the pudding arrived, was circulated and eaten, and coffee was announced. But Francesca had still not returned and, in fact, John McLeish had vanished as well. It was perfectly possible that both were now deployed backstage, and Sarah forgot about them until everyone rose to file into her sitting-room for coffee.

'Sarah,' Alice Hellier said urgently from the shadows as she stood back to let the guests file ahead of her. 'I need to speak.'

Sarah waited, smiling, until all her guests had gone through and turned, enquiringly.

'Bad news, I'm afraid. There's been another attack, on a second-year: Clarissa Dutt. On her way back to her room.'

'Is she hurt?'

'Yes. Badly, I am afraid. She put up a fight and he stabbed her. Francesca Wilson and her husband have gone in the ambulance with her.'

130

9

Francesca sat in the overheated waiting-room of the West Middle-sex casualty, shivering uncontrollably. She was wearing her husband's jacket over her own good dark blue silk suit and there was blood down the front of the jacket, the skirt, her own hands, and her muddied shoes. This seemed suddenly intolerable to her and she got up to find somewhere where she could wash, then sat down again as the room went dark and she was assailed by nausea. No one was taking any notice of her at all; her husband had put her down in this hard chair without taking his eyes off the trolley on which the unconscious girl lay, and had left her without a backward glance, to follow the medical cavalcade through the swing doors. He had returned, briefly, five minutes later, to bestow his jacket on her and a bloodstained shirt which reposed beside her in a plastic bag marked 'Laundry: West Mx'.

She sat, waiting for the trembling and sickness to subside, unable to avoid playing back the events of the evening. She had been summoned from her position at the head of her table by a white-faced undergraduate to hear that a body, female, was lying in the college grounds and that an ambulance was on its way. She had sent the undergraduate waitress straight back into the dining-room to get John, and they had taken off for the gardens, escorted by the shocked and trembling young man who had found the body. They had run, she trailing behind the other two in her straight skirt and high heels, so that she had arrived to find John on his knees in a pool of blood beside a bejeaned figure lying face down. The young man was standing helplessly at his side.

'She's breathing,' he reported. 'Handkerchief?'

Francesca produced a clean one, mutely, and the young man a

less clean one, both of which John accepted, winding one at elbow level on the girl's left arm and another on the right wrist and twisting the ends.

'Hold these,' he said impartially to them both, and they did so, the young man steadied by John's automatic assumption of authority. John felt his way quickly up the girl's spine and turned her over, infinitely gently, Francesca and the young man scrambling clumsily to keep from obstructing him while hanging on to the impromptu tourniquets. Blood flowed from the girl's chest as she was turned over, soaking her already sodden sweater, and John McLeish cursed, quietly, tearing off his jacket and shirt, to use the shirt as a bandage.

Francesca, trying to recognize the girl – a big, dark-haired young woman in a sweatshirt and jeans, pale as death – drew breath in sharply in horror, as blood trickled from the corner of the girl's slack mouth.

'John,' she said, on a rising note of panic.

'Yes,' her husband said, matter-of-factly. 'He got her lung. Where's that ambulance?'

They all listened, and heard the sirens.

'He can't get in,' Francesca said, galvanized, and, handing her tourniquet over to the young man, hitched up her silk skirt to knicker-level, kicked off her shoes and ran across the grounds to the gate by the car-park where the porter was ineffectually trying to find the key. She paused, helplessly, but the ambulance driver, a burly tough in his forties, sized up the situation and prised off the lock by brute force with a screwdriver produced from his cab. Then he drove his ambulance at breathtaking speed across the gardens, using the last of the light to avoid flower beds, trees and the college fountain, with Francesca, eyes tightly shut, bumping between him and his co-driver.

She took back her bloodstained handkerchief from the young man and watched as the girl was loaded on to a stretcher, John's fingers on the pulse in her throat and an oxygen mask over her face.

'Hurry,' he said, just once, and everyone speeded up, not questioning the necessity. Francesca scrambled into the ambulance too, still clinging to the tourniquets, her hands aching. The ambulance did a swerving course between the obstacles in its path, then swung, sickeningly, out of the college car-park on to the road, its siren going full blast to scatter any student bicyclists, who might be expecting the normal courtesies of the road.

They had arrived at the hospital in very short order. As she had got out, stiffly, Francesca was elbowed aside by a medical avalanche of three nurses, a doctor, and her own husband, who was telling the young doctor to get the heart-and-lung-man out of his cot now – there was a lung puncture, possibly two, and probably a graze on the heart muscle as well.

She looked up now, deciding to have another try at getting to the Ladies, to see Neville Allason and Louise Taylor bearing down on her, their steps involuntarily slowing as they took in her appearance. Just at that moment, the swing doors opened and John reappeared, in a hospital white coat that failed to meet over a bloodstained vest, and a mask, loosely attached to one ear.

'The consultant's started,' he reported. 'Assuming he's any good, the girl's got a chance. The knife missed her heart, but she's got a collapsed lung and she's lost a lot of blood.' He stared coldly on a drunken customer, who, sunk down in the seat next to Francesca, rose and stumbled away. He then bent the same cold eye on Neville Allason, who was explaining that he had been sent to see in what way he could help, and that Dr Taylor was here to stay by the injured girl, who turned out to be one of the undergraduates for whom she had tutorial responsibility.

'Good,' John McLeish said, unsmiling. 'Then I'd be grateful if your car could take Francesca back to the college now, Sir Neville. And you could send your driver back with something for me to wear – there's some kit in the boot of my car, Fran. Here are the keys.'

Neville Allason blinked, but fell in with these plans, volunteering to wait at the hospital with Louise until his car came back again. Francesca, unable to rise to the standards expected of a policeman's wife, gazed longingly at her husband.

'I can't come back just yet,' he said to her gently, squatting unselfconsciously beside her chair. 'I'm sorry, but I rang Alan Toms's lot and he's coming to meet me here. Dame Sarah will look after you at the college, darling. You need a bath and a sleep.'

Louise Taylor sat down on her other side. 'Would it help if I came back in the car with you?'

'Yes,' Francesca said, unequivocally, feeling about six years old, and found her way to the car with her husband's strong arm around her, just noting that Sir Neville's driver was obviously having the best time he had had in years.

By seven thirty the next morning, Sarah was awake, dressed, made up and organized, knowing that it was going to be a difficult day. She had been in bed for precisely four and a half hours, having had an active night ringing the Dutt parents, encouraging Francesca through a bath and putting her to bed in the spare room in the Warden's lodge, and driving herself back to the hospital to find that Clarissa Dutt was out of the theatre and in intensive care, recovering from a successful operation on the chest.

She collected a clean handkerchief and applied perfume, feeling that all the armour she could put on would be useful for morale. She decided to go and eat breakfast in the college dining-room, as a sign that the captain of the ship was on the bridge, but checked on her way out as the phone rang.

'It's Alan Toms here, Dame Sarah. Just to let you know we have a young man helping with our enquiries. The uniformed lot picked him up early this morning.' His tone invited her to marvel. 'Drunk in charge, they thought, then they wondered. So my lads took over and young Fields recognized his name from the lists we talked to when you had your last spot of bother.' He was sounding cautiously pleased with himself, and Sarah, mindful of Francesca's strictures, hoped privately that the detective force was not overstepping the limits of reasonable behaviour.

'Mind you, his solicitor's there,' Alan Toms said, dismissively, 'and his father. Banker of some sort.' He made it sound like an undertaker. 'But I think he's our man – I've got that feeling.'

'It would be an enormous relief to everyone here if the man were caught.'

'Victim's holding her own, I hear. I've got a man there, in case she can tell us anything.'

'Yes. Yes, the hospital did her very well.'

'Well, they would, wouldn't they? It didn't take young John long to make his presence felt.'

Sarah agreed that John McLeish was undoubtedly an effective

representative of the Metropolitan Police, and rang off, with Alan Toms's promise to keep her up to date.

Fellows of the college clustered round her at breakfast and she told them quickly what was happening. 'But what do we *do*?' Alice Hellier was badly upset and did not care who knew it.

'The police are questioning a young man, Alice. However, until we are sure I think we must warn all our undergraduates to go in pairs anywhere outside the building.'

'How?' It was a fair question, even if the note of hysteria was unwelcome. There was no recognized way of summoning a meeting of Gladstone's 400 undergraduates and 100 graduates, and there was in any case no time: many-tongued rumour was already doing quite enough damage.

'We'll have to draft a notice and put it up on all the boards. I'll talk to the president of the Junior Common Room and the graduates' convener personally, and get the notices up as soon as possible. Alice, had you not better rest this morning?'

'No, no, Warden, I must teach. This is the final supervision for one of my groups.' Given Alice Hellier's shaking hands, it did not seem that it would be a rewarding experience for young women already themselves nervous and Sarah sought for a stronger way of discouraging her.

George Hellier, looking tired and battered, leaned forward. 'Come and have a coffee with me, Alice. I need your eye over the library account for just five minutes.' He steered her away gently but firmly.

'Good old George,' Hazel Bradford said approvingly. 'He'll calm her down. She's a good teacher, and the girls will benefit if she can just get a grip. Warden, as soon as you have a draft notice, I'll gather my flock and read it to them, several times, in a monotone, so they will get bored with it.'

'Not too bored to heed the warnings about going in pairs.'

'No, indeed. All the time, or just after dark?'

'Oh surely, just after dark. He needs cover, whoever he is.'

'Clarissa didn't see anything?'

'No one has been able to ask her yet.'

Sarah walked back to the lodge, drafting in her head, and dictated three paragraphs before the phone rang.

'John McLeish. Have you got my wife there?'

'She is in the best spare room, sound asleep, John.'

'I'll come and get her at lunchtime. You can have her back tomorrow.' He choked off, without discourtesy, her attempt to thank him on Clarissa Dutt's behalf, and was about to ring off when she had the bright idea of reading her draft notice to him. He listened carefully, and offered two small amendments. Her respect for him increased; he was absolutely clear despite having been up all night.

'I wouldn't be too confident West Drayton have got the bloke – or that if they have they can hang on to him,' he warned. 'The suspect's Dad got Sir Richard Brown out of his bed and down to the station.'

'Sir Richard Brown?'

'You've led a sheltered life, Dame Sarah. Top criminal solicitor in London – specially good with hopeless cases.'

'You mean you think this young man really may be guilty?'

'Either that or Sir Richard is the only criminal brief the boy's Dad has ever heard of.'

Sarah digested this, thoughtfully. 'What else ought we to do, John?'

'Alan Toms regards this second attack as a personal insult. He'll find him, if he hasn't already got him. But he doesn't have the manpower – or rather his uniformed colleague doesn't – to patrol all your grounds after dark. You're down to a couple of lads with torches, so you really need to make sure your girls don't go out alone after dark. And not just your girls – your Fellows as well. This one's a nutter and he's not going to discriminate on grounds of age. You be careful.'

'I hope you're not too worried about Francesca?'

'If she needs to work evenings, I'll be there too.' The response was swift and uncompromising, and Sarah felt a pang of jealousy. Fortunate Francesca to have a man so openly protective of her. 'She thinks she can manage anything,' John McLeish said, 'even a nutter. The fact is, no one can and she hasn't quite grasped that. See if you can get the rest of your young women to take it on board. See you at lunchtime.'

Sarah made the amendments he had suggested to her draft, and dispatched the secretary to make twenty copies and round up all senior student representatives or nearest reasonable substitutes. Then she would have to go to the hospital and talk to the Dutt parents. For Clarissa to be all right was now the point – far more important than other young women not doing as well as they might in their exams.

The day wore on, with endless phone calls that were confusingly divided between distinguished guests, ignorant of the night's events, ringing to congratulate her on the Raab Lecture, and reports from various college fronts. A student visiting the third-year nervous breakdown who, it had been hoped, would manage to take her finals from the hospital, had idiotically told her about the latest events at Gladstone, and the girl had promptly relapsed. So the procedure for organizing a medical certificate, and the delicate business of negotiating an arrangement with the University, would, after all, have to be undertaken. It should be possible, Sarah thought, with a flicker of returning animation, to package the request for an aegrotat – a certificate that but for this breakdown this particular student would have passed her finals – with the much easier request that Clarissa Dutt, blamelessly recovering consciousness in hospital, should be exempted from the second-year exams.

Apart from that, quite unnecessary, nuisance, the college was reasonably calm. It had been impossible to prevent gossip, but so close to the exams, most undergraduates were working to tight revision schedules and had little attention to spare. One of the more articulate third-years, having heard all the warnings, had observed that she could not imagine who these fortunate people were who had planned to go out anywhere in the next two weeks. Alice Hellier had recovered and taken two supervisions, appearing both exhilarated and steadied by the experience. Sarah, meeting her by chance, crossing the gardens, expressed her warmest appreciation of George in general, and his support over the events of the last twenty-four hours in particular.

'He *is* kind, and supportive, and helpful.' Alice Hellier's anxious expression softened. 'I just wish more people would recognize it.'

The problem was, of course, as Sarah did not feel like articulating, that in an old, proud University these were not the qualities that secured the highest academic rewards. Nor were Heads of Houses drawn from the ranks of the kind and the supportive; they were either high-flyers resting on their laurels, or people like her, with good connections and distinguished public careers. Alice Hellier was not stupid, but she was not worldly, and

137

George was her husband; it was none the less a pity that she should still be banging her head against that particular brick wall.

Sarah's reflections were disturbed by the sight of Michael Taylor pushing his bicycle into a rack at the side of the student building that housed Dawn Jacobson. It was extraordinary how clearly any man engaged in some sexual misdemeanour telegraphed his intentions. Everything about Michael, from his quick glance round as he padlocked his bicycle to the elaborately jaunty way he hurried to the door, shouted that he was up to something. Sarah compressed her lips. Whatever the troubles in the Taylor marriage, Dawn Jacobson was in her charge and needed to get a good pass in her examinations. This was indeed exactly the kind of thing – a man using a young woman to ease his own problems – from which membership of a women's college ought to insulate its undergraduates.

'Michael?' she called commandingly, stopping him in his tracks. 'Have you a minute?'

'Of course, Warden. I'm just doing some last-minute coaching.' He dropped the padlock of his bike, picked it up, and succeeded in spilling the contents of his briefcase; he had apparently planned to conduct a supervision with the aid of two paperback novels and a bottle of wine.

'I have not seen Louise today, but I take it she is sleeping in after her most successful lecture last night?' Sarah enquired, with a cold eye on his fumbling efforts to reorganize himself.

'She's not at home.' He had flushed scarlet and it was fading, patchily. He had been cornered and knew it, but was not going to give up. 'She felt it necessary to go and sit with the Dutt parents for a bit.' He barely managed to keep resentment out of his voice.

'Very good of her. I do not know what I should have done without her or Francesca.'

'Or Francesca's husband,' Michael Taylor pointed out, aggressively, looking down at her.

'Indeed,' Sarah agreed, wrong-footed, but recovering herself. 'Would you say to Louise, if you see her before I do, that I have a long list of people who rang to congratulate her, and us, on her lecture. It was extraordinarily good.'

'She is brilliant.' Michael Taylor suddenly looked wretched, and Sarah felt deeply sorry for him. The truth was that men still expected to be the stars in their marriages, and it was hard on an ambitious man to find it was his wife who was the one in demand. And it was doubly hard when the wife was making it blatantly clear that she preferred successful men like Neville Allason.

Michael Taylor cast one single, hopeful look upward to a second-floor window, but Sarah was implacable.

'Which of your pupils have you kindly come to see? I thought I saw the whole of your chemistry set on the lawn – it's such a beautiful day – together with most of the rest of the college? It seems awful to think that when it gets dark none of us will be able to go out alone.'

Michael Taylor, acknowledging defeat, followed her through the gardens, to greet a surprised group of his second-year students, and Sarah left him there. She had delivered a warning; she could hardly bar him from Dawn Jacobson's door, but he should have absorbed the message.

Occupied with these reflections, she went back to the lodge, conscious of increasing exhaustion. It had not been possible to sleep after lunch, but perhaps she might have a catnap now? As she sank into a chair, the phone rang.

It was Neville Allason's private secretary, followed, after an annoying two minutes, by the man himself. 'Sarah? I waited to call till teatime in the hope that you'd got some sleep during the day. How are you all?'

'Louise Taylor is at the hospital,' Sarah said, unmollified and irritable. 'I am all right, just a bit short of sleep,' she added, belatedly remembering that Neville Allason, for whatever reasons, had stuck it out till 2 a.m., deploying himself and a government car to good purpose, and had since presumably done a day's work.

'I managed a kip on the plane to Scotland,' he said easily. 'Apart from *that*, I have to tell you the evening was a wild success. *You* looked smashing, Louise spoke brilliantly, the college looked wonderful. I have received all sorts of unwarranted congratulations for my humble part in keeping it afloat.' Neville Allason, never one to be rattled by female moodiness, was exerting his full, very masculine charm, and Sarah was, as ever, warmed and soothed by it.

'It *was* a success, wasn't it? I was proud of us. Does this mean the tutorial funding is all right?'

'Yes, indeed – or it will be the minute you submit your accounts formally. My people have seen them, of course, and discussed them with Francesca Wilson. *That* was another good idea, wasn't it?'

'I have occasionally wondered if you planted her at the health hydro.'

'No, that was serendipitous,' Neville said seriously. 'And Superintendent McLeish is a formidable creature, isn't he? A future Chief Constable if ever I saw one. Bit priggish of course, just like all those chaps – when I congratulated him on saving that child's life, he implied that they were trained to do that sort of thing three times before breakfast if need be.'

So John McLeish had not been charmed by Neville; perhaps that direct masculine assurance worked best with women.

'A very distinguished turn-out too, Sarah,' Neville went on. 'Does you credit, particularly the Aberdeen people. But darling, *where* did you get that German historian you lumbered me with?'

The trouble with Neville, Sarah thought, as she regaled him with the antecedents of Herr Professor Günther von Eysenck, distinguished medievalist and world-class bore, was that when he was on form he made other men seem about as entertaining as cold rice-pudding. At the end of fifteen minutes' deeply refreshing gossip, conducted with the easy intimacy only possible between people who had reached the ultimate in physical closeness, she felt a great deal better, and ready to face dinner in college. Indeed, she realized as she put the phone down, she had quite forgotten that this delightful supportive man was the same person who was threatening to destabilize his creation by an ill-considered affair with a key member of her staff. Nor could she deflect him with the same efficiency she had displayed with Michael Taylor that afternoon; Neville was too old and too used to having his own way. In two and a half weeks, however, term would be over and the long vacation would start. Three months was a very long time indeed in any sort of extra-marital love affair, and the situation would, with luck, have resolved itself by September. A final phone call to the hospital before she made for dinner and an early bed reassured her that the news was good:

Clarissa was still in intensive care but improving by the hour, and it was hoped to move her out the next day into a side ward.

A decent night's sleep worked its usual magic and Sarah woke the next day feeling much better. The Dutt father was asleep in a spare room so, had any change for the worse come to Clarissa, phone calls would have woken everyone. Sarah had breakfast and read the paper in peace. Reassured that the outside world was still in place – she was in danger of losing all interest in it, so absorbing were the affairs of Gladstone – she went into her office, greeted her secretary and spent a happy forty-five minutes reading the notes of congratulation and thanks that were pouring in, mostly full of gratifying pleasure that Gladstone was in such good heart, and all full of well-merited praise for Louise Taylor. She gathered them all together in a folder and set off to find Louise. Whatever idiocies she was up to in her private life, this professional applause was hers by right.

Louise was sitting in her room reading a newspaper, so concentrated and tense that for a moment Sarah thought it must be bad news.

'Louise?'

'Oh Sarah. The *TLS* has my lecture. In full.'

'How marvellous.' Sarah peered over her shoulder since Louise appeared to be unable to let go of the paper. 'What a compliment.'

'The chap said they might print a bit of it, but it's *all* here. I was just checking.' Louise was trembling with excitement, on the edge of tears, and Sarah exclaimed and applauded.

'I have letters you will be pleased to see too,' she said finally, when the first pleasure was beginning to evaporate. She handed over the file, and Louise managed to let go of the *TLS* and fall on the letters.

'Crumbs,' she said faintly, after a silent ten minutes.

'Well deserved,' Sarah said firmly.

The phone rang, and Louise looked at it, longingly.

'I'll see you later.' Sarah went, closing the door to the sound of Louise's voice changing as she answered the phone. 'Darling,' Sarah heard her say, 'I've been longing to talk to you.'

Not her husband, indeed; Sarah knew only too well who it

141

was. She sighed and turned hopefully into the Bursary for comfort, where she found it. A triumphant Francesca was brandishing a letter from one of the livery companies, offering £20,000 towards the restoration of Tydeman.

'I thought it was worth trying,' she said smugly. 'I promised we'd redo one of the carbuncles with their crest of arms.'

'For £20,000 we could stand an engraving of the president, wife and mistress reworked as a classical set piece,' Sarah agreed. 'That does cheer me up.'

'Now for the bad news. Alan Toms rang John at breakfast time. He sweated the lad he fancied as our knife-man, all of yesterday, but he can't prove it. The chap's Mum – separated from Dad – is giving him an alibi, and what with his very classy solicitor Alan daren't charge him. He's hopping mad – he's sure the chap is guilty, but he can't hold him. His brief's applied for a writ.' She looked soberly at Sarah. 'Since Alan thinks he's right, that suspect will not move without a detective on his trail. But, of course, he may be wrong and the lad's Mum may be telling the truth – in which case our man is still out there, in action.'

'Mr Toms seemed terrifyingly shrewd to me,' Sarah said thoughtfully.

'That he is; it's scrupulous he isn't. In fairness, my John thinks he probably does have the right man, and if Sir Richard Brown wasn't acting for the man, Alan would have got a confession. I'd have liked to have someone safely behind bars, I must say. Failing that, we'd better organize our own patrols for the grounds.'

'Francesca, we employ four men in all, of whom George Hellier is the only one who is remotely able-bodied.'

'That's true, isn't it? The gardener is 103, you'd never get Rumpelstiltskin on the gate to volunteer, and Peter the porter is nearly sixty and couldn't fight his way out of a paper bag. Not much of a vigilante group. Can we deploy people's husbands?'

They were discussing the problem in a desultory way when George Hellier, attracted by coffee, came to join them, followed shortly by Louise Taylor and Hazel Bradford. The conversation turned to the triumphs of the Raab Lecture.

'How much did we drink this time?' Louise asked idly, as the conversation ran down. She heard herself and laughed. 'I mean, you've had nothing else to do but count bottles, you and George, since the lecture.'

'We've done it, though,' Francesca said smugly. 'George and I checked the left-overs, counted them twice, and left a message on the caterers' answerphone so they couldn't argue, either. We had forty-three left over – three cases, seven loose, not to mention some half-empties which we gave the kitchen. So we drank 149 bottles all up, with drinks first, dinner-party in the lodge, and wine and cheese for the rest. Not bad at all.'

'It's very much less than last year,' Louise said, frowning.

'That's because George and I counted it. I told you, the caterers had most of it last year.'

'Can I have a look at the party accounts when you do them?' Louise was still looking puzzled.

'Of course.' The phone rang and George picked it up. He listened and held it out to Louise. 'Sir Neville Allason,' he said, his voice devoid of expression.

'I'll get it put through to your office,' Francesca said hastily, avoiding everyone's eye as she took the phone from George and told the DES to hang on while she transferred the call. 'Where were we?' she said briskly, putting the phone down again.

'You were going to do some work,' Sarah said obligingly and made her own excuses, leaving George Hellier still looking like a thundercloud.

The phone was ringing as she arrived.

'Dame Sarah? It's Alan Toms. We've had to release our suspect for the assaults on your young ladies.'

'I *am* sorry. You thought you had the right man.'

'I did have, I'd put my pension on it. He won't bother you again though, that I can promise you.'

Sarah struggled to find a formula that would not involve casting doubt on his judgement. 'It would be most helpful from my point of view – to reassure the girls and their parents, you understand – if there could be some visible police presence over the next three weeks. That would take us to the end of term.'

'The uniformed branch will provide a couple of blokes to come by at intervals. I don't know why they can't do more, they're not doing anything else worth a bugger, pardon my French.' Alan Toms sounded both weary and furious.

'I am most grateful for whatever can be done.' Sarah was

143

hesitating over a valediction, wondering whether 'Better luck next time' would be appropriate, when he bade her goodbye abruptly and rang off. She summoned as many of the Fellows as could readily be found to a room at the lodge, and explained the situation to them.

'Don't tell any of the undergraduates. It would merely alarm them.'

'It alarms me.' George Hellier, who had arrived with Francesca, spoke for the meeting. 'If they had the right man he is now out and able to do it again. And if, despite Mr Toms's conviction, they didn't, then there is still someone out there, only the police don't believe in him.'

'I agree that neither of these is a reassuring scenario, George.'

An awkward silence fell.

'We could patrol the grounds ourselves.'

'I knew you would want to be helpful, George, but we are very low on able-bodied men. In fact, you are the sole representative of the species in the employ of the college.'

'And *that's* ridiculous.' Alice Hellier sat up. 'We make this nonsense of managing our assets, we can't get enough people to teach the hard sciences and now we can't even muster a patrol to protect our students. All this because a third of our number – a minority – voted to protect an anachronistic vision of female education.'

'Alice, my dear . . .'

'Oh, for God's sake, Alice, not *again*.' George and Louise spoke simultaneously, both contributions acting as petrol on the flames of Alice Hellier's frustrations.

'And the way *you're* behaving, Louise, we're in danger of losing Michael too, and then we have virtually no chemistry supervision.'

Louise turned a bright, unbecoming scarlet, and Sarah reached out a firm hand to Alice Hellier. George Hellier looked helplessly embarrassed, and the rest of the Fellowship appeared to be struck dumb.

'Alice. Louise. We have a serious emergency here, and I would welcome support from you both as two of our senior Fellows. We are responsible for these children.'

This call to the colours served, as Sarah had hoped, to distract the participants. Alice Hellier went very pink and scrabbled in

144

her handbag for a handkerchief. Louise, the colour in her face slowly subsiding, sat still, looking down at the table.

'The answer is a private security firm,' Francesca said, coming to life, as if the acutely embarrassing scene had not taken place. 'That's what people do in this kind of situation. A couple of chaps at night until the end of term. It costs money, but it buys peace and reassurance.'

The Fellowship considered this diversion gratefully.

'Won't Mr Toms be offended?' Sarah asked.

'No, he told us he doesn't have the manpower himself. He expects commercial organizations, such as he thinks we are, to hire protection if we need to.'

A neat solution, Sarah thought wearily, and worth it, whatever it cost. The meeting agreed with her.

They dispersed: Francesca to ring up her husband to get a recommendation to a security firm, and the rest of the Fellowship to bring such semblance of normality as they could to the affairs of the college. Sarah waited, deciding there was no point in starting to do anything sensible, and presently, as she had expected, Alice Hellier appeared, looking plain and tired, her nose reddened.

'Sarah, I do apologize, you have troubles enough.'

'It is a tremendous strain for you too, Alice, particularly at this stage of term.'

'That is kind of you, but I should not have spoken as I did to Louise.' She pressed her hands together. 'I just could not bear to see her making a fool of all the men here.'

'Not John McLeish.' Sarah, who very much did not want to have a conversation about George Hellier, spoke in mock alarm, and Alice, taken by surprise, laughed reluctantly.

'No, no. Not only does that young man look like the Rock of Gibraltar, he behaves like it. Stands no nonsense – Michael Taylor should be firm too.'

'Alice, since we are having such an awful time anyway, may we talk about Loraine French? I understand that the hospital say there is no possibility of her being able to take finals and I need to work out with you how to present this to the University.'

'Oh dear.' As Sarah had hoped, Alice Hellier was deflected from the subject of the Fellowship's husbands. 'Yes, they are very bad about recognizing mental illness. We'll have to edit the medical report.' She was all professional competence now, even over a student right outside her own subject, and Sarah thought, as she had done many times before, what a refuge a proper academic training was from the demands of emotion.

The day went on, improving slightly as it went. Clarissa Dutt was still in an intensive care bed, but had been relieved of a substantial number of the wires and tubes adhering to her, and the Dutt parents, bright-eyed with hope, were at the hospital, getting in the nurses' way. Francesca reported that Securicor would be fielding two men as night guards, from the next day.

'I told them no guns,' she said, appearing at Sarah's desk.

'You were offered a choice?' Sarah said faintly.

'We could obviously have hired the Guards Armoured if we had felt like it, yes. I was made to feel rather insignificant with my humble request for two sensible men with torches.'

'So if everyone's careful tonight and tomorrow we should be fine,' Sarah said, thinking it through.

'Absolutely. I'm here tomorrow, anyway, till late. The wonderful Caroline is taking William to visit her mother, and John's working, so I thought I'd catch up.'

'Don't you dare go out into the gardens alone, Francesca. John would never forgive me.'

'Don't worry.' Francesca smiled at her indulgently and disappeared into the Bursary.

Louise Taylor was hurrying: she was late and she was still raging over the scene she had left at home. She turned her ankle on a bit of uneven pavement and laddered her tights so that she arrived on the doorstep of the neat flat-fronted Pimlico house in a state of some agitation. The door opened before she could ring the bell and Neville Allason, looking tired, bustled her through the tiny hall into the familiar flat.

'Darling,' he said, kissing her. 'There are limits to how many official dinners I can duck at the last minute, longing to see you though I was.'

'I expect you found a way.' Louise was in no mood to be rebuked, however obliquely. 'May I have a drink?'

146

'Darling, of course. We can't go out, I'm afraid – I have a nasty stomach upset. That's why I'm not at the Clothworkers' this evening – so I've got eggs and smoked salmon and things.'

'Very nice too.' Louise remembered the state of her kitchen at home after Michael, sullenly acknowledging that it was his turn, had put together the children's supper. It had been difficult to see how the preparation of baked beans on toast and poached eggs could have caused so much disruption.

'You're looking tired after your triumph,' Neville Allason said, leading her through to the tiny sitting-room and placing her carefully on the sofa. 'What's happened to your cheek?' He touched her gently and she winced.

'It's not been my day. I was hurrying to get out and I walked into the kitchen door.' She hesitated, insensibly relaxed by the pretty room and the company of her lover, who was prowling round the small room tidying away small amounts of clutter.

'Neville, I needed to talk to you. I've had a job offer. I've been . . . well, not promised exactly, but near enough . . . a Reader in the University and a Fellowship at UCL.'

He stopped, checked, for a moment, then came and sat beside her. 'Well, congratulations, darling. But is the journey from West Drayton not rather long for you?'

'I'd have to move.'

The sudden silence in the little room could be felt, and she watched as he put his glass down carefully, and got up to go through to the kitchen.

'How would your husband feel about that?' he asked, from the kitchen.

'He wouldn't be coming with me, or rather with us. I can't leave the children, and he won't want them. He's very bad about looking after them.'

Neville came back into the room slowly, carrying the bottle of wine, his face unreadable. 'It's always a mistake to decide these things too quickly,' he said carefully, and she thought with a pang that suddenly he did look his real age, this was a man in his fifties, nearly twenty years her senior.

'If I were in central London with the children we could meet more easily,' she said, standing up to kiss him.

He felt stiff and uncomfortable, she realized, and she slid her hands up his back muscles, then into the waistband of his

147

trousers and he started to unbutton her blouse. She smiled to herself in triumph and gave way to pure sensation and the feel of his back muscles under her hands and the growing warmth spreading all through her.

'Come on, darling, I can't go on standing up.' He bustled her through to the bedroom and they ended up as they always did in a tangle of bedclothes. Afterwards, when both of them were dressed again, she sat in the kitchen watching him arrange smoked salmon neatly on two plates, with lemon wedges and black pepper; he had claimed, laughing, that this was his sole culinary skill.

'Darling,' she said, uncomfortably conscious of the aching bruise on her cheek which she had forgotten about in bed, 'shall I take that job?'

'If you want it.' He was not looking at her, and she waited out the silence. 'Louise,' he said, sitting down opposite her. 'It would be wonderful to have you closer than Gladstone, but I have to say I'm not sure if we could find a lot more time to be together. And we'd have to be extremely careful.'

She reached for the bread, trying not to acknowledge the chill feeling in her stomach. 'Does your wife know anything about us?'

'I hope not,' he said flatly, looking at his plate. 'Oh, God,' he said, to the smoked salmon, then looked up and reached across the table and took her hands in his. 'Darling Louise, you know how I feel about you, but we have to be patient. I've been married for thirty years, unbelievable as it seems. And I, too, hope to get the top job one day; now is not the moment to rock any boats.'

Louise removed her hands, suddenly cold to the bone. 'If your wife knew about us, I suppose, she would make a fuss.'

'I would not like her to find out about us.' He had stopped trying to eat and was looking at her directly, and Louise, whose gifts and talents had hitherto taken her over all barriers, stared back, the taste of the smoked salmon greasy in her mouth. 'My love,' he continued, coaxingly, reaching for her hand, 'don't try and do everything at once. Take your decisions in order – if this job is right for you, take it, although Sarah will kill me for saying so. Then consider what you want to do about your marriage. You're rushing at it.'

True, she thought, momentarily relieved, and tried to eat some more, but found she could not swallow.

'Does your husband – does Michael know about us?' Neville asked, carefully, and she set her teeth, pushing her plate aside.

'I haven't told him, if that's what you mean. He may suspect, but he's fully occupied having it off with one of my students. He's probably with her now.' She managed to look at him and was taken aback; he was expressionless but intent and she understood that a variety of calculations were taking place. 'I'd better go back,' she said wearily. 'I can't eat, and we don't seem to be much pleasure for each other.'

'I'll drive you,' he said disconcertingly, making no attempt to persuade her to stay. 'Oh damn, I can't. My own car is in the country and the official car went to the dinner with the chap who substituted for me. Sorry, darling – I'll get you a taxi.'

'More discreet too,' she said bitterly. 'Colleagues might wonder about the official car.'

He got up and leant over her to kiss her cheek. 'Come and have coffee while I call a cab. We'll both be better tomorrow.'

Sarah arrived, in style in the DES car, in the car-park of Gladstone at eleven thirty that evening. Under the lights of the porter's lodge she saw Francesca and John McLeish grinning at her.

'Good party?' Francesca asked demurely. 'I finished the accounts for the Raab Lecture – Louise borrowed them to look at – and have started to sort out the kitchen account up to when we arrived. It's *worse* than last year, if anything.'

Sarah looked at them with affection. 'Have you just arrived, John?'

'Two hours ago. I have just got her out. I'll walk you to the lodge,' he offered.

'Thank you,' she said, noticing that even with the events of the past week fresh in her mind, she had nearly declined all assistance to cross fifty yards of darkened garden. The confidence in their own abilities that had been painfully instilled in women had to be equally painfully eroded when it came to physical violence.

She turned to accompany John McLeish, just as Michael Taylor, riding a battered bicycle which was missing a back light, raced into the car-park in a shower of gravel.

'Warden, sorry. I've come to find Louise.'

149

'She isn't here,' Francesca said, surprised. 'She left for home at about six o'clock.'

'I know. Then she left again, saying she had work to do. But it's now twenty-five to twelve.'

'She's not in her office,' Francesca pointed out, as they all turned to look at the corridor of small offices. 'No lights.'

'What time did she leave your house?' John McLeish asked and they all turned to look at him, drawn by the urgency in his voice.

'Oh, about seven thirty,' Michael said.

'Are you sure she was coming here?'

Michael stared at him. 'Where else would she go to work?' he asked stupidly.

'The university library? The library here?' Francesca suggested. 'I'll look.'

'*Not* through the garden,' John McLeish said in tones brooking no argument, and Sarah felt a cold chill invade the comfortable warmth engendered by good food and wine.

Francesca gave him one startled look and took off down the corridor, just not running. Sarah opened her mouth to speak, but a look at McLeish, methodically fetching a torch and jacket from his car, discouraged her and she stood wordless beside Michael.

'She's not there.' Francesca, running this time, was back. 'Nor in the Bursary, George was there – he's been in and out all evening – and says he hasn't seen her either. He's coming.'

'Right.' John McLeish hunched himself into a jacket, the line of his broken nose prominent under the lights, the dark, almost black hair, cut too short, standing up at the back of his head. He looked carefully at Michael Taylor, who was still standing clasping his bicycle. 'Dump the bike.' He handed him a torch. 'Have we got another of these?'

The porter, who had been watching with mounting fascination, twittered off to look in various corners.

'Over there. To your right. Under the paper.' The man dithered and found the big torch that McLeish had spotted.

'I'll come then,' Francesca said hopefully.

'No. This torch is for George Hellier.'

Sarah, feeling increasingly swept away by a tide, looked up to see George arriving at a fast walk, his face a map of anxiety.

'Wait in the Bursary,' McLeish said impartially to both women, and plunged out into the car-park, making for the gate that led into the gardens, with Michael Taylor and George Hellier.

Francesca turned back. 'Sarah, you're looking stunned, but don't – that's just Metropolitan Police language. It uses only the imperative form and has no words for "please" or "thank you", or "would you mind". Where can Louise have *gone*?'

Sarah hesitated. 'I think I know.'

'What?' They were in the corridor, out of earshot of the porter. 'Oh, you mean she's with the Golden Oldie? . . . Sorry, sorry . . . Can you find him?'

'I would have to ring Jennifer, his wife. But I do know that he cancelled an official engagement at the last minute tonight. I got a ride home in his car with the chap who substituted for him.'

'Oh dear.' Francesca, not herself without experience in these matters, was appalled.

'Perfectly all right to ring if he is at home,' Sarah was thinking aloud, 'impossible if he isn't. I beg your pardon, Francesca, I seem to be using Metropolitan Police speak too.'

'As well you might. Very difficult phone call, given that it's already . . . what . . . quarter to twelve.'

They looked at each other helplessly. Then Francesca's eyes widened, and Sarah heard the noise too – running feet. Francesca rushed to the door and threw it open to admit George Hellier, who was fighting for breath. 'We've found Louise. Get an ambulance. John says she's alive. Oh, God, her head.' He was scarlet with exhaustion and wheezing. Sarah seized the telephone while Francesca was opening windows and loosening George's tie. 'Breathe steadily, George, or we'll need an ambulance for you too. And give me that torch. I'll go and see what else John wants. Where are they? Over by the tennis courts? I'll find them. Sarah, you stay here to direct the ambulance.'

It was the longest fifteen minutes of her life, Sarah thought, waiting for the ambulance to arrive, feeding George lukewarm coffee in the interval of holding a disjointed telephone conversation with one of Toms's acolytes. George was shaking and grey with shock, and she did not dare leave him, even though Louise might be dying outside. As her head cleared, she rang Alice Hellier, who was mercifully awake and working, so she could look after George. Then there was a desperately confused five minutes while, hindered by the porter twittering with anxiety, she found the keys to the big gate so that the ambulance could get in and bump across the college lawns. She saw torches flash in acknowledgement and the ambulance alter course towards them. Having no torch, she decided reluctantly against going over, but it was only about five minutes before the ambulance was bumping back through the gates to the car-park, slowing to drop Francesca from the cab, then accelerating as it sped silently down the drive. She heard them check at the lodge gates, then the siren wailing as they turned on to the main road.

'John's gone with them,' Francesca said, redundantly.

'This is becoming a habit for him. How bad is it?'

'The attacker cut her hands with the knife but missed anywhere important. The real injury is a fractured skull. He hit her with something heavy, John says.' Francesca was white under the lights. She leaned against a wall. 'She is alive, Sarah, take heart.' Her eyes widened and she looked past Sarah. 'Ah, hello, Uncle. Well, you were right, weren't you?'

Sarah turned to offer a more conventional greeting to Detective Chief Superintendent Toms, who had arrived accompanied by a driver, Detective Sergeant Fields and a young acolyte, all grim-faced.

'Not this time, as it happens. Good evening, ladies,' Toms said tightly. 'Our suspect signed himself into Otley Farm around eight o'clock this evening. *You'll* know it, Francesca.'

'But it's in Somerset, *hours* away! And Louise was alive and well at . . . what? . . . seven o'clock,' Francesca said in horror.

'Right you are, Frankie. So if my man was checking himself into a loony bin there at eight o'clock – with Fields here not far behind him – he didn't do this, did he?'

10

Sarah woke full of mindless anxiety, which focused itself all too quickly into the memory of the ambulance swinging out of Gladstone's gates for the second time in three days. She looked at her bedside clock; it was six thirty and she had been up until two. As she sat up, realizing she was not going to be able to go back to sleep, she heard footsteps in the kitchen and remembered that Francesca was there. John McLeish had rung from the hospital to decree that his wife should spend the night at Gladstone in the Warden's lodge behind locked doors and a burglar alarm system.

'Sarah, any news?'

'No.' She joined Francesca, who was standing watching the electric kettle which was slowly getting noisier.

'Can we ring the hospital?' Francesca's eyes were swollen and gummy with weeping and sleep, short dark hair in spiky disarray, the long nose and solid jawline very prominent. She looked like a caricature of herself, ten years older and heavily plain.

'I'll do that now,' Sarah promised, and let Francesca make coffee and toast for them both while she worked her way to the night sister. She covered the receiver to say to Francesca, who was watching her anxiously, that Louise was out of the theatre and in intensive care. John McLeish was, moreover, available to speak.

'John,' she said into the phone, her spirits lifting at the sound of his voice. 'We're both up, Francesca and I. Would you like to speak to her? Have you seen Louise?'

'I'll talk to Fran in a minute, please. Louise is doing as well as could be expected, the doc here tells me. Straight bloke. He says it is touch and go. He managed to relieve the obvious pressure points on the brain, but it was a bad fracture, and another collapse would not amaze him.'

'Is there any damage to the brain?'

'Some, he thinks. Maybe some paralysis. He says we won't know for days how much. If she lives.'

Sarah swallowed, wishing she had not asked. She found herself unable to speak for a moment, appalled by the vision of Louise Taylor damaged and mumbling, rather than quick-moving, beautiful and rousing an entire audience. Francesca was at her elbow, clumsy with anxiety.

'Can I talk to him?'

Sarah handed over the phone, wordlessly, and sat down with her cup of coffee, gratefully gulping it.

Francesca was listening silently; she looked up, met Sarah's gaze, and instantly averted her eyes. 'So Louise's Mum has the children?' she asked finally. 'Well, that will hold till tonight, and then we'll make a plan. I'll sit tight here. Talk to you later. No, I won't, don't worry.'

She put the phone down, looking shocked, and seized her coffee cup, dumped three spoonfuls of sugar in it and drank half of it, greedily. 'Sarah, John will come over shortly.' She paused, anxiously, and poured Sarah some more coffee.

'I'm all right, Francesca, do go on.'

'Sorry. Michael Taylor was carted off to assist Alan Toms's lot with their enquiries just as soon as Louise got out of the operating theatre, which was about four thirty. It was a long operation.'

'He was what?'

'Taken off for questioning. After all, Sarah, he's her husband.'

Sarah stared at her.

'Most murders – which this was meant to be – are domestic, and most of *those* are committed by husbands.' Francesca was trying hard to achieve a detached approach, but her hands were locked round her coffee mug, which shook as she tried to drink from it.

Sarah took it from her. 'I suppose I knew that,' she said drearily. 'Why did they let Michael stay at the hospital first rather than take him off straightaway?'

'Alan Toms would have concluded that Michael wasn't going to get very far if he tried to run from John, and he might well confess sometime in the watches of the night. And John, of course, would make sure that he got all that in order.' She seized a handful of Kleenex and blew her nose.

'A policeman's must be a very demanding life, emotionally,' Sarah said feebly.

'John doesn't get emotional any more. He's been in the force since he was twenty-two and he's been through things going wrong. The last time I heard him cry over work was well before we were married; a man he counted as a friend died in his arms, murdered. John always felt he could have prevented that if he'd been a bit cleverer. Me, now – I'm still being taken aback all the time by police practice.' She threw a ball of Kleenex at a wastepaper basket, missed, and got up wearily to retrieve it. 'On the other hand, if it was Michael who did that, who beat Louise over the head so savagely that it is touch and go whether she lives and functions, I would be happy to hang him personally. How could anyone do that to Louise – to that bright talent – even if she was fucking the whole of the top two grades at the DES and every husband in the college?' She put her head on the table like a child and wept, and Sarah patted her shoulder, waiting for her to get herself a little under control. It was only a few months ago that she had suffered a near-breakdown over a new baby, she remembered.

'This is too much for you, Francesca, with the baby, and with John involved so heavily as well. I think you had better take a couple of days' leave.'

'No, I couldn't – please not, Sarah. I couldn't bear to be at home, brooding. And John won't be involved further; he can't be. He's a bystander here – it's not his patch. He'll go back this morning to Notting Dale and Alan Toms will be doing it all. Anyway, it's Louise I mind about.'

Sarah sat helplessly, remembering the pleasure those two had taken in each other's company and Francesca's ungrudging support for Louise's triumph at the Raab Lecture. 'Oh my God,' she said, startled into blasphemy. 'Neville. I never rang him – it went out of my head.'

They looked at each other. 'Do you think she had been with him?'

'He ducked the dinner last night.'

'You could ring him now, and tell him what has happened,'

Francesca said, distracted from grief by the necessity for action. There was a long deadly pause.

'Unless we think he already knows,' Sarah said, slowly.

'Oh, Sarah, no – surely not. We all saw how he felt about her.'

'A lovers' quarrel?'

'Not any lover I've ever had.' Francesca stopped and turned slowly pink. 'God, I am sorry, I'll go out and come in again.'

'No, I have got rattled. I've never heard that Neville went in for hitting women.'

'Ring him up,' Francesca said firmly. 'It's ten to seven, he'll be up by now, and if you get his wife, it's not difficult to explain that you're ringing to seek professional help. He was here during the last attack, after all.'

'Yes.' Sarah reached for the phone, impelled by Francesca's logic, but it rang, making them both jump. They stared at it and Sarah, taking a deep breath, managed to get her hand to it, a cold chill in her stomach.

'Neville!' she said, in amazed relief. 'I was just going to ring you. We have further trouble here.'

'The police woke me with it twenty minutes ago. Or rather they woke Jennifer. She rang me – I'm at the flat in London.'

'I'm sorry, Neville. There was, of course, nothing anyone could do to help, so I waited until the earliest I thought I could wake you.' She avoided Francesca's eye. 'But why did the police come to you?'

There was a long pause while she reflected that if she were not so tired she might have found a less direct way of asking.

'They seemed to feel that I might know where Louise had spent the evening.'

'And did you?'

'We were together for a couple of hours. I don't know how they knew that.' Neville was furious as well as frightened, Sarah realized, and felt suddenly blazingly angry herself. How had he the nerve to be angry with her – or anyone else – because one of his little intrigues looked like landing him in real trouble?

'Well, the police didn't hear it from me,' she said sharply. She looked over at Francesca to see how much of this she was taking in, and got a shock. Francesca was sitting, transfixed, eyes wide, one hand over her mouth in a textbook illustration of guilt.

156

'Did you bring Louise back here afterwards?' she asked Neville sharply, on the basis that attack was going to be the best form of defence.

'No, I didn't. I put her in a taxi, and she rang me, as I had asked her to, just before eleven o'clock, to say that she had arrived safely at Gladstone. As I told the police.'

'Oh, you did tell them?' Sarah said, incautious in relief.

'Of course I bloody did. But I went to bed after I'd seen Louise off. Of course, I can't prove it. I'm in the flat, Jennifer's at home. I'm seeing Toms later today. I gather Michael Taylor and your Bursar's husband both spent the night at the hospital. He seems to be living with you – McLeish, I mean.'

'Michael Taylor is with Mr Toms now at the police station, helping with enquiries.' Sarah decided not to be drawn.

'Is he? Now *that* Toms did not tell me – well, he wouldn't, would he? I suppose Louise might have admitted to her husband that she was seeing me?'

Sarah, contemplating Francesca, decided to duck this issue. 'My part of the story, Neville, begins when I came back from dinner at eleven thirty to find the McLeishes just leaving, and Michael Taylor just arriving in search of Louise. It was John McLeish who thought of looking for her at all, I am ashamed to say. I was just thinking about getting to bed. I was back at a reasonable hour, because I got a ride in your car.'

'Oh, that worked, did it? Yes, well, I found I didn't need the car.'

'Because you were with Louise,' Sarah reminded him, and found herself, in an echo of twenty-five years past, exasperated by the way Neville Allason kept his life compartmentalized, effectively denying that any affair was actually happening.

'Yes,' he agreed, sounding injured. 'Yes. That's true.' He hesitated. 'I understand she is stable – what a word!'

'That's what we have just been told. But John McLeish is coming here on his way back to work – to his own work, I mean, at Notting Dale – and we may get some more details.'

'Ring me, Sarah, anyway.' It was a plea.

'Of course.'

As Sarah put the phone down, Francesca took her hand from her mouth.

'It was me who told the police about him and Louise. I told

157

John you had wondered if she had been with Sir Neville – and, of course, he passed it on. I never manage to remember that he is a policeman rather than my husband.'

'It's a vocation, isn't it?' Sarah said thoughtfully. 'It does not matter in the slightest. It can't be the first time that Neville has had to deal with an embarrassing situation without any warning. He is very tough.'

'I do not think I could cope with a husband like that,' Francesca said.

'Exactly my own view. Not that I was asked to, you understand.'

'Were you very sad when it broke up?'

'Angry as well as sad. He cooled off rather suddenly. With hindsight I understood that Jennifer had become suspicious and anxious so Neville had rushed back to the fold.'

'He might have told you.'

'No. It would have involved far too much clear thinking about what he was doing.'

Francesca considered her respectfully, looking very young, and Sarah smiled at her wryly. 'May you not lead such an interesting life.'

'John and I had a shot at being unfaithful to each other before we married. The other parties both left us.'

'You must neither of you have been serious about your lovers,' Sarah said, with conviction.

'What it did for me was to make me understand that what I wanted was a husband and children, rather than a lover and a set of brothers.' She stopped, and both of them heard the noise of car wheels on gravel and a car door slam.

'John,' Francesca said confidently, and rushed to meet him. They came into the kitchen together and Sarah saw them as a stranger would: two dominant people, just ceasing to be young, the woman tall, slim, vulnerable, expressive, hands flying as she explained about Neville Allason; the man almost a head taller, steady as a rock, taking in all the detail. He folded himself neatly into a chair.

'Coffee?' Francesca said busily. 'Breakfast?'

'In a minute. Are Alan's men here? They should be going over the grounds with a hoover.'

158

'Oh goodness,' Francesca rushed to the window. 'Now you mention it, yes.'

'They'll need coffee and encouragement, but we don't want people tramping about everywhere. Could you take out a tray – and watch where you put your feet?'

'Hover horizontally, perhaps?' Francesca was restored by having her husband with her.

'That would be good.' He grinned at her, watched while she filled half a dozen cups, and patted her gently as she passed him on her way out with a laden tray.

'What about you, John?' Sarah asked.

'I need to talk to you about your predecessor.'

'What? Sorry, why?'

She sank down into a chair and looked into the unwavering brown eyes, noticing irrelevantly that they were actually flecked with green. Irish blood, perhaps, like so many of the Scots?

'Look at it my way,' John invited grimly. 'Consider these three attacks. The bloke who nearly killed Clarissa Dutt knew how to use a knife: he got it up under the breastbone, which isn't easy to do, you have to know where you're going. It only just missed her heart, and he was strong enough to hold her still. She was bloody lucky to survive. Susan Elias we can't tell about, she had the sense not to take her attacker on, and he was frightened off before he could do any damage. But in this attack last night, the bloke tried to stab her, but the knife bounced off her ribs – she's got a couple of nasty cuts there and on her hands, but nothing like Clarissa's injuries. He had to hit her over the head in the end.' John lunged for the sugar and put in three spoonfuls. 'I'm not saying Alan Toms necessarily had the right man for the first two attacks, mind you, but I don't believe for a minute that the same bloke attacked both Clarissa and Louise. Last night's was an attempted copy-cat job, in my book – by someone who didn't know that the bloke who probably did the first two was already under lock and key at Otley Farm.'

'So where does that leave you, John?' Sarah asked, dry-mouthed.

'It leaves me – and Alan Toms, this is his manor – looking at who would want to murder Louise Taylor. A lot of people here knew that Alan had had to let his suspect go. And the same lot of people knew that by tonight you would have Securicor marching about the gardens. So someone took their chance, and tried to make it look like the other two attacks.' He took a mouthful of coffee. 'It also leads me to wonder, as I did not at the time, about the death in January, in my manor, of another Fellow of this college – the more particularly since Dr Symonds was also involved with Neville Allason. And *that's* why we got Sir Neville out of his cot at six o'clock this morning.'

Sarah sat still, feeling sick. Then she reached a decision. 'Francesca will, no doubt, have told you that I was also involved with Neville Allason. A long time ago now.'

'Jesus.' John McLeish, disconcerted, blushed scarlet. 'Sorry. No, she didn't. She said he was your greatest supporter, but . . . but . . .'

'But you remembered he is nine years younger than I.'

'I didn't think about it at all,' he said slowly. 'You are so obviously old friends and close allies. Francesca has that sort of relationship with several men, but not the ones she went to bed with. Those vanished.'

'Only temporarily,' Sarah said grimly. 'In twenty-five years' time, John, you may expect them all to be back again, trying to persuade her into taking jobs like Warden of Gladstone.'

John McLeish refused to be deflected by this disheartening vision. 'You see, Sarah, I ought to hand over any reconsideration of the Judith Symonds case to the plain-clothes boys at my station. Or we ought to agree that the whole thing goes to CI at New Scotland Yard – they come in where there are two forces involved. But we're all tired, and I want to think for a few hours.'

'Do you want Francesca out of here, John? I would understand.'

'To be frank with you, yes, for the time being. But she's a Fellow of this place and I'd not get her to leave here – or to leave you – in a time of trouble, unless I could tell her she was in physical danger. And I don't know that she is.' He paused and chewed his lip. 'You may be, however.'

'Because of Neville Allason? He has been having affairs for years without killing people, John,' Sarah protested. 'He's very bad at finishing his affairs tidily, I am here to tell you, but he runs for cover at the end, rather than hitting out.'

'Does his wife always know?' John asked.

'I believe she must at some level, but it's a very solid marriage.'

'Would a scandal matter to his career?'

Sarah sat back to consider. 'Well, you can't fire a civil servant. Not even this government has pioneered *that* yet. He might not get the final step – Secretary to the Cabinet. The competition is very fierce, and anything can tell against you.'

'How much would he mind?'

Sarah looked at him helplessly. 'If he really minded about that he would stop having affairs, surely?' She considered him; nothing had apparently moved in his face, but he was radiating disbelief. 'I suppose I don't know much about what drives men to affairs even when it would be much better not.'

'Oh, nor do I.' John McLeish beamed at her like a friendly bear. 'I'm a comfortable homely type myself, and I've got my hands full keeping one wife more or less satisfied and on the straight and narrow. But I've seen enough married blokes, who always have someone else on the go, to know it's not something they give up easily.' He glanced at the window. 'Fran's on her way back. I'll chase her off to the Bursary, since I don't fancy my chances of getting her to go home.'

Sarah agreed, shaken, to these plans and rose to greet Francesca.

'Kindly received,' Francesca reported. 'Here is the tray back, and we'd better do all that again in an hour or so. And then there's lunch. I'll organize the kitchen – or I will if we can agree what on earth we are going to say to the staff *this* time. Do you and old Alan have a view, darling?'

'Less of the old, Frankie. Good morning, ladies.' Alan Toms, moving like royalty, appeared behind her.

'What have you done with Michael Taylor?' she asked belligerently.

'He's still talking to Fields.' Alan Toms sat down heavily, declining an offer to take his raincoat, but accepting coffee. 'I expect you've got some work to do, Frankie?'

'I am part of the management of this place, Detective Chief Superintendent. Let us square what we are saying to whom, and then I'll push off. We have to say something, or send all our girls home. Maybe you feel that's what we should be doing.'

'No.' John McLeish and he spoke simultaneously, and Francesca looked at them suspiciously. 'No,' Alan Toms went on authoritatively. 'The chap who did the first two is in Otley Farm

– I'll do something about that when I've got the time. This last one was personal; young John and I both think so.'

'What are the police going to say? Officially, I mean?' asked Sarah.

'Oh, that a man is helping us with our enquiries, following another attack.'

Sarah considered this masterly example of economy with the truth.

'Alan, are you going to charge Michael Taylor?' Francesca persisted.

'I don't know yet, my dear.' Sarah watched Francesca grind her teeth at this piece of patronage. 'I need to talk to one of your young ladies, Dame Sarah, while I'm here.'

'Dawn Jacobson?' Sarah asked, her heart sinking.

'That's right. Michael Taylor says he was with her for a couple of hours, till ten thirty or so. Then he went home, according to him; didn't find his wife; and came back and met you. No witnesses to him leaving the college of course. He could have got into the garden any time. Dr Taylor – Louise, that is – was attacked about eleven fifteen, you reckon, John?'

'More like eleven thirty. Blood had hardly coagulated when I got there.'

Francesca, pale now, got up decisively. 'All right. Do we keep Securicor booked?'

'No need,' and 'Yes.' Alan Toms and Sarah spoke simultaneously, and Sarah, catching Toms's outraged expression, hastened to explain. 'I don't want parents in droves collecting their daughters. These exams are critical to their future.'

'Makes sense,' Toms conceded. 'You'd better have a few of the uniformed branch too, for the same reason. Presentation.' He said it with the air of a man speaking of Satanism.

Francesca hesitated at the door, considering her audience's closed expressions. 'I'm here if anyone wants me,' she pointed out uneasily.

'And very nice too,' Toms said heartily, causing her finally to leave, shutting the door a little too hard. Both men listened to her footsteps going crossly down the passage, then hunched forward, concentrating on Sarah.

'Young John told you about our worries, has he?' Alan Toms asked, and Sarah confirmed that he had.

162

'The problem I have', she confessed, 'is that, while I understand you suspect either Neville Allason or Michael Taylor of this last attack, I can't see why either of them was involved with Dr Symonds's death. Never mind how for the moment,' she added hastily.

'The question of how matters very much.' John McLeish got in ahead of his colleague by a hair. 'We didn't consider – the CID didn't consider – murder very seriously in Dr Symonds's case. The lads did wonder about suicide, but we tend to let those go at accidental death. She had taken, or had had administered to her, an overdose of Valium, but not enough to kill her. She suffocated in the pillows.' He paused. 'Or was suffocated, but there was no evidence. It was some time after 11 p.m. – I'll have to look again at the autopsy. She was cremated, of course, so we've lost the evidence.'

'Where was Allason that night?' Toms asked broodingly.

'In London, at his flat. That I do remember.'

'Were Allason and Louise – Dr Taylor – already on the go then, would you know?' Toms asked.

'Neville came to see me at the health hydro and Louise was with him then. I could see he was interested in her, but I really don't know what was going on then.'

A dispirited silence was finally broken by Sarah. 'I forgot to ask whether Clarissa Dutt told you anything useful when she was able to talk?'

'She can only talk for a few minutes, but she said that he wore a balaclava and was strong. She's a big girl, Clarissa, and she fought, but it got her nowhere. She told Fields she might know the man's voice again, but nothing else about him. What we got, though, tallies with what the other lass, Susan Elias, said. It's certainly the same man.' Alan Toms rose. 'I must go and see my blokes out in the garden. I want to talk to the lad, but he'll wait in Otley Farm. It's quite a good place, Francesca tells me.' He flicked a glance at John McLeish. 'I checked, he was sectioned, it's not voluntary. So he'll be there when I want him. I'll be back, Dame Sarah, and then I'll want Miss Jacobson. You off, John? Ring me when you've talked to your guv'nor.'

Toms walked heavily out into the garden, his raincoat flapping behind him in the breeze.

'John, what *is* this about Francesca and Otley Farm?'

'Alan can't resist a dig. Fran's brother Tristram – you met him, he's one of the twins – spent several months there just at the time we were getting married, paid for by Peregrine. The lad was deported from America for using drugs, but he's been clean since, he's doing well. Alan is disconcerted by the whole thing.'

'And Francesca can't bear him in an avuncular mode.'

'That's right.' McLeish went off to his car, leaving her to reflect that Francesca had chosen wisely in John McLeish; a sure and present defence against the volatilities of her own family, a man balancing easily the demands of two lives.

The Bursary, at eight in the morning, was deserted as Francesca had hoped. She sat down to get her world into order, starting with a note of the things that had to be done to disseminate the news of the attack on Louise Taylor in the least alarming way. She put a draft on the word processor, cleared the result with Sarah, made twenty copies, went off wearily to distribute them, then returned to the Bursary to find George Hellier rifling through a filing cabinet.

'Good morning, George.'

'Not much good about it.' He was red-eyed and his hands were unsteady. Francesca considered him uneasily.

'I agree. I imagine we are going to spend the day on the phone, George, not doing accounts. Give it up, whatever it is.'

'I was looking for last year's accounts for the Raab Lecture – I can't see them anywhere.'

'I had them last night. Louise had had a look, but I wouldn't let her take them away. Here.'

'I haven't looked at them yet. I mean to; the comparison with this year's will be interesting.'

'Leave it now, George, please. I've just distributed a note about Louise – here's a copy. Sarah and I have agreed that calls go to her, or your lady wife as Deputy Warden, and failing that, to us here, the next most senior bodies. Since Sarah is with the police, and Alice, I know, is lecturing this morning, we'll get most of the calls. And you are very good indeed at reassuring distressed mothers, which is who we'll be getting.' She studied him anxiously; he looked old and broken, and worn out. 'George? Are you OK? I mean, are you hearing me?'

164

'Yes.' He sat down behind his desk, staring miserably out of the window, and Francesca watched him with pity. 'Louise has a chance, George,' she said gently. 'John says they have managed to lift the bone, so though she is unconscious, she is stable.'

'I cannot bear to talk about it.'

'Sorry.'

A long silence fell, then Francesca, disconcerted and distressed, decided to start working down her list, while George either recovered himself or went home.

'What about her children?' George asked a few minutes later, sounding human and reasonable again.

'That's the next problem,' Francesca said, relieved. 'They are in their nursery school until three, then we have no plan. Unless the police have finished with Michael by then.' She met George's look. 'I haven't done anything sensible about the Taylor children yet, because the first priority is the children here – the bigger ones who are taking exams. Three o'clock still seems a long way off.'

'The whole day is going to be an eternity,' George said drearily.

It was unfair, Francesca decided, to be impatient with George, who also loved Louise and who had known her longer – and better, or at least differently – than she had herself. The phone rang sharply and she squared her elbows to cope. The senior tutor in charge of one of the student halls of residence was on the line requiring amplification of the notice, consolation, the latest news, and support. It was, as George had observed, going to be a long day. Francesca saw with relief that he had picked up the other phone and was being soothing to someone who was plainly on the verge of hysterics.

By nine thirty the first wave of phone calls had broken over them, and a brief lull gave them time to drink more coffee.

When the phone rang again, she was about to pick it up when she heard raised voices in the secretary's office. She waved to George to take the call, deciding that he did not yet look ready to deal with personal callers, and put her head round the door. Susan Elias was there, pink and anxious.

'I take it you have heard the news, Susan?' Francesca said quickly. 'We are flat out here, as you can imagine.'

'Please may I ask you something? I'm sorry but I don't know what to do.'

This was another victim of a murderous attack – and one of Louise's pupils, Francesca reminded herself, shocked that she had forgotten so quickly. 'Of course, come in. Have a chair, and speak a bit quietly. I'm sorry, all this must be very upsetting for you.'

'How is Dr Taylor?'

'No different, I am afraid, unconscious but stable.'

The girl hesitated. 'Miss Wilson, I know you're busy, and you'll probably think I'm quite mad to be bothering with social things, but I'm so worried I can't work, and I thought you'd help.'

'If I can.'

'It's the concert. Our concert, the student one. Week after next, after the exams. I know you probably couldn't care less about that at the moment, but we've sold all the tickets, and I got a letter this morning to say he couldn't come.'

'Who couldn't?' Francesca asked patiently.

'Michael Miles.'

'The baritone?'

'Yes. He was doing two sets of solos for us. Without him it's just us – the college and St John's, I mean. We've sold the tickets under false pretences, and I don't know what to do.'

'Why can't he come?'

Susan sighed, looking a good deal older than her years. 'He has to go to Germany. They're paying him, we aren't.'

'Yes, I see. He shouldn't have agreed to sing for you on that basis. And above all, he should have cancelled earlier, not now when it's too late to substitute. Spilt milk, however. You'll have to cancel the concert, Susan; I'm afraid you can't really go on. Don't you think so, George?' She explained the circumstances, briefly, to George, who had just come off the telephone.

'We haven't got everyone's address,' Susan said helplessly. 'We sold 350 tickets.'

'One advertises,' Francesca said briskly. 'Susan, that's the answer – now stop worrying about it, go and do what work you can; and much, much later this afternoon we'll get together and draft that advertisement, OK?'

She waved Susan out of the office and turned back to her desk, to find George watching her, frowning.

'I hate to add to your troubles, Francesca, but all the catering is

166

already ordered for that concert. It will cost us money to cancel it.'

'Did we pay a deposit?'

'No, we don't do that. We've been dealing with these people for a long time.'

'Too long. We'll cancel and let them sue us for it, if they have the nerve. They've been taking us to the cleaners for years, and if I ever get my head up again I may even sue *them*.'

Dawn Jacobson, summoned to the Warden's lodge, had taken the obvious way out of a difficult situation and was weeping, copiously but prettily. Alan Toms confirmed Sarah's view of him by appearing unmoved by this display, matter-of-factly passing her a box of Kleenex.

'Come along, my dear,' he said briskly. 'Dame Sarah here has told you what's going on. There's one of your teachers very seriously injured, and one of your friends here lucky to be recovering the way she is. What we need is some sensible help, not all these tears.' The patronage seemed to have much the same bracing effect on Dawn as it did on Francesca.

'What Chief Superintendent Toms needs to be clear about is times, Dawn. He needs to know precisely when Dr Taylor arrived and when he left,' Sarah said firmly, hoping to indicate that there was no need at all for her to specify why Michael Taylor had been there. She got one swift, intelligent look of recognition from behind the handful of Kleenex which Dawn was pressing to her face, and watched, interested, while the girl collected herself, and explained that Michael Taylor had been with her from eight thirty to about ten forty-five. She was confident he had gone shortly after ten thirty, because he had waited to leave until the evening exodus from the television room after the ten o'clock news had finished. In order, Sarah mentally supplied, not to be seen coming out of the room of a young woman whose tutor he wasn't. Alan Toms had taken her over the timing again, but she was clear; Michael Taylor had left her room at ten forty-five at the latest. Finally he had given up and sent her off to sign her statement.

'Little madam,' Toms had observed sourly.

'I would, at her age, have been more daunted by all this than

167

she seems to be,' Sarah said, as temperately as possible, 'but she wasn't going to lie or fudge the time to protect him, at least.'

'She wasn't, was she? Tough little piece.'

'Are you going to charge him?' Sarah asked.

'Taylor? Not yet. One of my lads is doing a house-to-house in the street they live in, to see if anyone saw him come back to the house as he says he did. He told us he left here around ten forty, same as his young lady says; went home, hung around for twenty minutes, then thought he'd better find his wife and make peace.'

'You don't believe him?'

'I don't see why he was bothered about his wife after he'd had a couple of hours with the alternative, as it were. More likely to let the wife stew, and come home in her own time, when she got tired of wherever she was.'

'He might, of course, have decided to find out whether she was working, or whether she had gone off with – someone.'

'That's much more likely.' Toms sounded approving, and Sarah felt immediately anxious. 'You know that Louise Taylor was with Sir Neville Allason? I'm seeing him later. So young Taylor might have seen her come back in a taxi, understood that, wherever she'd been, she'd not been working, and started up another argument.'

'She apparently rang Sir Neville, with whom she dined, to say she was safely back in college.'

'Did she?' Toms was checked but not deflected by this. 'Well, Taylor waited till she made the phone call, then had the argument with her.'

'I hope you are not getting fixated on this solution, Mr Toms.'

'No, I'm not. There's Sir Neville Allason to consider too.' He beamed at her, and peered out of the window. 'I'll just go and see what my lads have picked up out there.' And he went, moving briskly, leaving Sarah depressed and frightened.

The phone rang, just as she sat down.

'Me, Francesca. You haven't forgotten, like I had but George hadn't, that we have a special governing body meeting at two thirty. To approve the bloody accounts? Today of all days!'

'Oh, Francesca, could we not postpone it?'

There was a moment's pause at the other end, then Francesca came back. 'Sarah? We have to have it, George reminds me. Our agreed extension of time runs out tomorrow. The University might well be prepared to stretch a point, given our troubles but . . .'

'I agree,' Sarah said wearily. 'No need to compound our problems.'

At 2.30 p.m. the governing body gathered, many of them red-eyed and pale. Alice Hellier was looking particularly shaken, but, Sarah reflected cynically, her distress would be tempered; without Louise Taylor's opposition the near two-thirds majority who wanted to admit men to Gladstone might reasonably hope that one more push would get them what they wanted.

Sarah opened the meeting by explaining why it had been necessary to hold it, and that she welcomed the opportunity to give everyone a chance to discuss the tragic and frightening events of the last two days. Without permitting any such discussion to take place, she then called on Francesca to explain about the Securicor hirelings.

'They and the police may well be falling over each other in the flower-beds tonight,' Francesca concluded, 'but I hope the governing body feels that, even if a lot of it is presentational, we and the undergraduates are entitled to reassurance in this particularly stressful week. The police will inevitably go away in a day or so.'

Alice Hellier rallied sufficiently to ask what it would cost, but seemed to be unable to do anything with the astronomical answer supplied without comment by Francesca.

'It is a grossly expensive precaution, but somehow today it does not seem so,' Sarah said simply, and the governing body roused itself to murmur approval.

'Warden.' It was Alice Hellier, looking desperately tired and frail. 'I understand the student concert has to be cancelled.' She leant her head wearily on one hand, pushing the fading grey hair back off her high forehead. 'Must we do that? Everything seems to be going wrong.' Her voice had suddenly faltered and gone out of control, her face puckered and tears started to flow uncontrollably.

'Alice, my dear . . .' Sarah started up, but Alice was on the

169

other side of the long table and it took Sarah a minute to get round. By that time Alice Hellier was weeping aloud with raw, gasping, painful sobs, which were all too plainly fraying the overstretched nerves of the Fellows.

'I'll take her home,' Hazel Bradford, who was young and strong and always a little detached from the affairs of the college, volunteered, and Alice Hellier allowed herself to be led out.

Sarah saw Hazel Bradford out of the room with the weeping Alice Hellier and turned back to deal with the Fellows, who were milling around aimlessly. She braced herself to give a lead. 'Could we resume for a minute? This is a very difficult time for us and for the college, and I would ask you all to spend as much time here as possible and be available to your students. They are going to need a great deal of steadying.'

The Fellowship settled down, and she swept the meeting on, dealing with detailed questions, feeling the Fellowship returning to something like normal as the usual argument about the college library, hours of access to, broke out. The accounts, as she had assumed, went unchallenged, and she watched with a sense of real achievement as Serena Copley, the college secretary, recorded the formal decision.

'Warden, sorry, but what *about* the student concert?' asked Hazel Bradford, who had returned to the meeting. 'I understand the lead singer has cancelled.'

'Yes. You felt, Bursar, that we ought in that case to cancel the whole concert? I must say, I fear that is right. How are the students going to communicate with ticket holders?'

Francesca was looking shifty. 'I had been hoping not to do any of that until tomorrow. It is a great disappointment for the students.'

On that note Sarah ended the meeting, keeping to herself the reflection that the students had had a good deal worse to face than a cancelled concert. She stood up, to find Francesca at her elbow.

'Francesca,' Sarah said, with the last of her strength. 'Thank you. Can you manage cancelling the concert?'

'Mm. We may not need to. I've got an idea.'

'What?'

'Perry. An excellent classic tenor before he became a rock star. *Much* better known than Michael Miles, and no one is going to mind that he is a tenor rather than a baritone. He may not be able to do it, but it would help us if he could, wouldn't it? Restore morale of staff? Cheer up students? Raise a lot of cash?'

Sarah sat down again, heavily, and looked at her. 'Yes, all of that. Would he do it?'

'If he feels like it,' his sister said coolly. 'We'll just have to see whether he does. Don't *breathe* to anyone yet.'

Sarah got back to her office to find the telephone ringing; with all the Fellows having been immersed for an hour and a half in a governing body meeting, there would be a lot of pent-up calls.

'Detective Sergeant Fields, Dame Sarah. Mr Toms asked me to tell you that Dr Taylor has completed his statement and is on his way home.'

'Oh good,' Sarah said, thinking of the Taylor children for whom arrangements would not now need to be made. Then she realized the implications. 'He is not being charged, then?'

'No.' Fields paused. 'We found two of his neighbours who saw him getting out his bicycle just after eleven last night. It makes it that much less likely that he could have been involved.'

Sarah sighed with relief, then remembered that the man on the other end of the line might not wholly share her views.

'It was you who found the neighbours?'

'Yes.' Fields sounded irritable and busy, so she thanked him, said goodbye, and sat in contemplation. Relief gave way to dull discomfort. If not Michael Taylor, then who? She thought of the expensive Securicor patrol and felt, marginally, better. The phone rang again, on her private number.

'Sarah?'

'Neville. Hello. How are you?' Idiotic thing to say, she thought.

'Only fair. I've just had an hour with Alan Toms. I am threatened with another hour at Notting Dale, and I am due to see my Secretary of State at seven in the House.' He was sounding rattled. 'Can I persuade you to come out and have tea with me here at the Holiday Inn, right now before I go back to the Department? I understand I can't visit Louise at all.'

'No one can visit in intensive care, except family. Yes, you can. I'm longing to get out of here for an hour or so – I'll meet you.'

When she walked in she found him instantly, sitting under a

potted palm, long legs folded under a small square table, and two waitresses dancing attendance. He leapt up to kiss her, rocking the table dangerously.

'They want to talk to me about Judith Symonds,' he said, these minimum preliminaries concluded, and Sarah summoned her nine years' seniority.

'Neville, tell me what is on your mind. We are short of time.'

'Yes.' He looked at her hopefully, to see if she was going to be helpful; and Sarah understood that one of the reasons he had stayed married to Jennifer Allason was because she looked after him like a mother.

'Tell me about Judith. How long did it go on, and were you still close when she died?'

'Oh, two years or so. And no, I was – we were moving apart. We weren't meeting very often.'

A familiar pattern, Sarah thought, feeling the shadow of an old pain. Neville Allason did not go in for clean breaks, because that would have involved accepting that he would always have an extra-marital affair on the go and that, in the nature of things, each one would have to end. So when he tired of a particular affair, or it became difficult for him, he would become busy and leave longer intervals between meetings in the hope that the woman would receive the message he only half knew he was delivering.

'Had you started up with Louise by then?' she asked bluntly.

Neville stared at his cup, looking a good deal older than his years. 'No. That is pretty recent.'

'I understand that the police thought it possible, at the time, that Judith had committed suicide.'

'Well, I don't see that it could have been over me. I mean, she knew I've been married for nearly thirty years. She could have been married herself – she must have had lots of chances. She just didn't want to.' He looked charmingly rueful, and Sarah reflected that there could be no more infuriating sight than a married man, who had used all his charm and romantic *élan* to get an affair started, running for cover when he found the other party had taken him absolutely seriously and was expecting the romantic passion to lead to real consequences.

'Judith had no reason to kill herself,' he was saying decisively.

172

'She was doing a job she wanted to do and the academic results were always good.'

'Life at Gladstone is not without its stresses,' Sarah said drily.

'Sarah, I'm sorry. You are having a terrible time, and don't think we don't all know it. Without you we'd have had no choice but to close or amalgamate this place.'

'You may yet have to. Or give it to Francesca Wilson to run.'

'Too young,' he said, apparently giving the proposal serious consideration. 'I could wish, Sarah, I must say, that Francesca was not married into Notting Dale.'

Nor, Sarah reflected, to a policeman who was quite so immune to Neville's charm. 'So they are reopening the case, as it were?' she asked cautiously. 'Judith's death, I mean?'

'As I understand it, McLeish has now convinced himself, and to some extent Toms, that there may be a link between Judith's death and the attack on Louise. I know they think the attacks on your two students are unrelated to Louise's death – they told me so.' He stared out of the window. 'I have to say they're probably right about that. Anyone who knew how to use a knife, like the chap who got your student – what's her name? Clarissa – would have killed Louise outright.'

She watched him pour tea, remembering that, like her, he was trained and would have had to kill, without fuss and ruthlessly. But if the victim were someone with whom you were emotionally involved, might the hand not lose its cunning? Sarah brought herself up short. Judith Symonds, she reminded herself, had died in her bed, stifled. The room turned cold as she had a sudden vision of Neville's strong hands holding Judith's face into the pillows. She had seen the death of Desdemona on stage recently and been totally unconvinced. Anyone trained would have pushed Desdemona's face down into a pillow rather than holding a pillow over her mouth and leaving her arms free to fight off her attacker.

'Sarah? You're looking terribly tired all of a sudden. Ought I to take you home, so you can rest?'

'Don't be silly, Neville,' she said acerbically, shaking off the vision. 'What are they actually going to do at Notting Dale? Did they say?'

'They told me they are reinterviewing everyone they spoke to

173

when Judith died, for a start. I was one of those. I had gone to Notting Dale to make a statement without being asked.'

'Why?'

He gave her a rueful, sideways, small-boy look. 'I was trying to make sure that there was nothing that would upset Jennifer.'

'Or embarrass you. And was there?'

'Nothing in her flat.' He did not write love letters or encourage the writing of them, Sarah remembered – but, of course, Judith might have kept a diary.

'So they want to talk to me again now. And to George and Alice Hellier, who identified her. And the Taylors – we all had coffee together after dinner at that university funding party.'

'I was at that party, but left early because I was still not at all well.'

'I remember. I expect they'll want to talk to you then unless they already have? No? I wondered, what with John McLeish being at the college such a lot.'

'Neville, you do know that Louise is not out of the woods? That she is as likely to die as to live?'

'I do know,' he said, quickly and sulkily; and Sarah understood that, as usual, he was pushing away an unwelcome reality.

'Why do they think you, or anyone else, would have wanted to kill Judith and Louise?'

'I suppose they think I was having problems with each of them,' he said irritably. 'It's *not* the way I would solve that.'

'How would you solve it? If one of them had threatened to tell Jennifer?'

'I'd have found it *very* difficult if anyone had told Jennifer,' he said, glancing at her sideways.

Sarah nodded, chilled. He was utterly dependent on the quiet, determined Jennifer Allason, who had brought up his three children, held his household together, and supported him every inch of the way. At the core of Neville Allason was that marriage, and in its defence he might have done anything.

'So that Louise, too, was just a romantic interlude,' Sarah probed cautiously.

He looked at her, eyes narrowed in the way she remembered very well, working out what to say to her. 'And I was for her too, I expect,' he said lightly. 'We ought to go.' He helped her up, looking at her carefully to see that she was still on his side, and

174

took her back through the tiles and the palms to her car, leaving her to drive soberly back to college where she narrowly missed running over Francesca.

'I've got Perry!' Francesca opened the door of the car for her. 'He will sing for us.'

'Oh, wonderful. Are you sure? But is the student orchestra good enough for him?'

'You haven't understood about Perry. He's rather grand now, but he's been performing since he was six. He can sing anywhere, accompanied by anyone, including me on a piano with half the notes missing, if need be. I'll say that for him.' It was an elder sister speaking. 'Susan Elias, who plays better than me, is dying to accompany him where he needs a piano, rather than the whole shooting match.' She paused. 'The plan is, Sarah, not to tell anyone that it's Perry and not Michael Miles until the audience is in place. If it gets out we'll get Perry's terrible fan club, who are twelve years old and scream and throw their knickers at him. No, I am not making it up. They'll do that whether he is singing the Mass in B Minor or his latest hit, it makes no odds to them. We have sworn everyone to secrecy and the concert is less than two weeks away.' She beamed at Sarah, justifiably pleased with herself. 'You're looking worn out. Was it Sir Neville who finished you off?'

'No. Or not directly.' Sarah paused, wondering whether to keep it to herself. Deciding that the news that the circumstances of Judith Symonds's death were now being reviewed would be round the Fellowship fast enough, she brought Francesca up to date as dispassionately as possible, mentally giving John McLeish full marks for professional discretion as she watched Francesca's mouth drop open.

'Sir Neville gets about a bit, doesn't he?' she said, when she had got her breath back, and Sarah was relieved to be interrupted by the phone.

'Dr Brewster from the West Middlesex,' her secretary said, anxiously. Francesca checked on her way out, catching the tone if not the words.

'Just to let you know we are going to transfer Miss Dutt to Manchester tomorrow. She's doing very well; be as good as new in a week.'

175

'That's good news.' Sarah drew a careful breath. 'Have you any more news of Dr Taylor?'

'No, no. She's still unconscious, but she's holding her own. Sorry – there's not a lot more to say. It's very early days yet, and this could go on for months.'

Or end at any time, Sarah silently supplied. 'Thank you, Dr Brewster. I will try and get over to the hospital later tonight.'

'And we'll try not to bring them any fresh business,' Francesca said, watching her put the phone down. 'Sorry, bad taste. The Securicor mob are on their way, all both of them. I am waiting to see them, just to make sure they have not given us a couple of enfeebled grandfathers.'

Sarah decided not to ask what her resourceful associate would do if the Securicor personnel did not fulfil her expectations, for fear of the answer. Just at that moment George Hellier put his head round the door.

'Sorry, Warden, I was looking for you both. Alice is resting. I got Dr Smith round and he's given her some tranquillizers to go on with, but I must get to a chemist. Hazel Bradford is kindly sitting with her.' He made a small, helpless gesture, which sat oddly on his competent, burly frame. 'I'm sorry that she should have collapsed just now.'

'Everybody is under a lot of strain,' Sarah said, meaning it. 'We'd better forget about your doing anything other than the procedures absolutely necessary to keep the Bursary functioning.'

'Well, Francesca, perhaps I can take some of the load from you? Shall I tell the caterers that we must cancel the concert?'

'Aha.' Francesca told him her news. 'So no cancellation. If you're feeling virtuous, though, you can have the staff Christmas party accounts to go through, or rather, the odd bits of drink-stained receipts which constitute all the data we've got.'

'Go away, both of you,' Sarah said, smiling. 'George, go home. Francesca, bring me the Securicor men when they arrive, then you, too, go, or John will never let you come here again.'

'I don't expect him home,' Francesca said, with a glance at George.

'I've had a phone call from Notting Dale,' he confirmed heavily. 'I'm seeing them there tomorrow.' He left, reluctantly, closing the door behind him, and the women watched him go.

'In a men's college he'd be Dean of Students and a Fellow, wouldn't he? Much steadier than his wife,' Francesca said sadly.

'Well, he isn't an academic, that's the difficulty. And that's silly of us – in future we are going to have to abandon the idea that bursars, deans and administrators generally should be academics. We just don't do it well enough. Look at you.'

'I trust, Warden, you are not suggesting that I would not have been a successful academic?'

'You have the ability,' Sarah said, 'but not the patience, and you're much too practically inclined.'

'Nonsense, I would have been jolly good. I can see me peacefully minding my own business, doing my research into Phoenician trade-routes – oh, there's the Securicor van now! Let's find out what we've got.'

She went, precipitately, leaving Sarah laughing. This day had ended a good deal better than it had started, she thought, as she peered cautiously out of the side window to the heartening sight of Francesca leading two large, young, uniformed toughs in her direction.

177

11

Francesca was having breakfast in luxurious state, sitting in her sunny kitchen at the large round table which had been the first piece of furniture she had bought. It was the day of the concert, five days after the exams had finished, and it was fine and bright and warm. On the floor beside her William was sitting, crowing, as he played with the assortment of toys strewn underneath and around the table. Tiring of this, he tugged at her skirt and she reached down to scoop him on to her lap, pushing her tea away to a safe distance. He pulled her hair reflectively and being disentangled, turned and lunged for her toast which she decided to let him have. The bell rang, and she carried William with her to the door, noticing how heavy he was getting.

'Uncle Alan,' she said, surprised. 'What are you doing here? Come in.'

'I was passing and I knew you were here, Frankie – I phoned the college. Yes, I'll take a cup. Hello, young man.' He touched William's cheek with a swollen forefinger.

'Not more trouble?' Francesca clasped William tighter.

'Well . . .' Toms said thoughtfully. 'Who is it who does your catering, Francesca?'

'Greenlees Limited. How nice of you to take an interest, but why do you ask?' She led him through to the kitchen and reboiled the kettle to make him tea as she knew he liked it, very strong and lots of milk.

'They were raided last night by my colleagues in Customs and Excise. And us.'

Francesca stepped back in shock, narrowly avoiding William, who was playing at her feet. 'Alan, how *could* you? And us with a concert for 400 tonight. At £50 a ticket including dinner, which

Greenlees are catering. Have we not got troubles enough with you failing absolutely to find out who has been lurking in the gardens, bashing people?'

'It's only been a couple of weeks, Francesca.' Toms was driven on to the defensive. 'And I could hardly tell you we were after Greenlees – or rather, that Customs and Excise were.'

'Why? What can Greenlees have been smuggling?'

'I'm surprised to have to remind *you* that Customs and Excise collect VAT.'

'Ah, of course.' Francesca remembered that Greenlees, like all providers of services, collect VAT from their customers on behalf of the government. They are, of course, expected to collect all that is due, and to pass it on when asked. 'You only had to remind me because you've given me such a nasty shock,' she said, rallying. 'So Customs took a detachment of the Metropolitan Police with them to remind Greenlees of their obligations. Were you all carrying machine-guns? Here's your tea.'

'Now, now, Francesca. Customs deal regularly with people who evade taxes, whether it be border taxes or VAT.'

'Whatever next? The Inland Revenue arriving in helicopter gunships? But are Greenlees still functioning? They're supposed to be arriving in a couple of hours with dinner for 400. Between ourselves I was going to get rid of them – I agree with HM Customs, I'm sure they're bent. But we do need them for tonight.' And that severely understates the case, she thought, bitterly.

'They weren't looking too clever last night,' Alan Toms said cheerfully, scooping William on to his knee, and expertly keeping his tea away from the little fingers. 'The Customs lads took all their books and the general manager. We picked up six illegals and I don't know how much of their regular staff that was.'

'Illegals?'

'Illegal immigrants. People who shouldn't be working here. Four Polish, two Paki.'

'You've just made my day.'

'I thought you'd be better off knowing now than later.' Toms sounded injured.

'I'd have been better off knowing several days ago, Uncle Alan.'

'Well, I couldn't do that, could I?'

'No,' Francesca allowed, running her free hand through her

newly washed hair, so that it stood up in undisciplined spikes. 'No, you couldn't. Oh well, our Securicor lads can double as waiters – they're not exactly overemployed, and they cost a bomb. I must get to college, now. You could look after William, Uncle? No? All right, I can hear Caroline's car, you're excused.'

'I thought we had really had our share of disasters this term,' Sarah said, appalled, forty minutes later, when Francesca had shared her burden.

'If', Francesca observed, after a moment's silence, 'you can keep your head while all about you are losing theirs, it is just possible you have not grasped the seriousness of the situation.'

'We can't cancel the concert now,' Sarah said firmly.

'No, we can't. Even if people have to have Twiglets and bread rolls rather than the decent dinner they have paid for, we can't. Look at all that lot.'

It was a remarkable and heartening sight, Sarah thought, looking affectionately at a student working party, engaged in moving chairs. Somehow the exams had passed without more than the usual unexpected casualties. Certificates of exemption had been secured without difficulty not only for Clarissa Dutt, just now leaving hospital in Manchester, but for the third-year nervous breakdown and for an anxious, lightly balanced first-year linguist. The pregnant second-year geographer had sailed through, buoyed up by her hormones and Sarah's brisk assurance that child-care arrangements would somehow be arrived at, so that she could continue next year. Susan Elias, to whose papers a note had been affixed explaining that she had been attacked, had done quite well enough.

Dawn Jacobson, by contrast, had struggled, but was probably clever enough to have got by. Sarah had tried to draft a note to attach to *her* papers, but had given up in the end. The facts were against them. It was entirely reasonable that Dawn should have been upset by a murderous attack on her supervisor. But the truth was that what had really rattled Miss Jacobson was the suggestion that her lover, husband to said supervisor, was responsible for the attack, and Sarah and Francesca had agreed that any rendering of these facts would make examiners less rather than more sympathetic.

180

'No news from the hospital?' Francesca's mind had also been running along lines which led her to Louise Taylor, who lay in intensive care, still unconscious.

'None. I did ring and spoke to her mother, who is there a lot of the time, poor woman.'

'What are Louise's parents like?'

'Pa is a rather dim clerk in the local authority somewhere. Her mother is the real character, but it is still difficult to see how they hatched Louise.' Sarah sighed. 'A colleague, now at Durham, who interviewed Louise for LMH told me she had come out of a house without a book in it, except for the Bible, and she was not sure anyone read that.'

Francesca turned her head, and Sarah saw tears in her eyes.

'Sorry. Tired. And rattled by this catering mess, I can't quite think what to do.' She reached for her coffee, uncorked a bottle of pills and took one, scowling.

'What are they, Francesca?'

'Valium. I don't really like taking them, but William is sleeping patchily again, and so am I.'

'And our problems can't be helping you.'

'No, I afraid that's so. Anyway, there's only a couple of days till full term ends and nearly everyone goes home, so I agreed it was sensible to take something to simmer me down until then. Don't worry, Sarah. What do we do about the caterers?'

'I suppose the important thing is not to panic,' Sarah said feebly.

'Depends on what our options are.' Francesca had recovered from the moment's weakness. 'Panic might be the best of them. We need to ring up Greenlees: if no one answers the phone, that'll tell us something after all.' She seized Sarah's phone and dialled.

'Is George Hellier in this morning?' Sarah asked.

'No, but I've talked to him. He's coming in later, but he's having a difficult time with Alice. She seems to be having some sort of breakdown.'

'I must go and see her again.' Sarah made a note. 'Don't look so severe, Francesca – different people are upset by different things.'

'I was actually thinking that Sir Neville must be a shrewd

operator – to get you for Warden here, rather than Alice, I mean. *You've* taken this lot without falling apart.'

'I am sure Neville would be grateful for your good opinion, Francesca. He is having a difficult time too.'

Francesca, as she sat listening to the ringing tone, gave her a considering look. 'Well, we'd have difficulty writing a note to go with *his* exam papers too, wouldn't we? One mistress dead and another unconscious, inside six months. Difficult to sympathize with. Ah, good morning, this is Francesca Wilson at Gladstone College, just calling to check the arrangements for tonight. You what? Well, who do you work for, then? Oh, I see. So what are you doing about commitments like tonight's. Yes, I'll hold on – find the partner, by all means.'

She looked across at Sarah, aghast. 'Worse yet. Greenlees went into receivership this morning, apparently. This is one of Smith Burney's men answering the phone. Mr Williams? You're the receiver? When were you appointed – before or after the Customs and Excise invasion? Oh, it's a small community here, I'm afraid, and I'd heard – not about you lot, but about the Customs. We have our own troubles here, as you kindly suggest, and that makes me the more anxious to ensure that you are keeping the catering business going. I do see it must be difficult without any management. Where's the managing director, in the nick? What?' She listened and scribbled a note for Sarah to read; the managing director and his wife had left, the day before the Customs raid, for an unspecified destination.

'All right. Look, you find out what staff and stores you've got, and we'll talk again in an hour. I'll have to look round for an alternative, but my best guess is that there isn't one, and we'll just have to manage with what you've got. Do your best – we've got every kind of grandee coming, and I will see the fair name of Smith Burney mentioned where it counts. OK?'

She rang off, shaking her head. 'The bank put them in. But they say there was nothing wrong with the books; it all looked all right, just rather unprofitable. So there's a second set of books somewhere, probably with the managing director – wherever *he* is.'

Sarah asked meekly if Francesca could very kindly explain to her what Greenlees had been doing that was criminal.

'Hiding turnover – diverting some of the incoming cash, and

understating therefore their liability for tax. They probably skimmed ten per cent off the top of all their contracts. And that's why they've run foul of Customs – VAT would have been payable on that ten per cent they've hidden.'

'Income tax too, presumably, on the profit they didn't report.'

'Very good, Sarah. Quite right. But the Inland Revenue sits in offices writing letters, and Customs and Excise comes out in force and raids you, apparently. I didn't quite realize that, and Greenlees obviously didn't either. You've got to be very criminal to be proof against ten strong men impounding all your papers and questioning all your staff. I thought they were just padding bills and half inching food and drink from us and everyone else silly enough to let them do it. I should have known better. Fraud appears everywhere once you've got it – like moth.'

'Will we be all right tonight?'

'They ought to have all the stuff they need for our dinner already in stock, as it were, and the receiver will want to carry out this contract, if he can.'

Sarah gazed at her acolyte. 'I never thought so much of your past experience was going to be so useful, Francesca.'

'Nor did I. Never thought to see a good fraud-with-bankruptcy again. Just like old times. They're going to ring back, but I must run. I have to move a piano.'

Sarah waved her off, reflecting that this term had revealed mercilessly how fragile the college's management structure was. With Louise Taylor gone, Alice Hellier no longer functioning, and George Hellier hamstrung by having to look after her, the active participants were now very thin on the ground. She looked up just as Francesca, with an entourage of six members of the college choir, went past the window carrying a table. She rose to remonstrate and sat down again; her table-carrying days were past and her energies better deployed in pushing another piece of the college machinery into place. She needed to visit Alice Hellier and she would do that now, in the lull before the storm of tonight's concert.

She decided to walk; she was increasingly able to cover distances, but she took her stick with her in case she got tired. George and Alice lived in one of the small, neat, thirties houses right on the edge of the college grounds, and much sought after for their views across the Gladstone park. She walked up the neat path, admiring the crisp white paint and olive-green door with its shining brasswork.

It was George who answered the door, looking drawn and tired. 'Francesca told me about Greenlees,' he said, barely giving her time to say good morning. 'I gather we're going to be all right for tonight? What a fool the man was.'

'Dishonest rather than foolish, surely? And Customs and Excise were less easy meat than the customers.'

'I suppose so.' George hesitated. 'I'm afraid Alice is still very shaky. The doctor is here at the moment.'

'Would you rather I went?'

'No, no. He'll be gone soon, and I know Alice wants to see you.'

Alice Hellier had been ill for two weeks now, and no one was even suggesting that the problem was physical. A conscientious Warden would need advice on how best to help her, and Dr Smith, who looked after the whole of Gladstone, in his fifties, quiet, and conservative in his ways and his prescriptions, would be a good person to consult later. George put her in the living-room with a sherry and she sat, drinking and contemplating the room. It was not large; none of the houses in this road had large rooms, built as they had been in the thirties, but it was pleasant and immaculately clean and tidy. The furniture was particularly good; Sarah gazed with pleasure on a very fine sofa table and display cabinet. The china in the cabinet, eighteenth-century blue-and-white, was carefully arranged. The curtains hung level and thick, as only expensive, hand-pleated curtains did. George's family must have been well off; Alice's parents had been elementary school teachers, and Alice herself had never earned much more than her academic salary, despite her distinction.

Dr Smith came in with George, and smiled on her, and she thought again how much she liked him.

'Don't go, please, Dr Smith.' Alice Hellier, looking old and frail, and haggard, with her hair wild and her feet in bedroom slippers, followed them into the room. 'There's no need; you know what I'm going to say. Sarah, it's good of you to come, and it saves me coming to you. George and I have talked it over, and we both feel that it is time for me to retire.'

'Oh, Alice,' Sarah said, distressed by her appearance more than the words. 'It has hardly been a normal term. There can be

184

no shame in being knocked off one's course by three murderous attacks on members of the college inside two weeks. What you need is a break and, after all, there is the summer.'

Alice shook her head vehemently, twisting her hands together in a curious washing movement. Indeed she could not keep her hands still; she alternated the strange pantomime of washing with anxious kneading of her skirt. Dr Smith watched her carefully. 'You certainly need a holiday, Dr Hellier,' he said gently.

'I must leave the college,' she insisted, her voice rising.

George was sitting, slumped in a comfortable armchair, looking defeated. Sarah found herself at a loss.

'Well, of course, you shall, Alice, if you really feel the time has come for you to retire. I should miss you very much – which is why I hope you will take a little time to decide.'

The restless hands clenched together convulsively, and Alice stared at her. 'Why should you miss me? You've got the job, you got what you wanted.'

Sarah was momentarily gravelled for a reply, but George put both his hands over his wife's. 'Alice, my dear.'

Sarah looked to Dr Smith, who gave an unmistakable jerk of the head. She summoned all her energies and touched Alice Hellier's shoulder carefully; she was rigid with tension.

'I'm sorry to see you laid so low, Alice. I'll come again later in the week, if I may.'

George followed her into the little hall.

'Oh George. Oh, poor Alice. Oh dear, I wish there was something I could do. I'm not taking her resignation seriously, of course.'

'I wish you would, in fact,' George said heavily. 'She did mean to go, even before all this happened, and I am sure I ought to be encouraging her. So don't plead with her, Sarah.'

'Of course not, if you are sure that is what she wants. But we can keep it open for a month or so – will you at least let me do that? No need to tell Alice.'

'That's kind, but I don't believe she'll change her mind. And I think it would be best if she didn't.'

Sarah hesitated. 'If Alice does decide to retire, would you want to go too?'

'Yes. Yes, we would want to move. I'm sorry, Sarah. I know

you are losing people rather fast, but you'll be able to replace a couple of old-stagers like us.'

'I don't want to stand in the way of your doing what you both want, George, but never underestimate the value of the old-stagers.'

He smiled, his gloom momentarily lifted, and Sarah patted his arm in farewell and went. She waited a few minutes, admiring the roses in the little front garden, and, as she had hoped, Dr Smith followed her out. She walked with him to his car.

'Alice was all right until a couple of weeks ago,' she said, in puzzled enquiry.

'Mm. Stress takes different people different ways.' He looked at her carefully. 'Now you, Dame Sarah, seem to me a person who knows when to stop worrying and get on with what you can do. So you are dog-tired, but you'll be fine with what we doctors call rest.' He gave her a small wintry smile. 'And that clever young Bursar of yours is a bit fragile – but in my view that's hormonal, left over from the baby, and it'll pass. But Dr Hellier, now, is seriously ill. If she doesn't get away from here she'll have a complete breakdown. I've no more idea than you why it has taken her like this, but you should not stand in her way.'

'Thank you, doctor,' Sarah said inadequately. 'That's very clear.'

'Good. I'll look forward to the concert tonight. I've heard Michael Miles on the radio. A fine voice.'

'Ah.' Sarah broke the news that it would be Perry rather than Michael Miles, and waited for Dr Smith's reaction with interest. He was reassuringly delighted. 'But I have the record still of Peregrine Wilson as a boy singing "Panis Angelicus". An angel's voice. I had no idea he was still a real singer, as it were. Can I get an extra ticket for my daughter? She'd never forgive me if I didn't.'

'Provided she promises not to hurl her knickers at the stage.'

'She's twenty-one,' he said, laughing. 'I hope she's passed that stage.'

He drove off, leaving Sarah reluctantly to recognize that she was in the street next door to the one the Taylors lived in, and she ought to visit that stricken household too. She walked past untidy overflowing dustbins, up an uneven path to the door, to be answered by a cacophony of childish shrieks. Michael Taylor, looking hopeful, opened the door to her, fielding a child with one hand.

'No, we're not going to the park yet. Please come in, Warden.'

He was pathetically pleased to see her, and Sarah found herself very sorry for him. He was patently depressed, and the children were being difficult. They were of course missing their mother. The girl crashed on to her not particularly welcoming lap, and explained in a barely subdued shout that Mummy was in hospital, very ill, so they couldn't go and see her, but she was getting better – searching Sarah's face for confirmation. The little boy was banging around with his toys, making a loud, tuneless, obsessive noise and all too obviously trying to shut out his anxieties. Michael Taylor, pouring a drink for her, turned and looked at them bleakly, and closed his mouth tightly. Not far from collapse himself, Sarah thought, alarmed, and moving three metal cars and two stuffed toys from underneath her right arm. No greater contrast with the Hellier household could be imagined; the living-room in which she now sat was about the same shape and conformation as the Helliers', but the curtains were thin and hung unevenly, missing a couple of rings, from a battered wooden rod. The fitted carpet, an unwise shade of beige, was heavily stained. Every available chair and the sofa – all of which would have been better for cleaning – were covered with a silt of toys and papers.

'I must clear up a bit,' Michael said hopelessly. 'They go to nursery school in the afternoon, which gives me three hours' peace. Our mother's help, Sally, is away this week – her holiday was booked – and my mother-in-law is spending a lot of time at the hospital.' He gave the children a biscuit each and settled them in the corner with the television. 'Thank God for *Playschool*.'

'You have no more news this morning?' Sarah asked, for something to say.

'No, nothing's changed. I'm going to the hospital this evening.'

If this young man had attacked his wife in a jealous rage, he was paying a heavy price, and Sarah found she could not think of him as a murderer. He seemed very ordinary, tall, fair and both harassed by and agonized about his children.

'You're not coming to the concert?'

'No. People are either avoiding me or being conscientiously

187

kind, as if I had suddenly turned up in a wheelchair. I couldn't face it. And anyway, the evening's the only time I can go and see Louise – my mother-in-law comes then, and takes over here.' He lapsed into silence, and Sarah bent to help the little boy with his puzzle.

'If we survive this, Louise and I,' Michael said suddenly, 'I'm going to get out of academic life and get a proper job. In a stockbroker's. They need people who understand what chemical companies are doing, and I'm tired of being poor and harassed all the bloody time.'

'Good idea, if you can get one of those jobs.' It would, she thought dispassionately, distance him from the world in which his wife was so successful, and give him the kudos of a successful breadwinner.

'They say Louise is a little better. I don't know how they can tell, she just lies there,' he went on.

'They said that to me too,' Sarah confirmed. 'The indications are better; she seems to be less deeply unconscious.'

'Mummy come home soon?' his daughter said hopefully, having abandoned *Playschool* and crept back to where she could get the news she needed so badly. He scooped her into his arms, resting his chin on the grubby fair hair, two shades darker than his own.

'She's very like you.'

'Mm. Andrew, of course, is Louise's boy.'

He was too, Sarah thought with a pang: that was Louise's dark hair above the same high forehead and bright blue eyes.

'Is there anything we can do, Michael?' she asked bravely.

'No, but thank you. We'll be – well, not all right, but in much better shape when Sally gets back tomorrow.'

'Sally,' the little boy said longingly, leaving the TV also, and his father scooped him up too; so that Sarah let herself out, leaving them huddled together like refugees on the sofa in the untidy room.

Sarah decided not to complete her morning by visiting Louise, or rather Louise's mother, in hospital. With a distinct feeling of playing truant, she stood herself lunch in a local Chinese restaurant. Feeling pleasantly overstuffed she walked back to college and stopped by Tydeman Hall to admire the preparations. It was a beautiful warm day; just for once the fine weather had endured beyond the end of the examinations and students were sitting around on rugs in the garden, eating whatever could be managed without knives and forks. Francesca was in the middle of a group, eating a sandwich and talking at the same time, in her element.

'We've sold the last tickets,' she reported feverishly. 'Susan and I had to tell people that it was going to be Perry, not Michael Miles, and the tickets simply went. The lad himself will be here by four o'clock to do a run-through. We could probably sell tickets for that too.'

'Do not get carried away, Francesca,' Sarah said sternly. 'We have enough to cope with.'

'I wish I could be confident that the roof will hold up,' Francesca said generally, to the group. 'I worry that any applause will wake the beetles in the beams, who will start to chomp, frantically.' She looked not much older than the undergraduates surrounding her, Sarah thought, with a sudden lightening of heart. Victory was going to be snatched from the jaws of defeat after all.

'There's George,' Francesca said, watching a familiar figure roll towards the Bursary. 'I must run; I've got something to tell him. Look everyone, you've been marvellous. Choirs do not usually have to line up 400 seats and manhandle pianos, and you've done wonders. You may have to serve dinner as well, but for now why don't you all get a rest?'

She rose from her rug and made for the Bursary. Sarah congratulated the students too, and caught up with Francesca as she stopped to consider, slitty-eyed, a large flowering rose bush. 'Just the colour we need for the dinner tables,' she said thoughtfully as Sarah and George arrived beside her.

'Look,' she went on, 'I need some guidance on policy from you both. I had a call from a senior chap I slightly know in Customs this morning: he wants us to help his minions with their enquiries into Greenlees.'

George Hellier put his head in his hands, in silent comment, and Francesca considered him uneasily. 'Well, I agree, George, we've got plenty to do without unpicking our records for Customs. My first reaction was to say no.'

'Mine is too,' Sarah agreed. 'Why don't we just do that?'

'Oh, because . . . well, we are all in some sense trustees of the college's funds, and if we make the effort we might be able to get some money back. And if we are going to do the work anyway, then we might as well take Customs and Excise along with us.'

'Greenlees are in receivership, aren't they?' George said slowly. 'Is there going to be any money left for us, or any other creditor, after the bank has had its pound of flesh?'

'Ah.' Francesca looked at him with respect. 'That I should have seen.' She turned to Sarah in explanation. 'As George has just reminded me, even if we got a claim together we'd only be an unsecured creditor. We'd never get paid.'

'That's the answer, isn't it?' George said, straightening up. 'We are not being derelict in our duty, because whatever we do we won't get any money. And we do not, surely, have to go out of our way to help Customs and Excise just to be good citizens?'

'That's right. I'll tell them it's no good invoking the Civil Service old pals act.'

Promptly at four o'clock a vast car drew into the car-park. Sarah downed papers to peep at it. The same elongated Rolls Royce that had come to the health farm was now disgorging Perry and two large men who were markedly similar in type to the Securicor hirelings and, presumably, like them called something brutally monosyllabic. Sarah returned to her papers reflecting that she was going through many experiences not usually vouchsafed to Heads of Houses.

At five o'clock she walked over to the Buttery for tea, to find most of the student body encamped just outside Tydeman Hall, from whose windows the sound of the college choir was issuing, going somewhat raggedly through a madrigal. She walked towards the door, closed and guarded by Perry's large friends, and greeted them cautiously, rather as she would have two large, fierce dogs. The door opened from the inside and Perry slipped out.

'There's a tenor sings half a tone sharp,' he reported, wincing. 'I'm sure it'll be all right later. I thought this was an all-female outing, Dame Sarah?'

'I'm sorry if you were disappointed, Perry. For concerts we combine with St John's Theological College. They sing.'

190

'They would, of course. *That's* better – he's on the note now.'

Sarah wondered aloud whether perfect pitch was not a handicap for a rock singer, and Perry looked surprised. 'No more so than for anyone else. You're born with it, you know, you can't grow it. There's a . . . well . . . famous operatic tenor I can't listen to, because he goes flat and doesn't even know when he's doing it. The group – my group – can all pitch, except the baritone, but he's too good to lose, so we just kick him when he goes off.'

He was a man totally in command of his craft, Sarah thought, and felt herself relaxing. As Francesca had known, this one would be able to perform in any circumstances.

'That's me on,' Perry said, listening critically to the music. 'Da, da-ah, de da,' he sang softly with the concluding notes, nodded to her, and disappeared.

She followed him in, drawn irresistibly to hear what he was like as a singer, and took a chair modestly at the edge of a row, behind the choir and orchestra, who were scattered over the first six rows. The orchestra was in place, in the sense that the piano, the chairs and the larger instruments like the cellos were all arranged, but people carrying cases were sitting all over the hall, rather than in their places. Perry was on stage with Susan Elias, who was sitting at the piano, pink and serious. He bent over the music, conferred with Susan, then straightened up.

'Fran? Susan and I want to change the programme a bit. We haven't got enough punch in the last section, it's all a bit samey.'

'What had you in mind? "God Bless the Prince of Wales"?' Francesca, sprawled in the front row, was plainly enjoying herself.

'In Welsh, do you think? No? What about "The Holy City"?'

'Not interdenominational enough,' his sister said, in ruthless disregard of any religious susceptibilities that members of St John's Theological College might be supposed to possess. 'If you are trying here for something that brings them to their feet, shouting and weeping, I must warn you that this may not be that kind of audience, Perry.'

'They're all that kind of audience,' Perry said, with dismissive confidence. 'And if the choir agrees, I'd like to sing something we can do together. OK, everybody, what can we do, on one rehearsal? Something where we sing alternate verses, yes? Don't you have a college song?'

'No,' Susan Elias said happily, eyes sparkling. 'What about "Men of Harlech"?'

'Rotten tune. The Welsh national anthem, now, there's a tune. Good for a tenor. Or something else ethnic – "The Wearing of the Green"? No, perhaps not. Well, shall I do the next two, while we think?' He walked to centre right of the stage, placing himself between the piano and the microphone. He glanced at Susan Elias, who started to play. Schubert, Sarah thought – and then all thought evaporated as Perry opened his mouth and sang – a high, clear, golden tenor, unfussed and unobtrusively well trained. The audience, all musicians, sat rapt and unmoving in absolute silence as Perry sang on, filling the hall effortlessly. It hardly gave the impression of a performance; this was a young man singing to communicate, and to share his pleasure in the music. One or two brave souls applauded at the end, and Perry smiled politely, but he was looking towards his sister.

'You lost Susan at 8D. And again at 9C,' she said, and Sarah saw that she was following a score.

'It was I who lost Perry. Sorry.' Susan Elias, Sarah observed with respect, was perfectly confident in this field. Untroubled, she played the offending sections, fast, half a dozen times and nodded to Perry, who sang them through at half-volume. The audience was watching them, wide-eyed and concentrated. She would have to go now, Sarah decided, for so compelling was the sight of these craftsmen making minute, patient adjustments to their work, unconscious of the spectators, that otherwise she would be here until they stopped.

She emerged from her bedroom an hour and a half later, bathed and changed and feeling ready for the fray. When the door bell sounded she opened the lodge door to George Hellier, who was carrying a case of wine. He was followed by both Securicor men and Perry's two bodyguards, similarly encumbered.

'Everything else is done, Sarah.' George was looking much better, no doubt for being involved in this creative activity. 'We just need to set up drinks here for your own guests.' He directed his crew and set them to unpacking.

192

'These glasses could do with a polish,' Bert, or possibly Jeff, from Securicor reported dourly. George, wordlessly, handed him a tea-towel. The guard looked momentarily mutinous, but Sarah snatched up another towel and began working alongside him.

'We gotta get back to Perry,' the other two heavies said hastily, and George lifted his head from unpacking bottles long enough to thank them.

Twenty minutes later the room was ready, with a table full of shining glasses. The four of them looked at it complacently.

'Let's start the party,' Sarah said recklessly. 'Crack a bottle, George, and we'll drink to the concert. Just half a glass?'

The Securicor team intimated that this would not break the terms of their contract, and they all drank, solemnly, to the success of the evening.

'It's been a nice job, this,' the senior man said shyly. 'Be sorry to leave. They haven't got your man yet, though, have they? Sorry,' he added belatedly, seeing their faces fall.

'No,' Sarah said resolutely. 'But tonight we rejoice. There we go,' she added, catching sight of summer frocks and sober suits at the edge of the lawn. 'Let joy be unconfined.'

And sitting in the front row, between Neville Allason and the Chairman of English Heritage, with the choir and orchestra uniformly dressed in black and white, nervous but concentrated, on the stage, Sarah did feel real joy and pride in the institution which had rallied to deal with near-death and disaster. Leaning forward to smile at a late-arriving professor, she noticed that John McLeish had not arrived, but a place had been left for him on the end of a row near the door, in a routine well established in the McLeish family.

George Hellier was two places away on the other side; he had been given his wife's seat of honour, and Sarah recalled, with a pang, that there were now three casualties of the term: Alice as well as the still unconscious Louise Taylor and the recovering Clarissa Dutt. Neville, she thought, was looking uncomfortable but stoic. He had arrived holding his wife's arm, and had stuck to her like glue, which Jennifer Allason had accepted placidly. Sitting beside her now, he was more or less holding her hand.

The audience was buzzing; they had been greeted on arrival

by a single piece of paper, explaining Michael Miles's indisposition and the substitution of Peregrine Wilson; those of the audience who had not recognized Perry Wilson, pop star, in this guise were being explained to.

The lights went down and Susan Elias, looking young and pale but perfectly composed, came on to apologize for the last-minute change, to express the hope of forgiveness, and to welcome Perry, who appeared from amid the ranks of the choir, to the accompaniment of his sister dropping her programme and muttering oaths. He moved to the left and the choir assembled around him, so that he was partly concealed among the tenors. A moment's pause, to greet the leader of the orchestra, then they launched into 'How Lovely Are Thy Dwellings Fair'. The choir sounded wonderful, Sarah thought. Perry was singing with the tenors, audible among them and holding the rogue tenor, who sang sharp, in line. She leaned over under cover of the applause to congratulate Francesca, who shook her head.

'He'll strain his voice,' she hissed. 'Trouble is he gets carried away.'

The choir stepped back; and Perry moved over to the piano, and held out a hand to welcome Susan Elias as his accompanist. He announced his intention to sing three songs, and started with a Handel anthem with which Sarah was unfamiliar, going on to the Puccini pop 'Nessun dorma', and the Schubert song she had heard earlier. The audience was justifiably enraptured. Neville Allason had been spellbound by 'Nessun dorma' and was leaning over to assure her urgently that the chap at Covent Garden had not been as good. Which was probably true, Sarah thought, wondering why this golden talent had decided to go for rock music, knicker-flinging teenagers and Japanese tours, rather than the prestigious life of an opera star. It was the money, she realized: the marks of a hard childhood were on Perry, as well as on her old friend. Neville Allason had gone for the top professional prizes; this young man had gone for cash. And for admiration, too. He had the audience in the palm of his hand and knew it. He retreated modestly into the choir to help out with the madrigals, but he was not, Sarah was relieved to see, superhuman – he was using a score this time. He went off stage, leaving the choir at the end of the group of songs, just touching his throat.

194

In the twenty-minute interval the students managed to sell huge numbers of raffle tickets to an excited audience who felt they had got more than they had paid for. Francesca vanished backstage without explanation or farewell and slid back into her chair just as the lights went down again.

'John not here yet?' Sarah enquired.

'No,' Francesca said, looking round, her attention reluctantly dragged from her sibling. 'He'll make it for dinner.'

The orchestra played a justifiably little-known short symphony by César Franck, then the choir sang a group of twentieth-century works, without Perry; the orchestra played the first movement of Beethoven's sixth, and then Perry appeared, as the final item.

'We left this a blank on your programme,' he said confidingly to the audience, 'because we were at the time still arguing about what we should offer you.' He waited out a ripple of sympathetic laughter. 'I am going to sing two songs, and then the choir and I will sing the last one with the orchestra.' He paused, and adjusted the microphone, as at home on stage in front of 400 people as in his own bathroom. 'The first song was written for a treble. I used to sing it as a boy, but I have to do it an octave lower these days.'

He moved back, marginally, from the microphone; Susan Elias started to play and the audience shifted and exclaimed in recognition. 'Oh, for the wings, for the wings of a dove,' he sang, effortless and relaxed, his throat right open; and Sarah decided, with tears just behind her eyes, that it *should* have been written for a tenor. He did the last verse in beautiful German, as a virtuoso flourish, and bowed in acknowledgement of the crack of applause.

'He's a parrot too,' his elder sister said, dispassionately, across the Chairman of English Heritage. 'Can do any language.'

Perry launched out on 'Panis Angelicus', another of his boyhood hits, pointing out that this one, by contrast, was written for a tenor but had worked very well for a treble. It was a clever choice, Sarah thought, listening to the beautiful, steady, high voice – much of his audience was middle-aged and would have heard him as a treble, indeed, many of the faces were soft with reminiscent pleasure.

His gesture brought the choir to its feet round him, and he

195

smiled at them all. 'And finally,' he said, to the hall, so that each member of the audience felt addressed personally, 'we are going to give you a song I first heard in Wales, sung by a Welsh choir, and have never forgotten. The English title is "Bread of Heaven".' He moved forward marginally and opened his mouth with the orchestra coming in behind.

It didn't sound quite the same as it would have done in Wales, Sarah decided, performed with a small choir and smaller orchestra with a lot of strings, when it really needed a brass band and a football crowd. But it was pretty good. Perry sang the first verse, superbly, and stepped back from the microphone while the choir sang the second. Then he moved forward for the third verse, with one slanting glance at the front row, and sang it in what Sarah recognized with a shock as Welsh, the choir humming behind him. Francesca's face cracked into a reluctant, enormous grin as Perry and the choir crashed together into the final, irresistible verse.

They had to do the whole thing again, all four verses, this time with Perry at his full, staggering volume, the voice soaring on top of the choir in the last verse with the audience on the edge of their seats, transported. They rose as one person to applaud as he finished. He bowed and smiled, and bowed again, and stepped back into the ranks of the choir, all of whom were beaming, transfigured. He stepped forward again and extended a hand to Susan Elias, who bent her head in acknowledgement from her seat at the piano, so that, laughing, he went to fetch her and brought her to the centre of the stage, holding her hand as she bowed with him, then stepping back, so that she herself received a crashing round of applause. He did the same with the conductor, then the leader of the orchestra. Finally, as the applause settled to a steady clapping, he nodded across to Susan Elias, who brought her hands down in the familiar rousing chords that had the audience bracing itself to sing all three verses of the National Anthem.

'We ought to be thankful Perry didn't do a verse of *that* in Gaelic, I suppose,' Francesca observed cheerfully, when the applause was over and they were all shuffling towards the doors. 'Still no John. Never mind, he's got held up somewhere. Let's get the buffet supper in.'

That went well too. Neville, still sticking close to his placid wife, was charming to students, and graceful about being so thoroughly upstaged by Perry, who was surrounded three-deep by admirers. As the party drew to a close, Sarah fought her way to his side to express her gratitude.

'I enjoyed it,' he said, with all of his sister's cheerfulness. 'No trouble in the world. Dame Sarah, I'm glad to have a word with you. I've told Frannie I've decided to underwrite your crèche for two years and help with the building. If it won't pay at the end of that – well, we'll all have to think again.'

'What a good brother you are, Perry.'

'I'm not the good one, I'm the rich one,' he said hastily, and she laughed at him.

'There's John, just made it,' he pointed out, indicating his tall brother-in-law standing in the doorway, looking round. Perry waved and jabbed a finger to indicate where Francesca was, but John McLeish came over to Sarah, moving with that unobtrusive speed which she had noticed before.

'Evening, Perry. Dame Sarah, We need a word.' His brother-in-law moved away after one single, startled glance sideways, and was replaced by Alan Toms, carrying his raincoat and looking like a thundercloud.

'Is it Louise?' Sarah asked, dry-mouthed.

'Yes,' Toms said. 'No, no, she's not worse, sorry to frighten you, Dame Sarah. She came round briefly about three hours ago, when her husband was with her. My lad was there too, and he reported that she was terrified. She kept saying, "Take him away, he'll hurt me," and had to be held down to keep the tubes in. So we hung on to Taylor. He's at the station with Fields, and we've got a statement from him.'

'So it *was* Michael who tried to kill her?'

'He says not. What he does now admit is that they had a row before she left, in the course of which he hit her and threatened to do worse if she continued carrying on with Sir Neville. So we've charged him. He'll be in court tomorrow.'

197

12

'So I told him,' Alan Toms said, in full narrative swing. '"Listen, sunshine," I said, "if you hadn't got in the way every time we asked a simple question, your client might have been able to tell us something which would have meant he could go home to his kids. But you weren't going to have that, so now we've had to charge him. And we're going to oppose bail, squire, don't be so bloody stupid."' Alan Toms checked to glare at a young man passing close by, almost invisible under piles of duvets, pictures and miscellaneous objects, who altered course nervously to avoid the small group.

When Toms and John McLeish had appeared at the lodge that morning, Sarah had been organizing breakfast for Louise's father, who had just arrived to support his wife, and for the Bishop of Norwich and his lady – not an easy occasion in its own right. She had decided to remove herself and the police presence to the gardens, it being mercifully a fine, warm day. The college was packing up; it was the final day of term and parents were everywhere, collecting their daughters. With luck they would all be gone before the news that Michael Taylor was now in custody could get around.

'This was Michael Taylor's solicitor you were talking to?' Sarah asked, in the interest of clarity, and Toms nodded.

'You had no argument from the bench?' McLeish said.

'No. Well, I had the advantage there. It's a stipe, and I'd had a word.'

'What's a stipe, Mr Toms?' Sarah did not really care, but he had paused.

'Stipendiary magistrate. A professional, not a JP . . . Jackson.

He knew what happened last time Sir Richard Brown's mob took a defendant away from us.'

'Brown's firm are looking after Taylor as well as the boy in Otley Farm?' John McLeish said. 'They cost a fortune to get out of their cot.'

'Michael Taylor is another one with a rich father, it turns out,' Alan Toms said, with displeasure. 'Anyway, old Jackson wasn't having any; looked at Brown's man over his glasses and told him he could apply again in seven days' time.'

'The magistrate felt Sir Richard Brown's firm had obstructed you over the previous attacks?' Sarah asked, hoping for some clarity.

'He didn't feel, he knew, Dame Sarah. Well, I mean Brown's firm are solicitors who act for criminals, not criminal solicitors, if you take my meaning. I was going to talk to a doctor at Otley Farm, anyway – under the old pals act. He used to work for us, when I was in Hackney. But I didn't have to make the call, because he rang me. Said he'd been given permission by Sir Richard Brown's lot. The young man they have will be there forever, or as near as makes no odds. Mad as the proverbial. Schizophrenic – paranoid, you name it. He'd have been unfit to plead if we'd got him, my pal says. And not to worry about letting him loose to prey on society – Otley Farm is one of the places where only the paying customers are round the bend: the staff are all right.'

'And the young man at Otley Farm didn't – he couldn't possibly – have attacked Louise?' Sarah asked, unhopefully.

'No, he couldn't. That was why Sir Richard Brown's lot were so accommodating about my mate there having a little chat: nobody wanted more on their customer's slate than there should be in case he ever comes right again. These people get better sometimes, apparently. He was in Otley Farm by eight o'clock that night, heavily doped, with my mate sitting beside him. There is no way he could have sneaked out and driven 250 miles back to his old hunting-grounds to assault Dr Taylor.'

A depressed silence ensued, while all three of them gazed at the scene in front of them, with streams of undergraduates and their adherents walking through the gardens, laden like mountain porters.

'Are you not working today, John?' Sarah asked, for something to say. 'I thought you wore uniform?'

'I am on duty, but I'm going in – I'm going to see someone.'

Alan Toms's head moved sharply, and Sarah understood that she had asked a question John McLeish did not want to answer.

'Mr Toms,' she said, ploughing firmly back to her main problem, 'do I take it that the police are now convinced that it was Michael Taylor who attacked Louise?'

'Depends which bit of the police you're talking about,' Toms answered, with a sharp sidelong look at McLeish. 'Me, I'm reasonably happy with the evidence of the victim, and the fact that the accused doesn't have an alibi. We let him go last time because he'd have had to rush to do it – a neighbour saw him around ten past eleven. But he did have time – just. John, now, he's still worrying about your predecessor; and both Taylors have an alibi for that, don't they?'

'Yes, they do.' John McLeish appeared, uncharacteristically, to be sulking.

'Well.' Alan Toms gathered himself to depart. 'I'm sorry you've had this to bear as well, Dame Sarah. A couple more of your people planning to leave, I hear?' He looked at her thoughtfully. 'My first station was like that, you know. The CID had gone native – joined the criminals, I mean – and half the uniformed branch were having breakdowns, or were spending all day in the pub. It came right in the end, with patience.' He extended his hand in farewell and Sarah saw him to the gate, waving him to his car.

She came back and met John McLeish's eye. He was, she saw, trying very hard not to laugh.

'I'm sorry,' he said, abandoning the effort. 'I must tell Frannie, that's one for her collection of the sayings of Alan Toms. It was kindly meant.'

'Of course it was,' Sarah said, feeling a good deal better. 'And it *is* the same really: an institution is only people, and academics just choose different ways of ceasing to function effectively.' She caught his expression. 'No, I suppose that's wrong too. My academics *are* having breakdowns, or going sick; I feel it can only be a matter of time before I discover that a couple of them are spending all day in the pub. And Michael Taylor does seem to have joined the criminal fraternity.' She looked at John McLeish

200

ruefully. 'We have absolutely nothing to feel superior about here.'

'Oh, I don't know. Last night was a triumph, and your students did it.'

'And your brother-in-law. And your wife. Speaking of whom, I hope she's not coming in today? She is very tired.'

'She is coming in, but late. She slept in, and she's going to nip into the hospital to see Louise, on the chance she catches her when she's conscious.'

'She won't get in,' Sarah warned. 'Only family.'

'I'm afraid she'll think of something.' He yawned suddenly and jaw-crackingly. 'Sorry.'

'You look worn out too,' Sarah said.

'I'm all right. Bit short of sleep. William's teething – I mean, that's why he's not sleeping; it's nothing to do with Fran, I don't think. But she gets wound up and needs the pills to get her off to sleep afterwards, then feels terrible when she wakes up. Don't you worry about it, Sarah,' he said hastily, seeing her face. 'Frannie will be all right. It was the concert too; she always gets overexcited when her brothers are around.' He hesitated, fiddled with an overhanging branch and let it go again. 'I'm out of line here, Dame Sarah, but I need to talk to you.'

'You managed to call me plain Sarah once this morning, John. Could you not go on doing so?'

'Sarah. Yes. I am not a happy man. I've had these – well, I suppose instincts – all my life, and I think I – we – missed out over Judith Symonds's death. But it was not Michael Taylor who killed her – not unless two people not related to him are lying. However, I'm going to have to stop worrying at this one. The CID at Notting Dale are only doing anything at all about it because one of the sergeants there, Bruce Davidson, is someone I've worked with for a long time.' He looked at his hands. 'I think – I don't know, but I think – that I'm going to find myself moved somewhere else.'

'You mean, they're cross with you at Notting Dale? Because of this case?'

'No, no. I'm not in uniform today because an Assistant Commissioner at the Yard wants to see me. Well, I haven't blotted my copybook, so far as I know, and I've now done three years at Notting Dale. He wants me to do something else – it has to be.'

'Promotion?' Sarah asked cautiously.

'Don't know. Probably. I won't be able to say no, whatever it is.'

'I take it people do not say no, in the police?'

'You *can* sometimes say no, and I have done it in my time. I wouldn't transfer out of London because of Fran's job. She doesn't know that, by the way,' he added warningly. 'That's all right, or has been so far, because there aren't enough people to fill the senior jobs in London – half the force are trying to get a posting outside the city so as to cut down their travelling time. No, it's likely to be a secondment to look at another force, where there's been trouble.'

'Oh, John.' Sarah was distressed, as she thought it through. 'That would mean that both you and Francesca were the rescue squad in exhausting jobs.'

'I'd thought of that. Fran needs the challenge, though, she'll never settle to something routine. And she's better when she's fully occupied.'

Sarah smiled at this masterly piece of understatement. 'Where does that leave you, John?' she asked.

'Like I said, unhappy. I'm not happy about Taylor, though Alan Toms had no alternative but to charge him. But I've seen these bang-on-the-head cases before: the shock often wipes out the most recent memory altogether. So Louise Taylor may well have woken remembering the fight with her husband – and there he was, sitting there – and have forgotten everything that happened after that.'

'Or, I suppose, Alan Toms might be right,' Sarah said reluctantly. 'He realized that she had gone off with Neville Allason and really lost his temper. It is clear he suspected there was an affair and to have it confirmed might have been too much. Even though he was doing the same himself.'

'Oh, *that's* never stopped anyone from clobbering the wife,' John McLeish agreed.

'I suppose she may change her view as she recovers?'

He shook his head doubtfully. 'She's still very ill. I'd not use words like "recover" just yet. Her skull hasn't mended.' The matter-of-fact statement chilled Sarah, though she knew it to be no more than the truth. 'Look, Sarah, humour me, all right?

Can we think about Judith Symonds? Who benefited from her death?'

'Me, I suppose. I have her job.'

'You didn't expect it.' It was a statement, not a question.

'No, I didn't. I thought I was going to Durham.'

'Who did expect it?'

'Oh heavens, John. Alice Hellier, I suppose. She was the natural candidate. But people don't murder each other in order to be Warden of Gladstone.' She thought involuntarily of Alice's bitter, unguarded comment of the day before.

'In my manor, people murder each other for a good deal less than that. Why didn't Dr Hellier get the job?'

'You mean, why was I preferred? My experience is wider, but at least in educational administration it's no better. And I am five years older. But given a choice between us, I think you would have taken me.' Sarah gazed into the gardens, too accustomed to this sort of assessment to feel any embarrassment. 'I suppose, looked at that way, Alice had bad luck. I missed the Durham appointment because I was ill, and had I got Durham I would simply not have been available for this job. But I do not see why she would have attacked Louise Taylor – there was no point in that. Why not have had a go at me?'

'Ah,' John McLeish said. 'Dr Hellier has got something against Louise Taylor, too. My wife, dear girl that she is, managed last night to tell me that Louise had a walk-out with George Hellier eighteen months ago. According to Louise, it was now over, but that young woman's been leading a complicated life. It could easily still have been on. I mean, George is still around, isn't he?' He considered, wryly, her astonished face, and waited while she assimilated the information.

'All right, it sounds far-fetched,' he said, after a minute. 'But Alice Hellier has cracked up completely – wringing her hands, your Dr Smith told me. It's a classic sign of guilt, real or imagined.'

'But the Helliers were together at the party before Dr Symonds died,' Sarah remembered. 'Don't they alibi each other?'

'No, curiously enough they don't. Dr Hellier went off afterwards to see an old colleague, stayed an hour there, and went home about 11 p.m., she says. George Hellier had a bite to eat, he says, went to a cinema, and then made his way back about midnight. She has no witness to her activities between nine o'clock and midnight; he between eight thirty and midnight. Thereafter they alibi each other – but Dr Symonds was probably dead by midnight.'

He let silence fall again, watching her.

'I did not, and do not, understand quite why Alice has collapsed, but nervous illness is like that,' Sarah said slowly. 'Some current event strikes an echo of a buried trauma, and the personality disintegrates. I've seen it before, and you must have too, John?'

'Yes.' He did not sound convinced. 'I've passed all this on to Alan Toms. He's not convinced; he always thought it was Michael Taylor who attacked Louise, and he doesn't believe her case and Dr Symonds's are linked. But he's indulging me. He's looking at both Helliers' statements now. And at Allason's; he's very much in the frame, Sarah.'

She decided to ignore this warning for now. 'I suppose the police suspect George, too, now – given that it was he who had an affair with Louise.'

'I can't see why he would have wanted to get rid of Dr Symonds,' McLeish objected.

'So his wife could be Warden?'

'Mm. And perhaps so that he got his chance at being Bursar. Alice Hellier always believed the Fellowship should be mixed, yes?'

'Yes, Alice did – does – believe we should mix. Both our senior physicists do. But then so did Judith Symonds; she just failed to get the necessary change through the Fellowship. I am sure we have to mix, but I am not confident that I could get it through either. Alice would have found the same difficulty, and she knows it as well as I do. Perhaps I, too, should be careful?'

'You should.' Sarah had meant it sarcastically, but McLeish's response was instant and uncompromising.

'I'm surprised you feel able to leave Francesca in post, if you are so uncomfortable with the situation,' she said, when she had got her breath back. She was aware that she sounded peevish.

'This is an old trouble that's surfacing at the college. If I'm right, it dates back before Francesca ever heard of the place, and she's not Warden, nor is she involved with Neville Allason.' He looked at her sadly. 'I've made your day, I can see that, but I wanted you on warning.'

'I know you mean well.'

'I mean to see the right person, man or woman, taken for this one,' he said slowly.

'A useful distinction,' she acknowledged. 'You mean to see justice done. I will try to look after myself and Francesca for you. Good luck with your interview.'

'Thank you, Sarah.' He hesitated, bent to kiss her cheek in conventional farewell, and straightened up, looking pleased with himself.

'Have a good day,' she said, amused, and waved him off to his waiting driver.

Sitting down at her desk again, Sarah realized that the morning's visitor had left her with a sense of some vital task unperformed. Michael Taylor was evidently well furnished with legal help; Alice Hellier had Dr Smith; Francesca was visiting Louise Taylor, and would, no doubt, find out what needed doing there. What she herself wanted was an undemanding contemporary to buy her lunch – and with that she remembered with a sinking heart the task she ought in kindness to be undertaking. It was unlikely that anyone on the police side would yet have told Neville Allason about Michael Taylor's arrest, and it would be the part of an old friend, and one who had need of Allason's good will, to do so.

She was put through to him at once, the private office obviously recognizing her as a person with a legitimate claim on his immediate attention. She told him what had happened and, to give him time, added Alan Toms's revelations about the two attacks on Gladstone's students.

'Well that's a relief, I suppose,' he said. 'That particular lunatic won't trouble you further.' There was a long painful pause. 'Are they sure about Taylor, Sarah?'

'He has been charged.'

'Well, thank you for warning me. I don't have anything more to tell them. Louise *did* ring me at eleven o'clock; she was perfectly all right and just going to go home, and there was no sug-gestion that she was afraid to do so.' Neville sounded thoroughly rattled, and Sarah hesitated, wishing she had left this to the police after all.

'I understand that Michael told the police he had had a row with Louise before she went out to meet you. In the course of that row, he had threatened her.'

'A row because she was having dinner with me?'

'She appears to have told him only that she was going to work,' Sarah said carefully.

There was a heavy pause. 'I suppose he may have become suspicious,' Neville Allason said heavily. 'In fact, now I come to think of it, that's probably right – that the row was about me. She never told me.'

It was a cry of resentment, and Sarah could find no words at all with which to reassure him.

'I can hear what you're thinking,' Neville said balefully. 'But nothing even remotely like this has ever happened before.'

'No jealous husbands?'

'There haven't been *that* many women in my life,' he said, sounding injured, and Sarah decided that this was not the moment to insist on a roll-call. It was, in any case, likely that he believed what he was saying.

'Neville, does Jennifer know?'

'No, no. Nothing at all.'

She waited out another silence.

'You think she may have to?' he asked reluctantly.

'If Michael Taylor comes to trial, you will presumably have to give evidence.'

'Oh Christ.'

'Well, what *did* you think, Neville?'

'I suppose I still thought it was our lunatic, and I'd never be asked. But it couldn't have been, could it?'

'No, not possibly. Or not *that* lunatic.'

'I may be in trouble, Sarah, but I do know that two random lunatics at Gladstone would be too much to hope for. Damn, damn.' He drew a deep breath, audible across several miles of telephone wire. 'It was good of you to ring me.'

'Not at all,' she said conventionally. 'See you soon.'

On her way across the garden, she thought about her old friend. He would put off letting his wife know anything until it became unavoidable; then he would appear as a penitent boy

206

and throw himself on her mercy, banking on the long years of marriage and her identification with his life. And this he would do, even if it had been he who had tried to kill Louise.

Three miles away, Francesca hesitated in the hospital's ugly reception hall, then advanced on the glassed-in cubicle in which sat the reception staff. She waited for a minute, and as none of the three occupants of the cubicle looked her way, being engrossed in finishing a conversation, she tapped on the counter.

'Where is my constable?' she barked. 'One of my men is watching over Dr Taylor.'

The group sprang reluctantly into action, one to answer a phone that had been ringing for some time, one to do some paper-arranging task, and one to explain elaborately where Dr Taylor now was.

'Out of intensive care?' Francesca asked, surprised, and the man consulted a list.

'Yes. In a side ward, but not allowed visitors except family.'

'I'll make quite sure my man understands that, thank you. No, I'll go up, never mind the phone.'

She arrived, triumphantly, at the ward and checked, recognizing the small, dumpy woman with Louise's black hair who was sitting, quietly looking into space, in a chair in the corridor. She looked past her to see the tail-end of a procession; that must be the ward round, and she had arrived in the middle of it. She found an unoccupied chair, carried it over beside Mrs Mason, and introduced herself, cautiously.

'Louise often spoke of you,' Mrs Mason said. She was pale and tired, but the same fire that burned in Louise burned in her. 'Now you can tell me: what is happening to Michael?'

'Ah.' Francesca drew a deep breath, but Mrs Mason had her eyes fixed on her. 'I'm afraid he has been charged with – well, with the attack on Louise. He was in court this morning and was remanded in custody.'

Mrs Mason stared at her. 'That means he's in jail?'

'Yes.'

'Why? Was Mr Mason there?'

'Yes.' Francesca wished she had minded her own business and gone straight into the Bursary. 'It was the police who opposed

207

bail. He has leave to appeal again – I mean, to be remanded home – in seven days.'

'And how are the children supposed to get on, without either of their parents?'

Francesca just managed not to gape at her, and produced a disjointed sentence about au pairs and neighbours.

'No, no.' Mrs Mason dismissed all this as impatiently as Louise herself would have done. 'They need their father – they must be frightened. I'll go there now – have you a car with you?'

Francesca, feeling about six years old, confirmed that she had and waited meekly while Mrs Mason explained to a young nurse that she would be back sometime in the day. She managed to recover her poise slightly as she installed Mrs Mason in the car and turned for Gladstone College.

'Can we – the college – help?'

'You've all been very kind,' Mrs Mason said flatly, the strong northern accent very pronounced, having judiciously reviewed their contribution. 'I should have been in court myself, but I thought I should be with Louise. She didn't mean what she said about Michael, you know, and I told the police that.'

Francesca kept her hands still on the wheel with an effort. 'You mean, you don't think Michael did attack her?'

'Oh, they may have had a quarrel, I'm not disputing that, and he may have slapped her.' Mrs Mason was searching her handbag for something. 'I've had to slap her many times as a child; she can be that annoying. But it is not in Michael to hurt anyone like Louise was hurt.' She found the handkerchief she had been looking for and blew her nose, thoroughly. 'Your husband is a policeman, Louise told me?'

'Yes, but this is not his patch. I mean it was not he who arrested Michael,' Francesca said hastily, feeling worse by the minute.

'What does he think?' Mrs Mason asked ruthlessly, ignoring these professional quibbles.

'He says people waking from unconsciousness very rarely remember the bit immediately before – I mean, they often lose that altogether,' Francesca said, deeply relieved to be able to tell a helpful truth.

'So she could have remembered getting a slap which was much earlier than the attack?'

You could readily, Francesca thought, see where Louise's genes came from. 'That's right,' she confirmed.

'Well, by all accounts, she deserved it,' Mrs Mason said, gazing out of the passenger window. 'Is this not the entrance?'

Francesca, who had been about to overshoot the familiar gates out of sheer surprise, apologized and swung the car left. 'Where would you like to go, Mrs Mason?' she asked, feeling the only safe role for her was that of deferential aide.

'We'll pick up Dad at the lodge, if that's all right, and if you'll be good enough to take us on, I'll sort out the young woman who helps and fetch the children back. Then I'll go and see the police about Michael.'

Sarah looked for her Bursar, but failing to find her, went in to eat lunch in the Buttery, which was a very pleasant experience. Parents who had come for the concert and stayed overnight to transport their young home, had made *en masse* for the Buttery and were all eager to meet Sarah and to congratulate her on the concert. The moments of pleasure and gratification in this job, as in life generally, being rare enough, Sarah decided that they should be seized when available, and she basked in the atmosphere of warm approval and gratitude for an hour.

When she got back to her desk, of course, she found that real life was back with a vengeance and returned George Hellier's call as being the least of the evils awaiting. He was sounding apologetic, harried and anxious; the nurse had been unavoidably detained, he could not come in until three and hoped that only routine business was being transacted. She reassured him, briskly observing that Francesca would be in shortly – and looked up from putting down the receiver to see her Bursar in the doorway, looking shaken.

'I'd better tell you,' Francesca said without preamble. 'I've weakened. My Customs chum has been badgering me, and I've feebly agreed to let him have a selection of our acounts with Greenlees. Apparently the runaway MD had a massive session with a shredding machine before he took off, and Customs are a bit short of documentary evidence. What they mean by that – I asked – is that they haven't actually got *any* documentary proof of the chap's *modus operandi*, as it were. They're dependent on getting evidence from the customers, and they know me, so they're using the civil-servants'-mutual-cooperation act, which I deny at my peril for the future. We're not committed to doing any of the work ourselves,' she added hastily. 'I made that a condition. It's just a question of our handing over papers.'

'Are these papers easy to find?'

'No, they're not. When we finished the kitchen accounts for last year, George took all the data away, and probably ate it. I've not told him all this – I'll break it to him when he comes in. I've got this year's stuff, such as it is, but it's really the back years they're looking for. I can give them the accounts for last year's Raab Lecture – I've got them on me. That will keep them quiet for a couple of hours. Then it's a question of what else George can find for last year.'

'Could we not postulate that he threw it all away?'

'Well, joking apart, you ought to keep all these things for a couple of years, anyway.' She thought about it. '*I* wouldn't have thrown them away. If he has, of course, that's the end of it. Oh, coffee. Could I have some?'

She sat down gratefully with a cup of coffee and fished a bottle of pills from her handbag. 'I wish I could remember how many of these I've taken,' she said irritably.

'Skip one, if in doubt,' Sarah suggested.

'Apparently, if you do that you might as well not bother taking any. My quack was rather firm on the subject.' She scowled indecisively at the bottle, then took one, washing it down with coffee.

'Are they helping?' Sarah asked, trying not to sound doubtful.

'Yes. A bit.' She brightened, momentarily and described her interview with Mrs Mason. 'She truly doesn't believe Michael did it, you know.'

'Nor does Mr Mason,' said Sarah. 'Let us hope they are right.'

A further silence fell and Sarah waited patiently.

'I am in a worry about John,' Francesca said finally.

'Why are you worried?'

'He is going to see a man at the Yard – an Assistant Commissioner, who thinks well of him.' She made this good opinion sound like a testimonial from the Furies.

'And may offer him another posting – is that right? I am a bit vague about the bureaucratic structure of the Metropolitan

Police.' Sarah thought it better not to reveal what John McLeish had already told her.

'Yes. The gossip is, according to Uncle Alan, that the AC in question is being dispatched to a really miserable trouble spot. My worry is that he wants to take John with him.'

'Where would it be?'

'I'll tell you, but you're not to breathe a word. It's every police wife's nightmare. Northern Ireland.' She looked miserably over the top of her coffee cup.

'John could say no, surely?' Sarah was as dismayed as Francesca.

'It wouldn't be a permanent job, that's the trouble. If it were, he could. It's an investigation – Alan's wife comes from Belfast, which is how *he* knows about it. It's the classic case where it's become clear that the local force has gone native.'

'Surely the religious differences preclude that?' Sarah protested.

'Gone native, in the sense of adopting criminal tactics just like their opponents,' Francesca said impatiently. 'Passing names of IRA supporters to the fanatics on the loyalist side. Not just conniving at murder, inspiring it.'

A discouraged silence fell between them.

'It would be very difficult for you both if John were there,' Sarah said, even more appalled as she thought about it.

'Yes, and I hope I'm wrong. But *that's* why I'm popping pills, Sarah – just so you know, and don't feel badly. I love Louise, I'm sorry she may never recover, I'm sorry that Michael may spend the rest of his life in jail, I'm sorry Alice Hellier's having a breakdown. But what has got me down isn't any of those things, it's the prospect of my husband being taken away from me to Northern Ireland.' She was very near to tears.

'When will you know?' Sarah asked.

'Tonight, presumably. At least, we'll know whether it *is* Belfast they're talking about.' She gazed bleakly out at the garden. 'Nothing to be done till then. Alan also saw fit to tell me that he was right about the first two attacks. So presumably we can now turn Securicor off? They are on notice to stop today, because it is the end of term. Alan's news and Michael Taylor's arrest make them doubly redundant, I thought?'

'I thought the same.' Sarah was relieved by the signs that business was proceeding as usual.

'I'll tell them,' Francesca said, briskly, getting to her feet. 'I've got quite fond of them really, but they cost a fortune, and they ended on a high note – useful above and beyond the call of duty, last night. Bert was trained as a silver-service waiter, did you know?' She paused in the doorway. 'I don't like to ask, but since we forgot last time . . . Did you ring Sir Neville, or did the police get to him first?'

'I got him before they did.'

'I hope he feels absolutely terrible.'

'He does. I know he is not one of your favourites, but he is not an insensitive man.'

Francesca was looking openly disbelieving.

'I must go and see George,' she said restlessly. 'He should be here by now. Is his time here pensionable, by the way?'

'Yes, but it isn't the riches of the east. I think he has private money, so I imagine they're all right. Presumably he'll be able to get another job, too. He's ten years younger than Alice.'

'It's bad luck on him, though; he likes it here. But it happens to women all the time – dragged by their husbands' chariot wheels away from occupations where they were established.'

Francesca went off to the Bursary, pausing here and there to say goodbye to an undergraduate. Her standing had been raised enormously by her star brother's mannerly, prompt and successful rescue job at the student concert, and she was amused, but pleased. If she was going to be in this institution for two years at least, it was nice to be popular. She entered the Bursary, smiling.

'George, hello?' she said, interrogatively. He was sitting behind his desk, preoccupied. 'Nice of you to come. Is Alice any better?'

'No.' He did not seem to be going to expand on that statement, and Francesca, eyeing him uneasily, explained the fresh demands from Customs.

'Nearly all that stuff is gone. I got rid of it.' He gazed at her hopelessly.

'Well, George,' she said cautiously, 'I have last year's Raab accounts and I was going to send them across by courier tomorrow. Perhaps that'll be enough? They only want to establish Mr Greenlees' *modus operandi*.'

'Why should we do Customs' dirty work?'

212

'I didn't think it would give us much extra work, and we are all citizens. If people like Greenlees don't pay VAT, the rest of us pay more – no?' She considered him. 'Let me try them with what I have here to hand, and *they* can come and search through the rest if they must.'

'Francesca,' he said heavily, 'please. Could we defer doing any of this for a couple of days? I am desperate about Alice – I am beginning to think she may have to go into hospital. I just cannot face that *and* a search through papers here.'

'I perfectly understand, George,' she said guiltily.

'And Francesca, I ought to look at those Raab accounts first. We cannot just hand them over without senior people being sure what we are saying.'

'Louise looked at them,' Francesca pointed out.

'I know she did, but only briefly. And you haven't had time yet, have you?'

'Enough only to be clear that there is something going on. With an hour and a phone call, I could probably tell you what.'

'I'll look at them first, then.' He took them in both his large capable hands and gazed at her severely. 'You'll kill yourself in this job, Francesca, if you try and do everything. Will you remember that when I'm gone?'

'I'll try,' she said, cheered by signs of returning humanity. 'I'll miss you. Oh, by the way – ' She looked anxiously at the phone. 'Sarah agrees we can turn Securicor off. I must ring them.'

'Really? On the basis that since we shall only have about a tenth of our students in residence tonight, the risks are much less?'

'No, George,' she said, laughing, 'that is not our calculation.' She explained quickly about the man in Otley Farm who was now known to be responsible for the first two attacks. 'And I suppose, with Michael now charged with the attack on Louise, we don't feel ourselves so much at risk.'

After confirming to Securicor that Bert and Jeff were no longer needed, she settled down to try and work. What she needed, she decided restively, was a short, contained piece of work, but everything on her desk had roots and tentacles going deep into the structure of the college finances, and was the work of several days. The Raab accounts would be just the right-sized job. She was getting to her feet to find them when the phone rang, and she picked it up, breathing short. She put it down, three minutes later, scarlet with relief. George had vanished, so she ran to Sarah at the lodge.

'It's *not* Northern Ireland!' she said without ceremony, tripping over the doorstep and all but landing on Sarah's knee. 'As so often, Uncle Alan had some of it right: the AC's drawn Northern Ireland, but he said to John he would not invite a father of young children to go with him.' She paused for breath. 'Had he simply been my husband, I suppose, no holds would have been barred, but let that pass. What the AC wants John to do is lead a team investigating East Yorkshire, where they've got thirty detectives suspended and half the uniformed branch disappeared on sick leave. East Yorkshire – two hours on a train! Nothing to it. Oh, *Sarah*! He's going up tonight, that's the only curse, but just for a meeting.'

'I have a bottle of champagne, a present from Neville Allason, if you can bear it. I was saving it for the end of term.'

'Oh, *yes*. Can we ask George too? He's so sad.'

'Why not? Will you go and get him? Three of us is about the right number for a bottle.'

They killed the bottle between them in half an hour. George, who Sarah had feared would be poor company, was in good form, and she admired him for it. It was not in its nature an easy occasion; Francesca, thinking only of Neville Allason, proposed a toast to 'absent friends', which forcibly reminded them of the Taylors and of Alice, but they managed to rise above that.

'Are you safe to drive home, Francesca?' Sarah asked, conscience-stricken as she rose to take her leave.

'With all these bits and pieces to soak it up?' The champagne had been accompanied by the best left-overs from last night's party. 'I'm fine. But I'll maybe take a cup of Bursary coffee first. Are you coming, George?'

'I am. I'll come and work the machine.'

'You must show me how to do that,' Francesca said seriously, as they went into the bright evening sun.

13

An hour later, Sarah decided to go for a walk round the gardens; she had spent the interval peacefully finishing a bottle of white wine, left over from the night before. At seven forty-five it was still warm and light, and she was pleasantly full of alcohol and canapés. She was also suffering the mixed guilt and relief of the survivor; somehow the college had weathered this term, most of her charges had taken their examinations in due time and the roof of Tydeman Hall had not fallen in. The appeal was going well, and Perry Wilson's efforts had certainly helped, not least in focusing the attention of present students. It might indeed be possible to present Gladstone College as the new smart charity, with Perry in support.

She blinked as she saw Perry's sister emerge from the gate that led out to the car-park. 'Francesca? I thought you'd gone home?'

'I had. I tried.' She looked white and her hands were shaking. 'I just bumped the gatepost going out, and when I reversed I bumped the other one. The damage is not serious, but I'm afraid I ought not to be driving. Come to think of it, the quack *did* murmur something about alcohol not being all that good an idea with these pills, but I just didn't listen. Stupid.'

Sarah gazed at her, trying to work out what to do. 'I'm afraid I'm not in any state to drive you either,' she said apologetically. 'I went on drinking where we left off an hour ago.'

'Ah. So did I. George and I had a small whisky, or maybe not such a small one. I'll ring up the wonderful Caroline and crawl, then I'll tuck into a college guest-room.' She leant decoratively against the wall of the porter's lodge; she was very pale and in no state to go anywhere.

'I'd like to offer you a bed in the lodge, but . . .' Sarah said anxiously.

'I know you have Louise's parents, and What's-their-names.'

'The Right Reverend the Bishop of Norwich and Mrs Jones?'

'It always sounds quite immoral, doesn't it?' Francesca pulled herself away from the supporting wall. 'No, don't worry, Sarah, I'll be fine.'

'Coffee? Join me on my walk round.'

'No, no. I think I'll just make a cringing phone call, and get to bed. Please, no one's to tell John, he'll worry. I'll have to confess, of course, but I'd rather do that tomorrow.'

'I'll come with you.'

'No, please not. I think I may be going to be sick and I'd rather do that in decent privacy.' She left hastily enough to add credence to her statement. Sarah hesitated, but was diverted by the sound of her own telephone ringing insistently. With two of the Fellowship seriously ill, she could not ignore a ringing phone, and she speeded to get to it, arriving breathless.

'Oh, Neville. No, I have no news. What? You want to come now?' She stared round her canapé-strewn living-room, which she had decided to leave alone until the next day. 'It will have to be coffee. We drank your champagne an hour ago. Indeed, Francesca McLeish is sleeping it off here.' She suppressed the thought that he could drive Francesca back home after he had said whatever he was coming to say; those two did not like each other. Tired and under stress as they both were, enough of that might surface to the detriment of their relationship and of the DES's relationship with Gladstone.

'Francesca's not with you, is she?' Neville was sounding alarmed.

'No, no, she's in a college guest-room. Well, do come, Neville. I'll expect you in about forty-five minutes.'

Which gave her time, just, to ring the hospital and talk to Louise's mother. 'She does seem a little better,' Louise's mother said, the northern accent very clear. 'She comes and goes. But she knows me, all the time, *and* she knows her Dad. She can move her arms, and they're going to do a few more tests tomorrow. She's not herself of course – she cries a lot.'

Sarah agreed that this was hardly in keeping with Louise Taylor's normal form but expressed pleasure at her progress.

'James is here too. Michael's father,' Mrs Mason continued. 'The doctor didn't think it was a good idea that he should see Louise, but he and I and Dad are going off for a bite.'

A remarkable example of family solidarity: it was devoutly to be hoped that nice Mrs Mason's publicly expressed trust in her son-in-law would be justified.

Sarah set out on a rapid clean-up of her sitting-room, eating canapés as she went, in the hope that they would act as blotting paper. She had restored a fair degree of order by the time Neville Allason's car drew into the car-park; not the official car, Sarah noted, so the conversation was not something that the DES were to know about. She watched the familiar blond head and blunt profile as he hauled a briefcase on to his knee, still sitting in the front of the car, and peered into it, irritably searching for something.

Her phone rang again, and she picked it up to find it was the porter's lodge, sounding flurried. 'A Mr Bourn is on the line. From Customs and Excise.' The porter's tone made it clear that nothing, including Sarah's imminent arrest for drug-smuggling, would surprise him, after what he had had to endure this term. He will have to go, she conceded; it was just too discouraging to have a personality like that as Gladstone's front-line receptionist.

'Dame Sarah, it's Stanley Bourn. Do you remember me?'

Yes, she did, Sarah realized. A capable Treasury man and a contemporary of Neville Allason's – not, perhaps, absolutely in the first flight, and most certainly lacking Neville's expressive flair, but good just the same. As this call confirmed, he was now a Deputy Secretary, and head of Customs and Excise, and he was asking for a favour.

'I know you must be under enormous pressure, and I do assure you we would do all the work,' he was saying, as she realized that this was the other half of a conversation she had had with Francesca. 'Your Bursar told one of my people that she was very doubtful about what help you could give. This is a big case for us, and we are in danger – or, at least, London West is – of falling flat on our faces for want of evidence.'

There was a hopeful pause, while Sarah tried to arrive at a graceful method of batting away this unwelcome demand. She waved to Neville Allason as he peered round her door, indicating that he should sit down and pour himself something to drink.

217

She had, in the event, relented and provided whisky as well as a thermos jug of coffee. He poured himself a generous slug.

'I do indeed remember you,' she said to the telephone rather more cordially than she had meant to. 'Let me start by saying that the Bursar is not being obstructive in any way; we discussed the question this afternoon, and I agreed with her that your people should be offered access to whatever records we have.' She drew breath, remembering the perilously understaffed Bursary. 'As you probably know, however, both she and I are new, and it has been a difficult term. I simply do not know what records we have, nor how difficult it is to give them to you. Perhaps we could talk about this in the morning?'

The phone recorded faithfully the sound-track of a man not at all sure that he had been favourably received. He embarked on profuse apologies for having disturbed her, and assurances that, but for Neville Allason's encouragement, he would not have felt able to do so. She slitted her eyes at Neville, who was restlessly leafing through the evening paper, and ended the conversation civilly. Then she went over and took the paper crossly away from her visitor. 'That call was your fault.'

'Stanley Bourn.' He had been listening, just as she thought. Not much going on in the same room would ever escape Neville Allason. 'Sorry. He rang me earlier today, not to complain, but to ask if I would help with you. I thought it much better for him to talk to you directly. If you can manage what he's asking, Sarah, do. Points with the Treasury can never come amiss, particularly in your situation. Or rather Gladstone's.'

'I told him the truth, which I do not think he recognized: which is that we will help if we can. Francesca is having to go very carefully with the Deputy Bursar.'

'George Hellier? Husband of Alice? Yes, poor chap, he has got enough problems.' He hesitated. 'I may have oversold you to Stanley, Sarah. Your predecessor, Judith, had become very involved with the college accounts, and would probably have known at once whether what Bourn was asking was possible.'

'She had to be involved with the accounts – she had a rotten Bursar.'

'Oh yes, that's the point. After three years of the college accounts falling apart at a touch, she decided to take them on, and spent far too much time and nervous energy on them.' He gave her one of his rueful, sideways, small-boy looks. 'At least my relationship with Judith saved you from Lady Trench. I knew that the Warden did not have proper support, and that's why I got you the admirable Miss Wilson.'

'I thought I got Francesca myself?'

'She came because of you.' One of the endearing things about Neville Allason was that he had always been able to accept areas where he had failed. 'But I did find her on a DTI list and serve her up to you.'

Sarah conceded that with good grace, and added that she would find the job of Warden intolerable if she had to do the accounts as well.

'Yes,' he said heavily. 'I know Judith was finding it so. She said that Hellier was extremely willing, but not really very good at matters financial.'

'Francesca feels the same, I know. She regrets his going, because he does know where things are and she really likes him as a colleague. But she is not at all downcast. She has a replacement in her eye, I understand. Oh well, you can just explain to your friend Stanley that I am not handing him off; unlike my unfortunate predecessor, I have not had to become familiar with our accounts, and I genuinely do not know how difficult all this is going to be.'

'But you are a person of good will, given to co-operation with the Treasury. I will tell him that tomorrow.' He reached for his glass and swallowed the contents. 'I cannot, Sarah, quite cope with where I might turn out to be.'

'Possibly responsible for the attack on Louise Taylor?' Sarah had had a long day, and astringency rather than sympathy had always characterized her relationship with Neville.

'Yes. That, and having to tell Jennifer about the whole thing.'

'Better sooner than later,' Sarah said ruthlessly, deciding it would be all too easy to let Neville talk himself into feeling that it would all go away if he sat tight and did nothing. 'You may otherwise find yourself in a position where Jennifer hears a bit of the story from other sources – the police, for instance.'

'Mm. Any more news of Louise?'

'She's had several patches of consciousness today, and she knows her parents. I spoke to her mother an hour ago. She has not, so far as I know, mentioned you.'

'Good.' He looked enormously relieved.

Sarah felt real impatience with Neville and the conversation, and her expression must have shown it.

'Sorry,' he said, 'you've got other things to worry about. Take me for a walk. Show me where the roof of Tydeman is about to fall, as Francesca seemed to feel it was going to. Then I'll go back. No, I won't have another whisky, thanks.'

It was a lovely walk, Sarah thought, forty minutes later; the gardens had received the afternoon's rain gratefully and everything shone in the late evening light. The scent of roses and honeysuckle was heavy on the evening air. They had toured the whole college, much of it walking rather faster than she would have wished, but the tall man at her side had always had a longer stride than she and was discharging accumulated tension. She had managed to get breath to keep up with him by stopping to point out places of interest, which were also mostly sources of future expense to the college – like the old laboratories, state of the art in about 1907 when a now long-dead donor had decided that the ladies of Gladstone were handicapped by the need to travel to the university laboratories in central London.

Neville was, as always, good company, amusing, creative and funny, and it was not difficult to see his attraction for Louise Taylor, even though he was twenty years her senior. Sarah looked at him as they halted by the substantial wrought-iron gates; he seemed calmer, but the lines round the corners of his mouth were tight and the eyes under the heavy bone of the brow narrowed. He was, she understood, bracing himself to perform an unwelcome but necessary task, and had sought exercise to clear his system for action.

Neville bent to kiss her cheek. He had always preferred small women, she reflected. She, Jennifer Allason and Louise Taylor were about five foot two inches, and Judith Symonds had been not much taller. Perhaps that was why he had not shown any sexual interest in Francesca. She accompanied Neville to his car across a car-park strewn with fallen rose petals, blown by the wind and rain of the day; she waved him off and turned back to the consolation of the nine o'clock news, thankful that the

Masons and the Bishop of Norwich and his lady wife were otherwise occupied.

But she was, disconcertingly, unable to concentrate. There was, for once, some real news, but it did not grip her. She switched it off and fidgeted restlessly round the room. It must be the end of term and the release of stress, but she had to acknowledge that she suddenly felt anxious and uncomfortable. She reminded herself that any bad news to come would reach her; nothing could be gained by ringing the hospital to see that Louise had not relapsed. Alice Hellier's condition was under control. She decided against another drink; that way, for a single woman, lay potential trouble. Indeed, she had heard before Christmas that Judith Symonds had been drinking too much.

She stopped, arrested, as the real source of her discomfort surfaced from the uneasy sea of consideration. Whatever McLeish had thought at the time about Judith's death, it had not then been 'his case' in the policeman's sense of the word. When it had become of real concern to him, because of Francesca's involvement, he had not believed his initial hypothesis: he had come to think there *was* a link between Judith Symonds's death and the attack on Louise Taylor, and was being frustrated from following it up.

She sat down, deciding that the only thing to do was to give herself seriously to consideration of John McLeish's hypothesis and try and make it work. If it wouldn't then she could perhaps dispel this unfocused nervous anxiety. She reached for a pencil and paper, then realized it was not going to work that way: it was better not to try to structure her thinking, but to let her disjointed, uncomfortable thoughts come to the surface.

She closed her eyes and in the darkness she saw the term's events in a series of cinematic shots, culminating in the night of the Raab Lecture: George anxiously hovering, counting bottles; Francesca looking for John as he slid into his seat with thirty seconds to spare, skid marks all over him as his wife had observed with disapproving love; Louise coming down from the platform into Neville Allason's arms. A worrying sense of something just outside her vision, something half seen out of the corner of an eye, nagged at her, and she was pursuing it when the phone rang.

'John, good heavens, I thought you were away?'

221

'I am. I gather my wife is also away. With you?' He sounded anxious and accusing.

'She's not with me, here, I'm sorry to say. She's in college, and I hope asleep by now. Is there something I can do?' The hesitation at the other end of the line puzzled her. 'John?'

'Could you go and look at her?'

Sarah looked uselessly at the phone in enquiry. 'Why?' she asked baldly. 'Of course I will, but why?'

'To see if she's all right.' John McLeish was embarrassed but uncompromising. 'I've got an anxiety attack,' he said unapologetically. 'I've had these all my life and they're usually right. Please, Sarah.'

'Of course. Shall I ring you back?'

'Bit difficult. I'm off my own patch. I'll ring you. Is anyone else there? I mean, are there people about?'

'Well,' she said, bewildered, 'not very many. It's the end of term.'

'You've got house guests at the lodge?'

'Yes, but they're all out,' she said, stupidly, then recovered. 'What *is* it, John? A pricking of the thumbs?'

'Yes. I've missed something. It's out of the corner of one eye – do you know what I mean?'

'I do,' Sarah said, wondering what a son of her own would have been like.

'Please go and see Frannie. And *please*, go carefully. Don't go across the grounds. And I'll ring you back in fifteen minutes. I'm sorry. I do not know what it is.'

'I've gone, John. Fifteen minutes.'

Sarah set out, then turned back, feeling less than sensible, to collect the stout walking-stick that had supported her everywhere through viral arthritis. Following instructions, she went through the building, not across the garden, and checked, dismayed, as she realized that she did not know what guest-room Francesca had commandeered. Despite her strictures, there were two that did not actually let water in when it rained. She tried the nearer, which was up two flights of stairs and empty, then stopped for breath, realizing that John McLeish's anxiety had communicated itself to her and was making her short of breath and inefficient.

The college was extraordinarily quiet. There was not a sound apart from the usual clunking noises from the plumbing. To the

222

uninitiated, this gave credence to the Gladstone legend of the young man who had lost himself in the labyrinthine and expansive corridors in 1897, had never been seen alive again, and still wandered as a restless ghost. Now, why had she chosen to frighten herself with that old piece of rubbish, Sarah wondered, and set off resolutely down the stairs. She glanced at her watch; it was seven minutes since she had spoken to John McLeish. She must hurry or he would worry himself into a frenzy in his present mood.

She walked as fast as she dared along the corridor to the next hall of residence. It was not safe to run, even if she had felt able to do so: Gladstone's founders had specified a floor tile which was intrinsically slippery, whatever anyone did to it by way of new finishes. Generations of dons and undergraduates trying to hurry had come to grief, with bruises and broken bones. She reached the foot of the twisting staircase that led to the next most likely guest-room, and as she put her hand on the newel post the corridor and staircase lights went out simultaneously, leaving her unable to see anything at all. She stopped, cursing Gladstone's early twentieth-century wiring, which was all too prone to deliver surprises like this.

'Hello,' she called. The college was absolutely silent. As her eyes became accustomed to the dark, she could just make out the first turn in the stairs.

She let go of the newel post and felt around for a switch. Able to see slightly now in the pale light let in by a heavily lozenged corridor window, she managed to turn on a light, not in the corridor but in part of the kitchen, so that she could just see where she was. Resolutely, she started again to climb the darkened stairs, holding on to the banister, carrying the walking-stick awkwardly in her other hand. There was a movement at the top of the stairs and a board creaked.

'Francesca?' she called hopefully, going steadily on up the stairs. There was no response. She stopped at the bottom of the last turn of the staircase, peering up into the darkness that was just barely relieved by the day's final light, heavily filtered by the little window. The boards creaked again, and she distinctly heard the click of a door handle.

'Anyone up there?' she called again. Someone moved on the

top landing, and she saw, just, a change in the quality of light. Then it was gone.

She froze, her heart banging and the hair on her head prickling in raw terror. There was someone up there who was not prepared to speak or to be seen, and whose only way out was down the staircase on which she stood. No sensible woman corners a burglar, Sarah told herself, before remembering that Francesca – for whose very presence in college she was responsible – was up there too, the only person officially in residence on that floor tonight. And this shadow was not Francesca.

Sarah, cold with terror, thought quickly: she had been in mortal danger before, and had been both resourceful and brave, but that was forty years ago when she had also been young and fit and trained. It would probably not have been sensible, even then, to rush the staircase single-handed against an unknown quantity; but at sixty-two, and unarmed except for a stick, it was simply impossible. The ony intelligent course was to proceed fast and noisily down the stairs and ring the police, without further challenging that shadow, in the hope that he would run. She turned slowly to do that, feeling unconfident and old and defeated.

The staircase window, slightly open to let in the warm June air, also let in the hum of traffic noise from the main road a hundred yards away, but there was something odd about the noise. It was now not a hum but a distant wail, growing abruptly louder as Sarah felt for the top step to go down. Sirens, several of them. Suddenly the sound checked, then, as she was two steps down, it started again more loudly and Sarah understood what she was hearing. Vehicles carrying the sirens had stopped at the gates of Gladstone, and the noise of the loudspeakers was much louder because the cars' engines were idling. So John McLeish had not trusted her – or he had remembered something and, excellent man, had called out his allies. Of course they had responded more sharply for a fellow policeman than they would have done for any other call. If God willed, they were even now persuading Rumpelstiltskin at the gate that they were real policemen and that he had better get the gate open.

Sarah hesitated, cursing her helplessness; but, whatever was happening above her, it remained the case that she would best help Francesca by getting down and finding able-bodied and determined help. She turned, tripped, caught the banister with her free hand, dropped the stick with a clatter and just saved herself from falling. Above her there came the sound of clumsy and agitated movement. She must get off these stairs, she thought frenziedly; she was blocking the intruder's only exit, and the police were far better able to deal with whoever this was than she was.

A shaft of light suddenly appeared above her and, blinking, she realized that a door had swung open.

'*Help!*' It was a husky, stifled noise, just barely translatable as a word. The light above wavered as somebody appeared in the doorway, then pitched forward heavily on to the landing, with a thump that shook the staircase.

'Francesca!' Sarah shouted, her own danger forgotten. 'Look out!' She plunged back up the three stairs down which she had painfully picked her way, and rushed up the last part of the staircase, whose steps were now just visible in the shaft of light from above. 'I'm coming, wait!' Every detail of the dimly lit carved banisters was suddenly crystal clear as she made it, her legs no longer hurting, on to the landing. She ran to get between Francesca, who was now on her hands and knees, and the figure in the patch of darkness at the other end of the T-shaped balcony.

The sirens were very clear now; Sarah could hear the sound check and change, as they bumped over the humps on the long drive. Help was at hand, and Francesa was blessedly, markedly alive – to prove it, she was being appallingly sick. The figure moved again, menacingly, and Sarah braced herself to fight, screaming for help and bitterly regretting the loss of her stick. It burst out of the shadows, a curiously deformed shape – but instead of rushing at her it turned down the stairs. The figure was unmistakably male, and appeared to be headless: seconds after it had taken the turn and was clattering heavily downwards, her brain caught up with what she had seen and she understood that whoever it was had pulled a sweater up over his head and was holding it in position until he got past her.

She saw him check and turn at the last bend in the stairs; then there was a disproportionate, ridiculous amount of noise, like a wardrobe falling, culminating in a heavy crunching thud. Getting to her feet, stiff and trembling, Sarah felt for the light switch. Two anxious, enquiring, undergraduate faces gazed up at her

225

from the floor below, and she snapped at them to come up and look after the still retching Francesca. She passed them on the stairs as she went down, holding tightly on to the banisters, to see what further disaster awaited her on the ground floor. As she turned the corner she saw a pair of grey-trousered legs, one of which was bent into a position that could not have been achieved without breaking the bone – indeed, blood was seeping on to the floor. Her walking-stick lay wedged between the legs, broken almost in half.

With a dry mouth, Sarah bent to look at the suffused face, which was still half covered with a heavy brown sweater. 'George?' she said, stupidly. *'George?'*

'I'll call an ambulance,' someone said, as she pulled down the sweater gently to feel for the pulse in the neck.

'Tell them his skull is fractured, and his neck may be broken. One leg has multiple fractures. They'll need blood.' Sarah, ice-cold now and totally concentrated, was just conscious of a gaping mouth, then the girl seemed to evaporate, and Alan Toms was kneeling beside her, silenced for once. 'He fell,' she said briefly, wadding two of her handkerchiefs into the groin where the femoral artery surfaces. 'That's better. Could you hold on, Superintendent, while I just check the rest of him?'

She sat back, painfully, on her heels, stripped off her jacket to cover George Hellier's back where the sweater had pulled clear, and went on gently to check his ribs. 'How did you get here so quickly? Did John McLeish ring you?'

'Yes, he did. But I was in the car already, on my way here. Where's his missus?'

'Upstairs, being sick.' Sarah felt carefully up the spine.

'Not hurt, then? Thank God for that. Thing is, we found Mr Greenlees with his girlfriend at Heathrow this morning. He gave us Hellier's name about . . . what? . . . twenty minutes ago. Fields got it – he's good, that lad. He sent me to tip you off.'

'I haven't understood, I'm afraid,' Sarah said, her hands busy. 'Where's the ambulance?'

'My lads are watching for it. It was Hellier who was Greenlees' contact here. They were both in it; making a nice little income between them.' He stopped as they both heard an ambulance scream to a halt outside the iron gates.

'Oh heavens, those gates are closed,' she said, recalling the time.

'Not any more. My driver took the bolt off to get us in. Here he comes.'

The clanging sounded painfully in their ears, then stopped abruptly. Two ambulancemen and a young doctor, half into his white coat, advanced purposefully on them and knelt beside George, studying him carefully without touching him.

'He's been breathing throughout, so far as I know,' Sarah volunteered.

'That's a start,' the young man said calmly. 'Femoral artery cut? OK.' He reached for a dressing and a strap and considered his angle. 'Right. Move your hand now, please.' Alan Toms did so gingerly, and the young man pushed the pad into place, released and handed Sarah's handkerchiefs, soaked with blood, to a uniformed acolyte who was left visibly wondering what to do with them.

'Can we leave them to it, Dame Sarah?' said Alan Toms. 'We'll need to get someone round to Dr Hellier.'

'I think she already knows,' Sarah said, suddenly exhausted, and unable to get up.

Alan Toms extended both his hands, and she managed to stagger up as the feeling came back into her feet and knees.

'Sarah?' Francesca, greenish-white, huge shadows under her eyes, was clinging to the banisters, her dark hair wildly and unbecomingly awry, barely decent in a short night-dress. 'Are you all right? What happened to George?'

'What happened to *you* is what your lad'll want to know.' Alan Toms, tight-lipped, was up the stairs in a flash, bundling her into his raincoat, doing up the buttons for her as if she was a child.

'I woke because someone was pushing my head into the pillows.' Francesca was shaking with cold and terror. 'I couldn't manage to call out, he was too strong. Then he went away.' She stopped, incredulous. 'It was *George*! Why?'

'Ah.' Alan Toms pointed like a retriever, nearly knocking Sarah over. 'I'm sorry, Dame Sarah. Here, you two lads, let's get the ladies sat down in the warm.'

He surrendered them to two of his detectives without a backward glance and plunged out of the door. In the bustle of getting to the senior common room and being settled into chairs

227

with hot drinks, they forgot about Toms until he swept back into the room and summoned his men around him in a huddle.

'He has a phone in the car, of course.' Francesca was still glacier-white and shaking, but her brains were engaged.

'He'll have rung John, then, I hope. It was he who sent us all this help,' Sarah said.

'I expect he will have done, but he'll have rung Notting Dale first.'

'Why?' Sarah asked, trying to control her own shaking hands.

Francesca edged her chair over and put a clammy hand over Sarah's chilled wrist. 'Your predecessor – that's how she died. Face down in he pillows.'

'Francesca!' The cup slipped in Sarah's hand and she just managed to retrieve it. 'Did you remember that?'

'Not while it was happening to me. I remembered when I saw George.' She paused. 'I've not even asked,' she said, in a voice breaking with hysteria. 'Is he dead?'

'No, but he's badly hurt. I didn't push him, he fell.'

'Thank God for that, I'd not have wanted him on your conscience.'

Sarah, drinking sugary, warm tea, thought briefly of the deaths in Holland for which she had so long ago been responsible; of Louise Taylor, still mortally ill in hospital; and of Francesca, her face pressed ruthlessly into the pillow. Also of the three small children who were dependent on her two young colleagues. 'I expect I could have lived with it. Finish that tea, Francesca, and ring John yourself.'

Epilogue

John McLeish woke slowly, and realized he must be off the motorway. The steady rhythm of the car's engine had changed, and there were houses at the side of the road.

'Getting close now, sir,' the driver said, observing him from the front. 'Do I take Newham Way?'

'Mm. Yes. That's right. No messages?'

'No, sir.'

McLeish reached for the phone, glanced out of the window and decided against it. He would be at the hospital inside ten minutes, and his time was better occupied having a cup of tea and waking up. The car turned into the familiar car-park and McLeish got out, stiffly, and glanced at his watch. Three hours from Hull was good going and the driver would have had enough. He told the man to go to a hotel and get some sleep; the combined resources of West Drayton and Notting Dale would provide him with transport. He walked into Casualty, and hesitated. Through a partly drawn curtain he could see Sarah Murchieson in profile, apparently asleep. He walked over, quietly, and put his head round. Sarah woke with a start and motioned him to silence, and he looked to her side where his wife lay, pale but breathing easily, on a trolley, a drip attached to her left arm. He went over and looked at the bag. 'Glucose?' he asked, and stood looking down at his wife.

'Yes,' Sarah whispered. 'She's here because her blood pressure dropped right down suddenly. I didn't like to leave her – they don't have a bed yet.'

'That happens to her.' He touched his wife's cheek, then offered Sarah his arm, wordlessly, and helped her carefully from her chair. She was moving very stiffly and winced as she placed her weight on her right foot. 'What did you do?'

'Nothing to worry about, John. Just a bruised hip – no, I promise, they did an X-ray.'

He settled her carefully on an even less comfortable chair. 'You should be in bed.' He considered her and bent over, shyly, to kiss her. 'Thank you for everything. She'd be dead without you.'

'Rubbish,' she said, embarrassed. 'You didn't trust me. You rang Alan Toms.'

'Yes, I did, but only when you'd had fifteen minutes. You don't agree that sort of thing and then go in early; or wait a bit in case you've got it wrong.'

'No, indeed,' she agreed soberly, seized by old memories of times when, after fifteen minutes, you knew something had gone wrong and you had either to attack or melt away to save your life for another day.

'In any case, your arrival saved her. Alan wouldn't have got there in time. Two minutes more, and Hellier would have seen her dead and got clean away.'

'But *you* would have known?'

'That she had been murdered? Yes, I would, because of Judith Symonds. And I would have known it was Hellier, because of the fraud. But there wouldn't have been any proof.'

No, Sarah thought silently, and you would have pursued George Hellier for the rest of his life – you couldn't have helped it. And that would have been your life ruined as well. She watched while he, without raising his voice, secured a hospital bed for his wife, and settled down to wait while he made sure she was comfortable.

Three days later, Sarah, Alan Toms and Francesca and John Mcleish were seated on garden chairs outside Tydeman Hall. The sun was warm, and the clanking of scaffold poles going up fast around the building only a minor distraction.

'John's not a happy man,' Toms said, his eye on McLeish. 'The Notting Dale lads have got nowhere with Hellier, even though we offered to roll all the charges together. Well, as I said to them, your victim died, didn't she. That makes it murder, not attempted murder. Hellier understands that very well, and they can't push him very much, as he's still very ill. You did a good job there, Dame Sarah. Two broken legs, couple of broken ribs and a hairline skull-fracture. All Hellier has to do is close his eyes, and the hospital staff throw us all out of the room.'

'You mean that you – the police – cannot charge George with Judith Symonds's murder? But he tried to do the same to Francesca.'

'It'll be a question of proof, won't it? Francesca can't identify him as the person who held her head into the pillows. In fact, she isn't going to be much use in the box. She was doped – that we can prove.'

'You'll have to try harder.' Francesca sounded cross. 'He tried to kill me exactly the way he killed Judith Symonds. He doped me with pills. We know that, because he forgot to clear up the whisky, and mine had crushed Valium in it. He met me after I left you, and helped me to a college guest-room. Then he waited till I had gone off, and tried to suffocate me.'

Alan Toms looked at her, eyes narrowed. 'Yeah? You'd been taking the pills anyway, hadn't you? Because of all this stress, and you've got a new baby? A good brief'd go straight through you.'

Francesca scowled at him; this was obviously an argument they had conducted before.

'And then,' Toms continued remorselessly, 'bless us all, you sicked up everything but your socks, and one of your little undergraduates mopped it all up and flushed it down the khazi before anyone could do anything sensible.'

'Being sick may have saved her life,' Sarah pointed out, seeing Francesca's lip tremble.

John McLeish reached for his wife and hugged her. 'Next time she'll wait for the stomach pump, I'm sure,' he said, ducking his head to look her in the face.

'Course I will,' Francesca said, rallying. 'I just forgot for a moment there that I was a policeman's wife. Please also remember, Uncle Alan, that without Sarah we'd have had nothing at all – no evidence, just me dead. Sarah and I both saw George leaving the college around seven thirty. The nurse who was looking after Alice welcomed him back at seven forty-five, and had no idea he'd gone out again.'

'No, but then *she* wasn't trying either. She was watching TV

231

and she was only listening for Alice Hellier. It was no part of her duty to keep an eye on the patient's husband,' Alan Toms pointed out.

'That's fair enough,' Francesca acknowledged, and shivered as she took her coffee cup.

Sarah, who was not at all sure that this conversation ought to be taking place with Francesca present, handed Alan Toms his coffee and passed him the sugar bowl automatically, knowing that he would load in two sizeable spoonfuls. In many ways she knew these two men better than the Fellows of Gladstone: it had been that kind of term. 'So what *can* be proved?' she asked.

'The fraud on the college. With Mr Greenlees' help, Hellier was getting something like £10,000 a year out of his deal with Greenlees Catering.'

'Enough to look like a private income, and make up the deficiencies in a Deputy Bursar's pay.'

'But Alice Hellier doesn't mind much about money, does she? Look at her clothes,' Francesca said.

'No, it was him that minded,' Alan said, and they fell silent.

'It is clear that Alice was in no way implicated, is it not, Alan?' Sarah said.

'Yes. She's talking about selling the house to repay the college. Are you going to sue her?' Toms asked.

Sarah was interested to see that Francesca, her financial rottweiler, was horrified at the idea of bankrupting Alice Hellier. 'No,' she confirmed. 'I have talked to Alice. We are not going to visit the sins of her husband upon her.'

'I thought she was too ill to make sense?' Francesca said.

'She was last week, because she was terrified. Now she has no reason to be frightened any more: the worst has happened.'

'Mm.' Francesca was watching her with uneasy respect. 'So George killed Dr Symonds because she had found the fraud?'

'Yes,' Alan Toms said. 'That's right. We're having trouble proving it.'

'And he attacked me because I hadn't. Come on, Alan.'

'You'd found the scam, Frankie, you just hadn't found out who was doing it. You were about to give all the papers to your mates at Customs and Excise, and the buggers would have got it in about ten minutes. George Hellier planned to have a field day with a shredding machine while we were trying to find out who'd killed you.' Alan Toms beamed at her ferociously.

'Thank you so much for that explanation, Detective Chief Superintendent.' Francesca went suddenly pale, but rallied. 'All right – but why Louise, then? Was that revenge, because she wouldn't go on sleeping with him?'

'No, that was the fraud as well,' Toms said. 'It's usually a better motive than sex, money is. Louise had had a look at the two sets of accounts for the Raab Lecture, hadn't she? Well, one was clean, one wasn't. My oppo in Customs got it straight away, looking at the two sets side by side. And who'd catered and organized both of them? George Hellier.'

'Louise must have spotted something was wrong,' Francesca said slowly. 'And I would have spotted what it was, but I was so busy doing other things that I never found time to look at both accounts. Though, to do me justice, George did keep taking it away from me.' She put her coffee cup down sharply. 'Why do I still think of him as George, who was kind and supportive and cosy – not as a man who killed, or tried to kill, whenever anyone threatened him?' She fumbled for a handkerchief.

Her husband found her one and put a big comforting hand on her shoulder. 'Because that's how men like that operate,' he said. 'They've found it works, being cosy and supportive. It gets them what they want.'

'I shall never feel the same about those chaps again,' Francesca said, and Alan Toms laughed.

'Time you learned a bit about the real world, Frankie.' He met her outraged glare. 'Now, don't look like that. You just come along and show me whereabouts you're going to put your little nursery. I don't want to find it's somewhere stupid, where every passing nutter can get at the kids.' He rose and stood, implacably, waiting for her.

Francesca looked at her husband, but he was grinning, so she followed Toms out with a suggestion of a flounce. 'Do you want her to stop working here, John?' Sarah asked apprehensively.

'Heavens, no. She loves you; she's at home here; and it's a challenge. I really do not want her either at home, or busting herself doing a full-time heavy-duty policy job back at the

Department.' He smiled at her. 'And I still don't have much luck telling her to not to do things she wants to.'

'Well, I want to keep her. We don't have many with her kind of drive and attack.'

'You'll get Louise Taylor back by the autumn.'

'Yes, yes, that is wonderful, and a far, far better outcome than we could have hoped. You know that against a lot of precedent the whole of the period before the attack has come back to her? She remembers quarrelling with Michael, him slapping her, and then going off to dinner with Neville. Where, I understand, she got a bit of a slap as well, figuratively speaking. She remembers that, now, too.'

'If she'd just seen George coming, we'd have been away. But he attacked her from behind and left her for dead,' McLeish said grimly.

Sarah judged it better to change the subject. 'I've been talking to Michael Taylor. He's a changed man; in thirty-six hours in the cells he seems to have sorted out his whole life. He's gone to see old friends in one of the big stockbrokers this morning. Of course, it was a great help that Louise's parents never thought for a minute that he was guilty.'

'Well, I'm glad somebody benefited.' Sarah noticed again how weary McLeish looked. 'I must get back, Sarah. I've got a good man – Bruce Davidson – taking turns with Alan's people to sweat Hellier in the ten minutes a day they're allowed. This is the tricky bit – we can all see what happened, but we've got to get it so a jury can do the same. And so no highly paid brief can derail us in the box. I'll just say goodbye to Frannie.'

She watched him with affection as he strode over the lawns to where his wife and Alan Toms were contemplating a space by the tennis courts.

She heard the phone ring in her office; she decided she must answer it and went reluctantly in out of the bright morning. 'Oh, Neville. How are you?'

'Have they charged Hellier?' Neville Allason, unusually, was prepared to forgo the civilities.

'Yes, they have. Only with the attempted murder of Francesca. He has not admitted to the attack on Louise.'

'What about Judith's death?'

'No, he hasn't admitted to that one either. As my police friends point out, the trouble is that Judith is dead and it would be a murder charge, which we still seem to take seriously. But they are not in any doubt about it.'

'Thank God for that.' Neville's clear voice was buoyant.

'I expect Jennifer will be relieved too.' She listened sardonically to the silence at the other end.

'I never quite had time to tell her anything about all this,' he said, with attempted briskness.

'And now you don't have to.'

'Don't sound so disapproving, Sarah. I know I haven't led a totally blameless life – any more than you have – but I don't see why I should worry Jennifer with it all.'

'I know you don't,' Sarah agreed. 'When are we going to see you again?'

'Oh, soon,' he said unhesitatingly. 'The week after next?' He made a date, and she put down the phone, amused and relieved. The truth was, a working relationship survived longer than the most passionate of love affairs.

She looked out of the window and laughed aloud. Alan Toms and John McLeish were standing thirty feet apart on the grass like matching bookends, watching sceptically as Francesca danced between them, making eloquent spreading gestures so that the projected nursery building somehow rose, complete, between her and her two observers. I have seen the future, she thought, rising to join them, and it looks like a crèche.